WELCOME TO WINTERVILLE

CARRIE ELKS

WELCOME TO WINTERVILLE by Carrie Elks

Copyright © 2021 by Carrie Elks

170921

All rights reserved.

Edited by Rose David

Proofread by Proofreading by Mich

Cover Designed by The Pretty Little Design Co (https://www.theprettylittledesignco.co.uk)

This book is a work of fiction. The characters, events, and places portrayed in this book are products of the author's imagination. Any similarity to persons living or dead is purely coincidental.

Welcome to Winterville
Where Every Day is Like Christmas

Holly Winter pressed the brake pedal of her rental car and took a deep breath, staring at the writing in front of her. The sign was faded, as though somebody had forgotten to paint it this year, and there was a thick wedge of snow laying across the top like a sleeping cat. In the distance, she could see the twinkling lights of the town as it nestled around the mountain.

Opening the window, the cold air rushed around her face. The air in the Allegheny Mountains was so different to the atmosphere she'd become used to in Chicago. It wasn't just that it was thinner – thanks to the elevation of the town, but because it smelled sweeter.

Like home.

Or as near to home as she'd ever been.

There wasn't another car on the road. She hadn't passed

one for the last hour since she'd begun her slow ascent from the interstate. No SUVs full of families, excited to spend the weekend at *America's Favorite Holiday Town*. No buses full of day-trippers, traveling to soak up the festivities at the Jingle Bell Theater. Instead, there was silence and the rumble of her engine, deadened by the layer of thick snow.

She pressed her foot down on the gas and the Jeep's tires gripped the roads – thankfully clear of snow despite the lack of travelers. That would be thanks to Charlie Shaw, who ran the Cold Start Garage in the center of town. For the past forty years he'd taken his snow plow out whenever Winterville had a hint of snowfall.

It was the first time Holly'd been back to town since her grandma's passing earlier that year. It wasn't just that she'd been busy at work – though Lord knew that was true – but she'd found herself finding stupid excuses not to come.

Winterville without her grandma was hard to imagine. Her grandma had been the heart of the town. She'd been the one who built it, after all.

Her phone started ringing through the car's speakers, and she hit the accept button, braking sharply as a white snowshoe hare bounded across the road. "Dammit!" she called out, and a low chuckle echoed back at her.

"Holly?"

"North." As her eldest cousin, North was the leader of their generation of Winters. "I nearly hit a damn hare."

"You've made it into the mountains then." His voice was warm and low.

"I just passed the town sign."

"You're close." He sounded pleased. "Are you heading straight to the Inn?" The Winterville Inn was the heart and soul of the small town. It had been built and owned by their grandma for more than fifty years. Growing up, it had been like a magnet for the Winter cousins. Holly had spent many holidays there with North and his brothers – Kris and Gabe – and her girl cousins – Everley and Alaska. A smile pulled at her lips as she remembered their epic snow fights.

"Yeah, I'm beat. I'm going to check in and veg out for a while. Are you at the farm?"

North owned the Christmas Tree Farm at the other end of town. Along with his co-owner, Amber, he lived in a sprawling set of lodges alongside the farm. Some of the buildings belonged to his brothers – though right now they were living elsewhere.

"Yeah. It's been crazy this week. But you, Everley, and Alaska should come over for lunch on Sunday. Gabe has promised to cook, which I'm hoping won't put you off." He chuckled, and it made her smile. Gabe was known for burning water. She kept her fingers crossed that he'd keep it simple.

"Lunch on Sunday sounds good." She nodded. She passed the Jingle Bell Theater, where her grandma had starred every year, pulling in fans from far and wide for her Holiday Shows.

Now it looked empty and alone. Holly pulled her eyes away and concentrated on the road ahead.

"We can work on our plans then."

Their plans to stop the town from being sold.

Not that Winterville was strictly a town. It was an unincorporated settlement, according to the legal description. The land had been bought by their grandma, the famous singer and actress Candy Winter, after she'd taken the world by surprise when she'd retired at the peak of her fame, and brought her family back to the wild mountains where she'd grown up.

"Our plans?" Holly echoed, knowing exactly what he meant. And she hoped to God he did have a plan, because she'd come up with nothing. Their parents – her mom and

3

two uncles – had inherited the town and wanted nothing to do with it. They were set on selling it to the highest bidder.

It was the reason she was here, after all. Driving a rental car from the nearest airport – three hours drive away, thank you very much – to a West Virginian town tucked into the side of the mountains.

North had this crazy idea that they could work together to stop their parents from cashing in on their inheritance. Even though the six cousins didn't have anywhere near enough money to counter the offer they'd been made.

Their grandma had been a force of nature. A woman in charge of her own destiny at a time when it was unheard of. And she'd had a vision for this land she'd bought – a vision that included building a town, brick by brick. Giving homes to the people she'd grown up with, along with jobs to replace the ones they'd lost years ago when the last local mine had closed down.

And she'd named it Winterville.

As she followed the bend, the Winterville Inn loomed ahead of her. It felt bittersweet, seeing the tall sprawling building and knowing that Candy wouldn't be waiting for her inside, her blonde hair swept up into her signature beehive, her eyes dancing because she adored her grandchildren.

Running the town had always been a family affair. Along with North and his brothers, and Everley and Alaska, Holly had worked here at Winterville every vacation as a teenager.

They would serve breakfasts at the restaurants and clean cabins, before they moved to manning the reception and, in the case of Holly's more talented cousins, starred in the annual Christmas shows that Candy would hold at the Jingle Bell Theater.

Pulling into the graveled driveway, she looked up at the Inn ahead of her. It had started snowing again. Thick, heavy flakes danced down from the dark gray sky and landed on the windshield.

Parking in the lot at the side of the Inn – almost empty, despite the season – Holly climbed down from her SUV and grabbed her purse, her feet crunching in the snow as she followed the path to the front door. Before she got into the lobby she could smell the sweet smokey aroma of the inglenook fireplace, and hear low piped Christmas music echoing through the speakers.

Despite the lack of guests, the lobby was still beautifully decorated. Garlands of holly and ivy were strung on every surface, fairy lights wrapped around them, twinkling in time to the music. Giant gold and red ornaments hung from the ceiling, and life sized wooden nutcracker soldiers stood sentinel at each doorway, holding drums or spears, their moustaches quirked up into permanent smiles.

But the focal point was the huge tree standing proud at the center of the lobby. The green boughs were weighed down with gold decorations and glittering tinsel.

"You made it!" A human tornado launched itself at her. Holly laughed as Everley almost tackled her to the ground. "You should have told me you were getting close. I've been annoying Alaska all day wondering when you'd get here."

"Sorry." Holly hugged her tight. "I'm here now though."

"Yes you are. And you're a sight for sore eyes." Everley dragged her over to the reception desk, where Alaska was typing into the computer. Their youngest cousin's eyes lit up when she saw them approaching.

"Holly!" She grinned, reaching over the counter to hug her. "How was your trip?"

"Not too bad. There was a bit of turbulence when we got closer, but nothing I couldn't handle."

"Ugh. I hate flying." Alaska wrinkled her nose.

"We know." Everley shot her an amused look. "That's why

you never leave Winterville." As the elder of the sisters, Everley was always teasing Alaska. She took it good humoredly.

"I can't help it. I love it here." Alaska shrugged, still smiling at them both. "And now that you're both here with me, it's even better." She looked down at her computer, then back at Holly. "I've put you on the fourth floor. Are you sure you don't want to stay with me?"

"The Inn is fine." Holly was looking forward to staying here. "Anyway, at least I'm not in the cabins." When they were teenagers, they'd always stayed in the staff cabins at the bottom of the hill. They'd been simple affairs – one room with two beds, plus a primitive bathroom. Though there was a basic heater, the best heat came from a fire they had to build themselves each night.

And yet they were so happy there. Back then, they'd been teenagers playing at being adults. She'd felt so grown up having a cabin to herself, while Everley and Alaska shared one a few cabins down. North, Kris, and Gabe had lived a few cabins away from that.

She'd had her first drink in those cabins – Gabe had let her sneak some whiskey from his hip flask.

"No cabins for you," Alaska said, smiling. "Not even if they were inhabitable, which they aren't. Those things were condemned years ago. You've got a pretty room that overlooks the town, with hot and cold water and a mattress to die for." She looked pleased with herself. "A *Great Night* Mattress. All our rooms have them now. I negotiated the discount myself."

"It sounds perfect. I'm going to dump my bags in there and take a shower if that's okay. Are you guys going to North's on Sunday?"

"Of course," Everley said, looking amused. "He just called and invited us. And you know that when North calls..."

"We come running," Alaska finished her sentence for her.

Holly grinned. "Yep. Some things never change."

"I'm so glad you're here," Everley said, hugging her again. "For the first time, I feel like we might be able to save this place."

"Exactly." Alaska nodded. "You and North will know what to do. You guys always did have the best ideas."

Holly's stomach twinged, because they were both staring at her with hope in their eyes. "Of course we're going to save it," she said, almost believing her own words. "We have to. For Candy's sake."

"I need you to sign these purchase orders,"

Josh Gerber turned his head to see his assistant, Willa, holding out a pile of papers and a pen. Josh took the papers, and looked at them, frowning at the words typed across the white expanse.

"Christmas invoices?" he asked. "*Already?*"

"It's December," Willa pointed out, biting down a smile as he sighed and scrawled his name across the line on each page. "We need to pay the deposits for the company party. Plus the gifts for all your employees. Holiday baskets, as usual. I sent out an email suggesting a change and you should have seen the replies I got back."

"People don't like change," Josh murmured, handing her back the signed documents. She picked a piece of lint from the lapel of his jacket, wrinkled her nose, and threw it in the trash can beside her.

"Will you actually come to the party this year?" Willa asked, slipping the signed orders into her to-do tray. "You could surprise us all. Who knows, you might even have a good time."

"Nobody wants the boss at the Christmas party." Josh grinned at her. Willa was one of his favorite employees. At almost sixty, she gave as good as she got. He needed that in his life. "They want to kick back and have fun without worrying about what they said to me the next morning. It's my Christmas gift to you all. An evening free of Josh Gerber."

"You could dress up as The Grinch," Willa said, ignoring his reply. "That would make everybody smile."

Willa was the only employee of Gerber Enterprises who could get away with talking to him like this. Some of that came from the fact she'd known him since he was born. She'd been his grandfather's secretary then, a fresh faced college graduate at the time. Josh had asked her to stay on when his grandfather had retired – or partially retired – and he'd taken over as head of the company.

She'd said yes, eventually. Thanks to a hefty pay rise and a promise that he'd let her tease him the same way she always had.

"I don't hate Christmas. I just don't understand it." Josh shrugged. "It's just another day, isn't it?" He glanced at his watch. He was already late for his next meeting. "Anything else I need to sign?"

Willa shook her head and glanced over at the board room. "No. And they're all in there waiting for you. I sent in some coffee and pastries, so they should be happy."

Josh winked at her and straightened his tie, pushing a lock of hair back into place. "I knew I could rely on you."

"Ah, one handsome smile from you and you'd be forgiven by them anyway." Willa shook her head. "You have the same charm your granddad has. One look and you always get what you want."

"I wish that was true. My winning charm has been sorely lacking lately."

"Well it will work this time," Willa told him, sounding certain. "Now go get 'em, tiger."

Josh rolled his eyes because even though she was cheesy, she also made him smile.

"Thanks," he said, walking over to the boardroom. Before he pushed the door open, he straightened his shoulders, lifting himself up to his full six foot three height.

"Okay," he said, walking into the already-full room and taking his seat at the head of the table. "I don't have a lot of time, so let's make this snappy. Who wants to start?"

"What do you mean there's a problem?" The meeting had been going on for two hours, despite Josh's best attempts to move it along. His back was aching and his stomach was rumbling, reminding him how long it had been since breakfast.

"We thought we were buying the land," Kevin Davies, the head of his real estate division told him. "But it turns out we've bought the town, residents, businesses, and all."

"How the hell did that happen? Didn't you read the deeds?" Josh frowned. Kevin was a veteran at Gerber Enterprises. He'd been working in Gerber Enterprises' real estate division for twenty years, and Josh had made him the department head a year after he'd taken over the reins.

"It was my fault," a woman's voice said. Josh looked over Kevin's shoulder to see one of the interns standing up. She looked scared to death as every member of the board turned around to look at her. Josh tried to remember her name. Ellie or Eliza or something? She was one of ten interns the company took on every year under their community outreach program.

"What's your name?" Josh asked, looking at her directly.

"Elizabeth Norton."

Ah yeah, *now* he remembered.

"Did you read the deeds, Elizabeth? Visit the land to do your research?"

She took a deep breath in, and Kevin shook his head at her. "It's my fault. I should have double checked. She's still learning."

Josh could remember Kevin talking to him about the new intern. That she had great promise. He exhaled heavily and looked around at the other twenty people in the room. "Okay, I think we can finish here. Kevin and Elizabeth? Please stay so we can discuss this."

It was amazing how long it took everybody to pack up their folders and leave the room. At least five of them asked for a quick word with him, and he pointed them all toward Willa to make an appointment. He didn't have time to talk. Hell, he didn't have time to deal with whatever the hell Kevin and Elizabeth had messed up, but it was his family's money, and it was his job to make it right.

"Okay," he said, when it was only the three of them in the room. "Talk. Tell me about this land."

Elizabeth grimaced. "I was tasked with finding some land in West Virginia that would be suitable for building a new ski resort. And this place looked perfect. It has main roads leading up to the summit, has all the utilities already installed, and there are towns nearby where we can recruit workers. I really thought it would work."

"But?" Josh raised his brows.

"But the only place we can build the resort is on the Main Street. And that's already full of businesses that lease their buildings. As you can imagine, there'll be uproar when we try to level all those places to the ground. And I know that you hate adverse publicity."

"Have you checked the leases?" Josh asked. "Can we evict the tenants?"

Elizabeth nodded. "We can, but I called a couple of the businesses last week, pretending to do a survey. I didn't tell them who I was or why I was calling, but all the business owners told me how much they loved being part of the town. That they weren't planning on going anywhere soon." She grimaced. "I can't see how we can evict them without there being a lot of backlash."

Josh sighed, leaning back to run his fingers through his thick hair. Bad publicity was poison for a business like his.

"I'm sorry," Elizabeth said again. "The owners said it would be no problem to level the ground and build a resort there. I took their word for it and assumed the buildings were all empty."

"Rookie mistake." Kevin shook his head. "Never believe anybody, especially when it comes to money."

"How much are we talking about here?" Josh asked, raking his hand through his thick hair. Kevin wrote a number on a piece of paper and slid it over to him.

"Shit." Josh looked at the zeros. All of them. "Can we pull out of the contract?"

"We already signed." Kevin swallowed. "The lawyers say it's water tight."

If his grandfather was here he would be shouting. Josh was cooler than that, but the fury was still pulling at his empty stomach. This was a mess of epic proportions. "So what do we do next?" he asked, as much as to himself as to them.

"I think we should visit the town," Elizabeth said, glancing at Kevin. Her hands were still shaking. "It's the only way to see the scale of the problem. And maybe there's an angle we can take to make it right."

"Yeah, I guess we should." Kevin nodded. "Not that I have time to visit Winterville right now."

"Wait, what?" Josh frowned. "We bought *Winterville?* As in the Candy Winter town?" An image of snow and twinkling lights escaped from his memories. The smell of hot chocolate and burning logs and soft lips that made promises against his.

"That's the one." Kevin nodded, his expression grim. "Although Candy has died. She left the town to her children. They're the ones who are selling."

Josh nodded silently, looking down at the paper with the numbers on it again. *Welcome to Winterville. Where Every Day Is Like Christmas.* He wondered if that sign still hung on the road leading to the town.

How long ago was it since he visited that little town nestled in the side of the mountain? He blinked, trying to remember. It had been right before he moved to London, and that was eight years ago. Damn, it felt like a lifetime ago.

He'd only been there for two days. And it was completely unplanned. He'd been driving from Cincinnati to Washington DC to deliver some documents before he left the US for London, and his car had skidded to a halt on the snowy roads.

It had taken an hour for a tow truck to come. Once it did, he and his car had been towed up to what looked like some kind of Disneyland wannabe, a little town covered with snow and Christmas lights, full of tourists and staff who made you feel welcome.

Including one very pretty receptionist who'd taken his breath away. At least, until his car was up and running and he could hightail it out of there.

Kevin and Elizabeth were looking at him expectantly, as though he could solve all their problems. He nodded slowly.

"I'll talk to Willa. Book a few days out of my schedule and we can go see what the hell's going on there."

Kevin did a double take. "You're coming too?" he asked Josh.

"Yes I am. I want this sorted out before the end of the

year." Not least of all because if his grandfather found out about it he'd throw a fit. Better to give solutions than problems. That's what he'd been taught from a young age. "Talk to the sellers and arrange a meeting with them as soon as you can, then liaise with Willa over details," Kevin said to Elizabeth, who looked almost green at the thought of it. "I guess we're taking a trip to Winterville."

"Darling." Josh's grandma wrapped her arms around his waist. The top of her head barely reached his chest. "You've grown again."

"I stopped growing at least a decade ago," he said, his voice teasing. "You must have gotten shorter."

"Hush with that kind of talk." She shook her head. "I hear you're going on a trip. Or at least that's what your grandfather tells me." She lifted her hands, cupping his cheeks. The way her arms stretched up it was almost like she was saying a prayer. "Oh, I've missed you, sweetheart."

It didn't escape his notice that his grandfather already knew he was going on a business trip. That's what happened when you took over the family company. The old man hated being retired, and somehow always knew what was going on at Gerber Enterprises. Josh had long since stopped trying to work out who the mole – or moles – were.

"Is that the boy?" a gruff voice called out, as if on cue. At almost thirty-two, there was nothing boyish about Joshua Gerber III at all. And yet that's what his grandfather always called him. Josh had no idea if that was because it gave him a power trip, or because he was jealous of Josh's comparative youth.

A little of both maybe. The old man had always been tetchy, ever since Josh was a young child. He'd moved in with his grandparents at the young age of three, when his parents had died in an accident. He could barely remember them, apart from when his grandma showed him photographs.

"Yes, Josh is here. I'm just making him a drink." His grandma shook her head. "And stop shouting. I can hear you perfectly fine."

His grandad grunted. "Send him in when you're done. I need to talk to him."

"Six years he's been retired, and he still thinks he knows everything." She rolled her eyes.

And didn't Josh know it. In the time since he'd taken over the business, his grandfather had tried to interfere at every turn. Josh had learned to fend off his efforts where he could.

Sure, he'd been trained to run the business from an early age. After his parents died, Josh had been the focus of all his grandfather's efforts. Working at the company during summer vacations once he was old enough, then during college, and finally being sent to run the London office for a year to prepare him to take over the reins.

Whether he wanted to or not. Because it was his birthright.

"What did you get him for his birthday?" Josh asked his grandma, as she fussed with the coffee machine.

"I thought about buying him a personality transplant," she said, deadpan. "But then I realized he'd have to have a personality to start with."

Josh bit down a laugh. "You're on fire today."

"Yeah, well. He's grouchy as hell today. Doesn't want to celebrate his birthday, doesn't want anybody here. Keeps telling me you're hiding something from him. He's not exactly a delight to live with."

"Then leave him." Josh gave her a pointed look. This wasn't the first time they'd had this conversation.

"You know better than that. I love the old grump, really."

She passed Josh a steaming mug of coffee. "Anyway, speaking of grouches, how's your love life?"

"Grouches?"

"Willa told me you're not going to the Christmas party this year. I don't know how you expect to find a wife if you don't socialize. Did you know that almost a quarter of people meet their future spouse at work?"

Josh leaned on the counter, shaking his head. "Okay, first of all, why are you and Willa discussing the Christmas party?"

"Because unlike you, I'll be going." His grandma gave him a pointed look.

"Well, second of all – and this is related – if I find a future spouse at work, then I'll be opening the company up to a lawsuit. And if you think Grandad is grouchy now, he'll be impossible to live with if I mess up at work. Remember what he always says?"

His grandma sighed. "I know. Never mix business and pleasure." She looked up, her eyes soft. "But I want you to find somebody. To be happy. You deserve it. And I deserve great grandchildren." She raised her eyebrows.

He pulled her close, pressing his lips to her hair. "You're way too young to have great grandchildren."

"And you're way too good at smooth talking your way out of trouble. So when are you going to settle down?"

He gave her a lopsided smile. "When I meet Miss Right, you'll be the first to know." It was a complete lie, but he hoped it soothed her anyway. It wasn't as though he had any time for relationships.

No woman liked being second to work. He'd learned that the hard way.

"Yeah, well don't take too long. Some of us have an expiration date, you know."

"Nah. You're going to live forever." Josh grinned. "It's all that champagne you drink. It's pickled you from the inside out."

Ten minutes later, after finishing his coffee, Josh walked into his grandfather's office. The old man was sitting completely upright in a wing backed chair. A cane was propped against it, though his grandfather hated using it.

Putting down the papers he'd been reading, he looked over at Josh, pushing his glasses up the bridge of his nose.

"Happy birthday," Josh said, carrying his gift over. It was beautifully wrapped, the dark blue paper shining beneath the office lights.

His grandfather looked at it. "Socks?"

"Gloves, actually."

"Willa always did have good taste. Put it on the desk with the rest of them. No doubt your grandma will open them later."

Josh didn't take offence at the casual dismissal of his gift. His grandfather hated birthdays and holidays. Anything that would once have taken him away from the office. Maybe that's why Josh put no effort into choosing a present. So much better to task his assistant with finding the perfect gloves.

"I hear you have a project in trouble." His grandfather looked up at him, his face impassive. The moles were obviously working overtime.

"It's nothing to worry about. Just a small snafu with a purchase. I'm heading there tomorrow to meet with the sellers. I'm confident it'll be cleared up within a few days."

"Hmm. Whoever started that project should be fired."

Josh ignored the bait. "I've got it covered," he said again. "You don't need to worry about anything."

"It's not me I'm worried about. It's your investors. *Our* investors. They've put a lot of money into this transaction.

People come to us because they can trust us. This is not a good look." His face was flushed, his voice animated.

Josh was unblinking. "It's okay," he told the old man. "Calm down or Grandma will be in with the blood pressure monitor."

"She needs to stop fussing."

"Maybe you do, too." Josh raised an eyebrow at him.

"Hmmph." His grandfather waved his hand. "You can go now. You've done your duty, and I'm getting tired. No doubt you'll need to get back to the office."

"That's where I'm heading now."

"Good man." The older man's voice deepened. He really did look sleepy. It wasn't a surprise, the number of medications he was taking. Pills to keep his heart beating, others to stop his blood pressure from getting too high, and then there were the painkillers and the diuretics that he always cursed.

"Happy birthday," Josh said, giving him a nod. He couldn't remember ever actually hugging or kissing his grandfather, and he definitely wasn't planning on starting now. The old man was right, he'd done his duty, he could leave with his head held high.

After another few hours at work, he'd go home and pack for Winterville. The last time he'd visited that place he'd been a different person. A younger man, with hopes and dreams of being something more than what his family thought he would be.

Now he'd grown up and he knew who he was. A business man. A bachelor. Somebody with a few close friends and a hundred thousand acquaintances. A man who drank too much coffee to keep himself going during the day, and one too many glasses of whiskey at night.

He'd long since given up thinking about the boy he'd once been.

Even if sometimes he didn't recognize the person he'd become.

"I can't believe we're all here together again." Alaska beamed at her cousins. "Apart from Kris, of course."

"And North," their cousin Gabe, pointed out, dryly.

"Yeah, but he'll be down in ten minutes. He just needs to take a shower." Everley grimaced. "He stank, didn't he?"

Gabe laughed. "You could say that."

Holly leaned back on the sofa, her heart feeling warm as she looked at her cousins.

It was good to be with them all again. The last time they'd all seen each other was at their grandma's funeral, and that had been such a difficult, sad time, they hadn't had the opportunity to reconnect.

It wasn't a surprise that it was near impossible to get them all in one place at the same time. Holly lived in Chicago, and though it was only a two hour flight away, she'd been crazy busy for the past few months finishing up a case she'd been working on.

Gabe was as busy as she was. He'd competed at the past two Winter Olympics as part of the US Snowboard team. The only reason he wasn't training this year was because of a surgery he'd had to undergo earlier in the year on his Achilles' tendon. He was slowly regaining his fitness, and after Christmas he was hoping to start up training once again, ready to compete the following year.

Everley didn't get to spend much time here in Winterville, even though it was her home base. She was a performer – a singer and actor like their grandma – and she went where the work took her.

And Kris – the youngest of the three boy cousins – was working in Paris, where he lived with his wife and their daughter.

Only Alaska and North were full time residents of Winterville. And from North's face when he stalked into his ranch house ten minutes earlier, he wasn't enjoying that fact right now.

Holly bit down a smile as she remembered how he muttered to himself before he headed to the bathroom to shower off the stench. From what she could make out, he'd discovered a huge pile of deer droppings in his Christmas tree farm, and while cleaning it up he'd managed to slip and fall straight into it.

And the resulting stench was terrible.

"I don't understand why he's so angry," Alaska said, her brows knitting. "White tail deer are common around here. And like us, when they have to go, they have to go."

"Because he fell and got peppered with deer crap." Gabe lifted a brow. "It ruins his image of being a cool mountain man."

North walked back into his living room, wearing a pair of faded jeans and a gray sweater, rubbing at his hair with a black towel. He was a good looking man, according to the adoring women of Winterville and beyond. Tall and built, with a light beard that enhanced his strong jaw, he'd broken hearts all over the Allegheny Mountains when he was younger.

He sat down on the edge of the table and looked at them, still rubbing the back of his neck. It was funny how they all turned to look at him.

Even after all these years he was still the ringleader.

"Feeling better?" Gabe teased.

North gave him a dark look. "Next time you get to clear up the crap."

Gabe pointed at his ankle. "I can't, I'm injured."

"I thought you were better." Alaska frowned. "You went skiing yesterday."

Gabe shook his head, widening his eyes in an effort to quieten her. Holly had to bite down a laugh.

"You went skiing?" North asked, his brows knitting.

"Just trying out the ankle. I'm gonna have to rest for a few days now. Don't want to overdo it."

"You're gonna have to help out in the shop is what you're gonna have to do. Have you seen my grocery bill since you moved in here?"

They were like a couple of old women. Really handsome, funny manly women. Holly met Everley's eyes and they grinned.

"Can't Holly help out at the shop?" Gabe asked, his voice wheedling. "She's got some free time on her hands."

"Hey, I'm taking some vacation time, buddy." Holly lifted her hands up, as though to fend him off. "Some of us *have* been working our asses off."

"I heard about your court win." North smiled at her. "Congratulations."

"It wasn't my win," Holly pointed out. "I just provided some expert testimony."

"They couldn't have done it without you," Everley pointed out. "I followed the court reports. Your testimony swung it."

As a forensic accountant, Holly was frequently called in to help with court cases. Especially high profile divorce cases, where money was being hidden in an attempt to lower payouts.

Her job was a lot more difficult than it sounded. Trying to find money that people had hidden behind long and complicated transactions through shell companies or in tax havens could take months. Months to track down. Months of scrutinizing spreadsheets and bank accounts until her eyes felt like they might drop out. And she didn't always have months to follow the trails.

Then she'd have to stand in front of a judge and testify that one complainant had been trying to screw the other over.

"Speaking of divorces," North said, looking at Holly. "Your mom's in town."

Holly pulled her lip between her teeth. "I guessed she might be. I haven't spoken to her in a while. What about her husband, is he here?"

"She's married again?" Gabe blinked. "When did that happen?"

"A few months ago. She called in the middle of the night from Italy to tell me."

"Who's this one? An Italian Prince? A French Playboy?"

"Some British guy. Son of a duke or something." Holly shrugged, trying to be nonchalant. Her relationship with her mom could be described as 'complicated' these days. The youngest daughter of Candy Winter, Susannah had inherited all of her beauty, but none of her empathy. She'd given birth to Holly when she was twenty-two, and unmarried. Holly still had no idea who her father was.

Their relationship had always been difficult. As a child, she'd been desperate to please her mom. She could be bewitching and fun, and when she concentrated all her charms on you, it felt a little like staring into the sun.

But she got bored easily. Not just of husbands, but of Holly, too. She flitted in and out of her life on a whim. Maybe that's why Holly had been so close to her grandmother. Candy Winter had been the one consistent person she could rely on growing up.

North shrugged. "I don't know if her husband is here or not. She's staying in the house she inherited from grandma. And that brings me to my other piece of news."

Gabe raised an eyebrow. "You're full of news today."

"Yeah, well this part isn't good. The reason she's in town is because all of our parents have a meeting with the new owners of Winterville."

For a moment there was silence. Holly blinked, trying to let the words sink in. "So they already found a buyer?" Her chest clenched.

"Yep. They were trying to hide it for as long as they could. Didn't want us to interfere. From what I can tell, there's a lot of money involved."

"I can't believe they went through with it." Alaska's eyes were shiny.

"Believe it. They've agreed on a sale with some company in Cincinnati for ten million dollars."

"We could never hope to match that," Holly murmured.

"Nope." North's smile was grim. "And no bank would lend us the money. Believe me, I've already asked."

"So what happens next?" Everley inquired. "If the sale has already gone through, it's over, right? What else can we do?"

"I don't know." North blinked, his eyelashes sweeping down. "But we have to do something. We can't let this place go without a fight. Our grandma loved this town. She built it brick by brick." He ran his tongue along his bottom lip, as though he was thinking.

"You think we stand a chance?" Gabe tipped his head to the side.

"I have no idea. All I know is that Grandma wouldn't want this. So we keep fighting until there's nothing left to fight for."

"And how do we do that?"

He let out a sigh. "I have absolutely no idea.

Holly's heart clenched, because he looked defeated before they'd even started. She knew enough about business and contract law to know he was probably right.

"Do you know who the new owners are?" she asked him.

"No. But they'll be here this week."

"Then let's see what they have to say," Holly suggested. "Find out who they are. We can't do anything until we know that, right?"

North nodded, his gaze meeting hers. "Right."

Gabe clapped his hands together. "In the meantime, let's eat lunch. I'm starving."

4

Holly pulled on her hat and gloves, looping her scarf around her neck before she pushed open the Inn door and stepped into the fresh morning air. It had snowed overnight but had since stopped, and a fluffy light layer carpeted the lawn in front of her. At some point in the early hours, Charlie Shaw must have plowed the roads, because the blacktop was gleaming in the early morning sun.

She'd been here for four days now, and she still hadn't been able to sleep properly. Maybe it was a combination of being in a strange bed, and the firmness of Alaska's beloved *Great Night* mattress. Whatever it was, she was wide awake at six a.m., and had tossed and turned until seven, before she decided to go for a walk.

Winterville was always at its prettiest at this time of year. The icy air was so still that the vapor from her breath lingered long after she exhaled. She made it to the end of the driveway and turned left, the sight of the Town Square warming her heart.

When her grandma had bought this town – or rather the land that now housed it – she'd wanted to carve out somewhere that she'd truly belong. Candy Winter had grown up about ten miles away, in a small cabin on the slopes of the mountain, where her family had lived a hand-to-mouth existence. She'd been discovered at the age of fifteen by a Hollywood Scout who'd heard her singing at a bar, and was whisked off to LA to be glamorized and trained. At sixteen, she was given her first movie role – a small supporting gig playing a maid in a musical. It was a blink and you'd miss her kind of part, but the director had seen something in her, because he'd cast her in his next movie.

By the time she was twenty-years-old, Candy Winter was in her first starring role. The movie itself – *Every Day Feels Like Christmas* – would have been forgettable if it wasn't for the pretty blonde with a voice like an angel. And the title song that gave her grandma her first radio hit.

For five years, she was America's first sweetheart. And then came her first scandal, when she became pregnant outside of wedlock. According to Candy, there was huge pressure to get married – not particularly to the father but to anybody who would have her. So many people in Hollywood had a vested interest in keeping her pristine image. It took a strong woman – one like Candy Winter – to avoid them.

And that's how Holly's Uncle Noel came to have Candy's surname. Two years later, Joe was born, also given Candy's surname, even though at that time she was living with a man – much to the scandal rags' disgust.

It wasn't until she was pregnant with Holly's mom – by a shocking third man – that Candy turned her back on Hollywood and came home to the mountains. She'd saved enough money to be set for life, and had looked for a place to settle down, away from prying eyes.

It took a lot of guts to build a town up from nothing, but Candy did it anyway, working with local architects and builders, with business owners looking for new ventures. And the public had loved her for her strength, eating up the newspaper reports on her progress.

By the seventies, Winterville was up and running, with people loving to visit the town and feel its Christmassy vibes. The Jingle Bell Theater had been added in the mid-seventies, and every year Candy would put on a Christmas Revue, from September to January, which always sold out.

When Holly's grandma had finally slowed down, North had helped her as much as he could – even though he had his own business to run. And Everley had stepped up to help with the Christmas Revue, using a recorded version of Candy to make sure she was always involved, even when she was too tired or sick to come to the theater in person.

But for the past couple of years, her grandma had been too sick to do much at all. The revue had stopped, and the constant gush of visitors had slowed to a trickle. Sure, the town had decorated the streets, but the sparkling lights and decorations didn't hide the peeling paint on the signs or the potholes filled with melted snow on the roads. If Candy could see her town now, she'd cry.

Holly blinked that thought away. Maybe whoever bought the town would repair it. Make it look modern and sparkling new.

Sure, and maybe the fake reindeer around the town square tree will sprout some wings and fly.

At the corner of the square was the Cold Start Garage. The sliding doors at the front were open, revealing an old car up on the ramp, over the pit. Holly walked in and peered down, trying to see if Charlie Shaw, the owner was there.

Then she heard a cough from her right.

Upon seeing her, Charlie's eyes widened. He quickly closed his hand into a fist, then let out a howl before opening it again. And a crumpled cigarette fell to the ground.

"Sheey-it." He grimaced, shaking his hand. "You didn't see me smoking, right?"

"That stuff is bad for you," Holly pointed out.

He looked down at the red mark on his palm. "You're telling me."

"I thought you quit years ago."

Charlie had worked at the Cold Start Garage for as long as she could remember. He had two sons that she'd grown up with.

"I did. Or at least that's what I tell them. If you see Dolores, don't tell her you caught me, okay?"

Dolores ran the local café. She was one of Holly's favorite people in town. "I won't tell her, if you promise to try quitting again."

He gave her a narrow-eyed stare. "I promise."

She grinned, because she knew he was lying.

"So how long you back for?" he asked Holly, walking back toward the car he'd been working on.

"A few weeks. Until after Christmas."

"It's nice that you're spending some time with your family." He pressed his lips together. "Candy would have liked that."

Holly's throat felt tight. "She would. And how's your family?" she asked.

"They're good. Graham made partner at his firm. He's going to Europe for the holidays. Asked if I wanted to go. Told him I didn't want to spend Christmas anywhere else but here."

"And Dylan?" Holly asked, referring to his youngest son.

"He's still working in Africa." Charlie pointed at some photos tacked to his wall. "There he is."

Holly looked at the photo he was pointing at. A tall, broad man was staring at the camera, surrounded by children.

He had a stethoscope around his neck, his face tanned and handsome.

"He looks good." She wondered if Everley had seen this photograph. Once upon a time, she and Dylan had been a thing.

"Yeah he does. He's a good man. Everybody says so." Charlie sounded full of pride.

"Will he be home for Christmas?" Holly asked him.

"Nope." Charlie shrugged. "I'll probably go over to Dolores' place for the holidays."

"That's nice." There had been rumors about a romance between the mechanic and the café owner for years. Holly had no idea if they were true or not. "And hey, if you don't go there, you could come to the Inn. We'll be having lunch there for anybody who has nowhere else to go."

"You're a good girl," Charlie said, patting her arm. "It's nice that you take care of so many people. I hear you're doing well in Chicago."

"Yeah, it's good there." She nodded.

"And do you have a special someone?" He wiggled his gray brows.

"Nope. I'm still single." It was a perpetual joke that she spent so much time on other people's divorces that it had made her jaded.

And like all good jokes, maybe there was a hint of truth there. Though it wasn't her job that made her guarded when it came to relationships. It was experience. Her mom was on her fourth husband in twenty years, her grandma had three baby daddies and goodness only knew how many failed relationships.

Maybe being bad at relationships was in her genes. And that was okay. She had a great job. She could take care of herself. Even if she got a little lonely sometimes.

"I can't understand it," Charlie muttered, shaking his

head. "A pretty woman like you. If I was thirty years younger, I'd take you out."

"If you were thirty years younger, I'd let you." Holly smiled at him.

"Ah, I can still take care of your car though. What are you driving at the moment?"

"A Jeep Grand Cherokee."

Charlie nodded, his face serious. "Good car for the snowy roads. Drop it over and I'll give it a tune up."

Holly smiled, because he really was sweet. "It's a rental. No need to tune it up."

He grimaced. "Those are the worst. People hammer the heck out of them."

"It drives fine. But thank you anyway." Impulsively she leaned forward to hug him. He took it stoically, patting her back like she needed a burping. "It's so good to see you." She released him, and there were two bright red discs on his cheeks.

He cleared his throat. "And you, too. Welcome home, sweetheart."

———

Holly spent the morning walking around Winterville, trying not to notice how shabby the Jingle Bell Theater was looking, or how empty the gift shop and bookstore were. It was early in December. Maybe things would get better as the month progressed.

When she arrived back at the Inn, Everley was waiting for her, stalking up and down the huge covered porch like she was on a mission. She was wearing a cashmere sweater, her long blonde hair cascading down her back.

"You're here, thank god." She threw Holly a pointed glance. "I've been waiting for you for hours."

"You sent me a message ten minutes ago." Holly smiled at her cousin's exaggeration. "I came right back. So what's up?"

"They're here."

"Who's here?" Holly frowned.

"The buyers. They're in the conference room with our parents. Which means this meeting is important."

Holly followed Everley to the lobby, where Alaska was behind the desk. "They got here about an hour ago, right?" Everley asked Alaska.

"Yep. They've been in the conference room ever since. The kitchen's already sent in two rounds of coffee."

"Have you over heard anything?" Holly asked hopefully. The door to the room was next to the reception desk.

"Not a thing. Damn walls are too thick." Alaska shrugged. "They looked nice though."

Everley laughed. "Only you would say something like that. Did you catch what the company is called?"

"Um, Garret something? Or Gurner?" Alaska pulled her bottom lip between her teeth, thinking. "There are three of them. Two guys and a woman. All dressed in business suits."

"Garrett something?" Holly repeated.

"Or Gerber," Alaska said, wrinkling her nose. "I can't remember."

Gerber. The name sounded uncomfortably familiar.

"Or maybe Garner."

Everley started to laugh again, covering her lips with the back of her hand.

Before Alaska could say another name, the door to the conference room opened a fraction, and voices spilled into the lobby.

"We can promise you there won't be any trouble," Uncle Noel was saying. "This is a quiet town. Folks around here do as they're told."

Everley's face wrinkled with disgust.

"And you'll arrange that meeting for tomorrow?" The voice was low. Smooth. It sent a shiver down Holly's spine, triggering a memory from deep in her past.

"Yes, at the Jingle Bell Theater. We're on it now."

"Meeting?" Holly mouthed at Everley and Alaska. They shrugged.

"At noon, please. I'd like to get this cleared up before we leave." There was that voice again. Like honey dripping in June.

"Of course. The town will all be there to listen. Now are you sure we can't persuade you to stay here at the Inn? We have some very beautiful suites. At no cost to you, of course." Uncle Noel chuckled. "And our chef does cook a fine dinner."

"We already have accommodations. Just out of town." A different voice. Female. It had to be the second of the three from Garner or Gurner or whatever they were called.

"And we'll be leaving the day after tomorrow." The third voice. "I have to be back for my kid's Christmas show."

"I understand. But if you need anything at all, just call."

"And if you change your mind about dinner, I'd be happy to host you." That was Holly's mom. "After all, you're giving us a heck of a lot of money."

Everley pretended to vomit, right as the door opened fully. She almost dislocated her arm at the speed in which she moved her fingers from between her lips.

Uncle Noel was the first to step out of the conference room. He did a double take when he saw his three nieces standing there, all eyes on him.

"Uncle Noel." Holly's smile was tight. "We thought you were in Florida."

"Where all the lizards are," Everley cough-mumbled, muffling her voice with her hands.

"I'm only here for a few days. To tie up a few loose ends."

His eyes cooly appraised them. "Is there something you need?"

"Oh no. We're just hanging around with Alaska while she works." Everley flashed him a bright smile.

"Girls, I didn't know you were here." Alaska and Everley's father followed his older brother out of the conference room. At least he looked embarrassed to be caught. He quickly hugged his daughters before taking a step back. "I left your mom in Florida. She would have come if she knew everybody was here."

"I work here, Daddy," Alaska pointed out.

"And I called you last week. You didn't return my messages." Everley raised her eyebrows at him.

"Yes, well, it's just a flying visit. I'll be going back home very soon. Let's arrange a video call some time." He couldn't meet their eyes. "I should be going. I need to... ah... make some calls." He shuffled over to the other side of the lobby and turned his back toward the girls.

"Well at least he has the good grace to be ashamed," Everley murmured.

But Holly didn't reply because a pair of cool blue eyes caught hers. Her mother was looking as beautiful as ever. Though she was fifty years old, she could pass for at least fifteen years younger. Her blonde hair was captured at the nape of her neck in a chignon, and her svelte body was encased in a black silk designer dress.

"Holly."

"Mom." She kept her voice even.

Her mom touched her neck with her hand, her huge diamond ring catching the light. "I didn't know you were coming here."

"I didn't know you'd be at the Inn either," Holly said pointedly.

Her mom faked a smile. "I guess we need to communicate better."

Or at all. That would be a major step forward.

"Well, we should go," Uncle Noel said, placing his hand on her mom's shoulder. Her mom nodded, looking relieved to be able to escape the silence.

"Yes, we should. My husband is waiting for me." Her mom glanced behind her, into the conference room. "Thank you again. It's a pleasure doing business with you."

"And you," Mr. Smooth talker replied. The next minute he was walking out of the door. All six foot two of him. Wearing a beautifully tailored gray suit, and a shirt unbuttoned at the neck, revealing tanned skin and a hint of hair.

Holly's gaze clashed with his and the air rushed out of her open lips.

Gerber. That was his name. *Josh Gerber.* Alaska had been right about the business name after all.

Recognition sparked in his eyes. He tipped his head to the side, his gaze scanning her face, before he looked back at her Uncle Noel.

"You haven't introduced us," Josh said.

"Oh I'm sorry. Girls, this is Mr. Gerber of Gerber Enterprises. Mr. Gerber, these are my nieces, Alaska, Everley, and Holly."

Josh curled his mouth into an easy smile as he held his hand out, shaking first Everley and then Alaska's hand.

Then he turned to Holly, his palm enveloping hers. It was soft and warm and made her body want to melt against him.

"Holly Winter," he said softly. "It's a pleasure to meet you. *Again.*"

5

I t had been eight years since she'd last laid eyes on Josh Gerber. Back then, she'd been twenty years old, and covering the reception desk while her cousins appeared alongside their grandma in that year's Holiday Revue when a tall, handsome twenty-four year old man walked in and asked for a room.

And she'd told him they didn't have one.

Somehow, she'd ended up suggesting he stay in her room. And for one night, she'd stayed with him. Even all these years later, she could still remember how his lips felt on hers. How he'd touched her in all the right places.

How they'd gone almost all the way before he pulled back.

The next morning, he'd left without a word, and she hadn't heard from him again.

And sure, she was fine with that. He hadn't promised her anything, and she hadn't asked for anything. But it irked her that he expected her to remember him after all this time.

As if he'd given her the most memorable night of her life.

Sure, he was still devastatingly attractive, wearing a perfectly tailored gray suit that enhanced his broad shoulders and strong chest along with a crisp white shirt that was unbuttoned at the neck. He looked like he belonged on the cover of GQ instead of standing in the lobby of the Winterville Inn.

She ignored the way her blood rushed through her body at the memory of him and tipped her head to the side, keeping her back straight and firm. "Have we met before?" she asked, her voice casual. "Surely not. I would have remembered."

Take that, Mr. Smooth talker.

Everley blinked, looking from Holly to Josh, like she was trying to figure out exactly what was going on.

The smile didn't waver from his face. "Yes. We met here eight years ago."

"I'm sorry." Holly shrugged. "A lot of guests pass through these doors. I can't remember them all."

His eyes dipped to her mouth. She dug her teeth into her bottom lip and he swallowed.

"You let me use your cabin."

Oh, she let him use far more than that. Even worse, she enjoyed it. Realization washed over Everley's face, and Holly shook her head almost imperceptibly. *Don't spoil it now.*

"I did? That old place?" Holly grimaced. "I guess you *would* remember that. Well, I'm sorry. And I hope you have somewhere better to stay tonight."

"We do," Josh murmured.

"Speaking of which, we should get back there," the man next to him said. "If you're ready, that is?"

Josh glanced at Holly again. "Yeah, I'm ready. Let's go." He nodded at Uncle Noel. "We'll see you tomorrow. Elizabeth will be in touch to discuss the arrangements for the theater."

"Of course. You have my direct number," Uncle Noel said. "I should be going, too."

It only took a moment for them all to leave. Josh Gerber and his co-workers, followed by her uncles and her mom.

Then the lobby was empty, save for Holly, Everley, and Alaska.

"Oh my god," Everley said, her eyes wide as she looked at Holly. "It's *him*."

"I know." Holly shook her head. "It's crazy, right?"

"Who's him? Who are you talking about?" Alaska asked.

"Josh. That guy who stayed in Holly's cabin that one time and helped us out with the Christmas Eve parade." Everley prompted. "You helped him with his Santa outfit, remember?"

Alaska's mouth dropped open. "The guy that North hit?"

"Oh god, I'd forgotten that." Everley grimaced. "He's not going to be happy about this."

Holly rubbed her face with her palm. "Ugh." She could remember it all so clearly. North had caught Josh with a pair of Holly's panties and assumed the worst, smashing his fist into the man's face before waiting for an explanation. After, she'd taken him back to her cabin, cleaned his face up, then he pulled her onto his lap and kissed her like his life depended on it.

Yep, he was the best kisser she'd ever met. And she hated that she remembered that.

Especially now that he'd bought the town her grandma built.

"What a weird family," Kevin said, as they climbed into Josh's shiny black Escalade. "How could they not know their kids would be in town?"

"I don't always tell my parents my plans." Elizabeth shrugged.

"Yeah, but they didn't even hug each other, or looked

pleased to see them. There's something going on there." Kevin frowned, shaking his head.

"Well, as long as it has nothing to do with the purchase, they can do whatever the heck they like." Josh started up the engine and pulled on his seatbelt.

He wasn't really thinking about the rest of the family. He was too busy thinking about Holly Winter and the fact she didn't remember him. Because he remembered those pretty lips and dark, tumbling hair. Not to mention those delicious curves that made his body ache.

Did she really not remember him?

It stung.

Sure, he didn't think that every girl he'd ever kissed should remember him. But they'd spent a whole day and night together. Her lips were swollen from their kisses, and her body warm and soft from all his attention by the time he'd left.

And he'd made her happy. Very happy. Three times, not that he was counting.

How the heck did she not remember that?

He drove out of the parking lot and around the main town square. Kevin glanced out of the window at the tree and surrounding buildings. "Do you really think the business owners are going to let us flatten this square?" he asked.

The square was the only part of the town that was suitable for the new ski village to be built. It was even and accessible, but close enough to all the slopes for the lifts to start there.

"They don't have much of a choice," Josh said, his voice even. "We own the land. We just need to give them notice." But he'd rather they left willingly. That's what the point of tomorrow's meeting was about. To persuade them that redeveloping the town was a good thing. That it offered opportunity, not pain. "The buildings have all seen better days. It's only a matter of time before they'd have to be torn down."

"Do you think the grandchildren are going to be a problem?" Elizabeth asked, her brows furrowed together.

"What do you mean?" Kevin asked.

"Didn't you see the look Joseph Winter gave those two girls. As though he was scared of them."

"Scared of his daughters?" Kevin asked. "Why would he be scared?"

"I don't know, I just feel like there's more going on than we know about. And I don't want us to be blindsided again." Elizabeth sounded anxious. "I messed up before, I don't want a repeat."

Josh looked at Kevin. He shrugged.

"We'll keep an eye on it," Josh said, steering the Escalade into the driveway of the house Willa had rented for them. It was picture perfect, with a low roof that stood against the backdrop of the snowy mountains. It was on the other side of the town limits, something he might be grateful for if the residents turned sour on him. Plus, it had a lot of space and great wifi – something they were all going to find useful.

Not that he was planning on staying here long. He'd try to keep the peace tomorrow before he headed home. And not think about a certain brunette who really should remember his name.

He parked in front of the house and looked at Kevin and Elizabeth.

"The thing to concentrate on is our town meeting tomorrow," he told them. "We need to tell these people that things will be changing around here, and somehow keep them on our side. We don't want any adverse publicity."

"Easier said than done," Kevin murmured.

"I know," Josh said, his voice low. "That's why we'll be working through the night."

North walked into his open plan kitchen and living area and wrenched open his refrigerator. "Anybody want a beer?"

"I'll take one," Gabe called out. North grabbed two bottles and twisted the lids, passing one to Gabe as he walked back into the living room. All five of them had gathered at North's ranch house again.

"We have wine," Everley said, smiling at him. "We started without you."

Alaska was sitting next to the fire, her legs curled beneath her. She'd been the last to arrive, waiting for her shift at reception to be over, and had made herself a hot chocolate rather than share Holly and Everley's wine.

"So, Holly has something to tell you." Everley was trying not to grin. She was finding the situation with Josh hilarious, much to Holly's embarrassment.

"You do?" North took a sip of his beer. "What?"

Holly swallowed hard, her cheeks flaming. "I know who's buying the town."

"We all do. It's Gerber Enterprises." Gabe shot her a weird look.

Everley rolled her eyes. "She means, she knows the CEO. Josh Gerber. The guy who met with our parents today."

Gabe blinked. "How do you know him?"

Holly cleared her throat. This was actually more mortifying than she'd realized. If only she'd actually not recognized him. That would've been so much easier.

"Actually, you all know him," she said, looking down at her hands. "He stayed here around eight years ago. Remember the Christmas my mom flew to Barbados to be with that guy and left me on my own?"

"When you were still in college?" North frowned.

"Yeah."

Gabe took a mouthful of beer, swallowing it down. "So wait, he was here for Christmas? With his family or something?"

"His car broke down. We were fully booked so I let him stay in my cabin," Holly said, shifting on the sofa. It was way too hot in here. "He stayed for two days. Helped us with the Christmas Eve charity singalong."

North's brows pinched together. He ran a finger along his jaw. "Wait," he said, his voice low. "This isn't the guy I..."

"You punched him." Everley was trying not to laugh. "Because you thought he was trying to take advantage of Holly."

North looked like he'd been punched himself. He looked at Holly, who gave him a shrug. "Are you sure it's the same guy?" he asked her.

"Certain." How could she forget those eyes? Or those lips, dammit. Ugh, what a mess. She had no idea why she pretended not to know him when they were introduced earlier. It was a split second decision. Maybe it was pride, but she didn't want him to know that she still thought about that night sometimes.

Or the fact that he walked out of her life on Christmas morning and never once tried to contact her.

"Damn." North leaned back on his chair, shaking his head.

"I can't believe you hit him." Gabe was trying not to laugh. "Why the hell did you do that?"

North's eyes flickered to Holly's. She swallowed hard. "It was a misunderstanding," she said, her voice thick. "He thought Josh had seduced me."

"He had your panties in his pocket. I jumped to conclusions." North grimaced at the memory.

"He had your panties?" Gabe's eyebrows shot up. "Why did he have those?"

Holly sighed. "It was Rudolph's fault." Rudolph had been the Inn's resident Saint Bernard. A shaggy, friendly, and surprisingly lazy dog who spent most of his time sleeping under Holly's bed when she stayed in the cabins. He'd passed over the rainbow bridge six years ago, but he was still a legend in town. "He found them under my bed and gave them to Josh. He'd hid them in his pocket so he didn't look like an asshole. But then everything went to hell and North overreacted."

"I did *not* overreact. You were twenty. I was protecting your virtue." North had the good grace to look ashamed.

Everley bit down a grin. "You did the opposite, actually. After you hit him, Holly took him back to her cabin and we didn't see either of them all night."

North frowned, putting his fingers to his temple like he was in pain. "I really don't want to know."

That was good, because Holly didn't want him to know, either. He was her cousin and she loved him but there was no way she was discussing her love life with him.

Holly exhaled heavily. "I just wanted to tell you that this guy has a connection with Winterville and with us. In case it helps."

"Do you think this is some kind of revenge?" Alaska asked, her voice soft. "For North hitting him?"

"I have no idea." Holly shook her head.

"What do we know about his company?" Gabe asked. "Gerber Enterprises, right?"

"Holly Googled it as soon as they left the Inn," Everley told him.

"They're a multi billion dollar company. Privately owned and funded." Holly moistened her lips with the tip of her tongue. "They have fingers in lots of pies, but their real estate division specializes in buying land to sell for development. Particularly large estates or resorts."

"So they're like a middle man?" North said, his eyes on Holly.

"That's a nicer description than I'd give them, but yeah, that's essentially it."

"What's a less nice description?" North asked.

Holly put her wine glass down on the table in front of her. "They're like corporate raiders for land acquisitions rather than businesses."

"You're gonna have to put that in words of one syllable," Gabe said, pointing at his chest. "Jock over here."

"Have you seen the movie *Pretty Woman*?" Holly tipped her head to the side. She had no idea if Gabe had even heard of it.

"The one with Julia Roberts?" Gabe asked.

She tried to hide her surprise. "Yeah, that's the one."

"Don't look so shocked. I've dated a lot of women. And some of them love chick flicks." He shrugged. "Anyway, I kind of enjoyed it. Especially that piano scene."

Everley sniggered.

Holly took a breath, ignoring Gabe. "So, Richard Gere's character is a corporate raider. He buys up companies, tears them apart, and makes a profit by selling them in pieces to other companies."

Gabe nodded. "Yeah, I remember. Except Julia Roberts persuaded him otherwise."

Everley grinned. "That's the power of the pu—"

Holly cleared her throat. "As I was saying, Gerber Enterprises is a bit like that."

"But how do you pull a town apart?" Gabe asked, shaking his head. Next to him, North was leaning forward, his fingers steepled. He was looking intently at Holly.

"They don't. They level it. Make it ready for development." Holly pulled her lip between her teeth. "Then sell it to a developer."

North's eyes met hers. He knew exactly what she was trying to tell them. She could see the clouds darkening his gaze. "Grandma should never have left this town to our parents," he said thickly.

Holly gave him a half smile. "No, she shouldn't have."

He closed his eyes for a moment. "Dammit."

"So, what do we do now?" Gabe asked.

Holly picked up the wine bottle and refilled her glass, passing it to Everley. "They've signed the contract. Technically, there's nothing we can do."

"But it's Grandma's town. Her dream." Alaska's voice wobbled. "They can't just raze it to the ground."

"We don't know they're going to do that," Gabe pointed out.

"What else are they going to do?" Everley asked him. "Paint a few fences and hope somebody gives them double what they paid?"

"Well there's nothing we can do right now." North raked his hands through his hair again, his eyes catching Holly's. "We'll go to this meeting they're holding tomorrow and see what they have to say."

❄ 6 ❄

The crowd outside the Jingle Bell Theater was lively and talkative. Old friends hugged each other, while long-timers gossiped about grandchildren and how much they were looking forward to seeing them at Christmas. Holly joined North and Everley at the edge of the hoard who were slowly entering through the open double doors, and rubbed her hands to get some circulation back into them.

"Where are Alaska and Gabe?" she asked them.

"Gabe's on a conference call with his coach," North told her. "I promised to update him afterward."

"And Alaska took an extra shift at the Inn." Everley shook her head, though her expression was soft. "But we all know she just hates conflict. She said she barely slept last night."

The three of them shuffled forward, saying hello to the town's residents that recognized them. Every single one of them asked how they were doing without their grandma. Their concern warmed Holly's heart.

"Why aren't they talking about the meeting?" Holly asked quietly, when they reached the foyer.

46

"Because they don't know about the sale." North shook his head. "Our parents haven't had the guts to tell them."

There were black and white photographs on the dusty, paint peeling walls, reflecting the various revues Candy had held over the years. Famous stars mixed with local actors and singers, all of them smiling at Candy as she stood in the center of them.

The three of them took seats at the end of the fifth row. There was a lectern on the stage, along with microphones and chairs arranged for the speakers.

"If they don't know about the sale, what do they think this meeting is about?" Everley whispered across to North.

"No idea." North shrugged.

"Those aren't our microphones." Everley frowned at the equipment on stage. "Unless Grandma bought new ones before passing."

"I saw an audio visual van parked outside the stage door," North said. "Looked pretty swanky."

Of course it did. It was paid for by Gerber Enterprises. Holly knew from her research that they only used the best.

Looking around the theater, she took a deep breath. Every seat was occupied. She could see Dolores from the Cold Fingers Café on the other side, sitting next to Charlie Shaw from the Cold Start Garage along with the owners of the Mistletoe Gift Shop and the Frozen Perfection Spa. Dolores lifted her hand to wave, and Holly waved back.

Folding her hands in her lap, she looked up at the stage, right as her uncles and mom walked out onto it. All three of them looked nervous.

The two businesspeople she'd seen at the Inn followed them. She couldn't remember their names but she knew they were with Gerber Enterprises.

And then *he* walked out of the wings, and her breath caught in her throat.

Josh Gerber stood stock still in the center of the stage. The conversation in the hall hushed completely as people's gazes were drawn to him.

He looked powerful standing there alone. And it wasn't his perfectly fitting navy suit, that only seemed to enhance the strong muscles that she knew lay beneath. Nor the way his gray blue eyes scanned the room as though he could read every thought in the auditorium. No, it was more than that.

It was charisma.

The first time she'd met Josh he'd been softer. Warmer. But this man exuded a raw strength that made her mouth turn as dry as the desert. It made her skin tingle, too.

She knew men like him. She'd met them over and over again in her job. Men who thought they were above the law, or social norms. Men who always wanted to win, no matter the cost.

He ran the tip of his tongue over his bottom lip, his eyes still scanning the room. And then they landed on her.

She held herself perfectly still, staring right back at him, unwilling to waver or show any hint of weakness.

His face was impassive, his body relaxed. But then she saw a tick in his jaw and she knew that he felt it, too.

This weird, unwanted pull. The knowledge that once upon a time his bare skin had pressed against hers.

"Hol, you're staring," North whispered.

"Of course she is. He's so damn beautiful," Everley said, sounding wistful. "And he's staring back at her."

Holly pushed her shoulders back, willing the heat to stop flooding her skin. Not once had anybody looked at her like that. Sure, she'd had boyfriends, and that one brush with marriage that they all wanted to forget, but never anything like this.

This was a pure power play.

The corner of Josh's lip pulled up. He was smiling? *Why*

was he smiling? Holly tried not to frown, but it was a losing battle. What had he seen in her eyes that amused him?

"Ladies and gentlemen, thank you for joining us today." Josh didn't lean into the microphone. He held himself straight and tall, keeping eye contact with the crowd at all times. "I'd like to introduce us all to you. Of course you know the Winter family. Noel, Joseph, and Susannah, Candy Winter's children." He flashed a smile at them, though it didn't reach his eyes. "And I'm so pleased to see some of her grandchildren have joined us, too."

Everybody turned to look at Holly, North, and Everley. Holly glanced at North. "Now they'll think we're involved in this, too," she said to him.

"I know." North's voice was grim. "He's doing it on purpose."

"My name is Joshua Gerber. I'm the CEO of Gerber Enterprises, and these two people are Kevin Carter and Elizabeth Norton, who both work for me at the company." He nodded at his employees. "We're here today to talk about the future of Winterville." He glanced at the young woman standing in front of him. "Elizabeth, can we run the promotional video please?"

She nodded, and whispered something to somebody in the wings. The next moment, the huge screen behind Josh lit up with an oversize blue and gold logo, Gerber Enterprises splashed across the white.

Then a voiceover began.

"Forty years ago, Candy Winter built this town from nothing." Black and white photographs depicting the town's construction flashed across the screen, an old 1970s recording of Candy was spliced in.

"Winterville isn't about looking back," she said, a distinctive southern twang in her voice. "It's about looking forward. It's about living a twentieth century life. I'm not sentimental,

I don't have time to be. I just want the best for this town and the people who live in it."

Holly swallowed. It was hard to watch.

"This is a good production," Everley whispered. "Expensive, too."

Holly nodded grimly.

There were more images. Of the town as it was in the 1970s. Of Candy's productions here in the Jingle Bell Theater. Of the cousins running around in the Inn. Of Candy laughing at her grandchildren.

"Our parents gave them these photos," Holly said, her brow pinching and eyes welling.

"Yeah, well we already knew they were traitors." North shook his head.

A recording of Candy came on again, but this time she was older. It could only have been recorded a few years ago. She still had that timeless beauty, though. "I never want time to stand still here," she was saying. "This isn't an old fashioned village that stands still. It's a living, thriving community. We keep moving on and we keep adapting."

"Elizabeth," Josh murmured. "Let's pause it here." The screen paused on Candy smiling out at them all.

Josh looked out at the residents. They were staring raptly back at him. "This town was built by a strong, visionary woman," he told them. "And though her loss is mourned, her work and her words live on. And we've been working with the Winter family to move Candy's vision into the twenty-first century. I'd like to show you a little of what that vision looks like." He nodded to Elizabeth again. Candy's face faded from the screen, replaced with a mock-up image of a ski resort on the mountain.

"I never want time to stand still here." Candy's words echoed out again. "We keep moving on and we keep adapting."

A fury washed over Holly. They were using her grandma's words to trample over her dream. And her mom and uncles were letting them.

She leaned forward, as though about to stand. North put a hand on her arm. "Be cool," he whispered.

She glanced out of the corner of her eye. Everybody was staring blissfully at the screen, as images of ski slopes and state of the art chalets flashed up on the screen, a smooth voiceover explaining all the details. No trace of the Winterville charm remained. It was clear her grandma's town had no place in their future vision.

"We invite you on a journey. A journey to the future of Winterville," the voiceover said.

Holly rolled her eyes. When she looked up, Josh's gaze was on her again.

The final image came on the screen. Her grandma, surrounded by her family. Then it faded away.

Everybody started clapping. Holly and her cousins looked around in horror. Why the hell were they applauding their town being destroyed?

Josh was smiling. "We have brochures that we'll be giving out to each and every one of you that will detail the plans we've made and the next stages," Josh told them. "And of course, we're more than happy to answer any questions. Maybe we can start right now?"

Charlie Shaw put up his hand.

"Yes sir?" Josh asked. Somebody ran down the aisle to put a microphone to Charlie's mouth.

"When will this be happening?"

"Well, that depends on a few things, but we want to start the build early in the new year."

Somebody else put their hand up, and the usher took the microphone to them.

"Will it still be called Winterville?"

Josh smiled. "Of course. We'd never want to change the name."

A third hand shot into the air. This time it was Dolores. "What are your plans for eating establishments?" she asked.

"That's still under consideration." Josh gave her an easy, reassuring smile. "But anybody who makes pastries like you do will always be in demand here."

"What a crock of shit," Everley murmured.

Swallowing hard, Holly shot her hand up. Moments later, the usher was holding a microphone toward her. Holly took it, standing and facing the stage. She watched as Uncle Noel leaned forward to whisper something to her mom, who shook her head.

"Holly Winter, you have a question?" Josh stared right at her. It felt like a challenge. She straightened her spine, and held the microphone to her lips.

"What will happen to the town square?"

His gaze was steady. "We'll be upgrading it."

"Does that mean you'll be knocking the buildings down? What will happen to the establishments there?"

"As I explained, there'll be some redevelopment going on. Some establishments will be rebuilt, others will be assisted with relocation. But we'll be working with all the owners to make sure we get it right."

There was a frisson between them. His stare was unwavering, making her feel heated. Needy. She blinked, trying to ignore the electricity.

"How long will it take for you to rebuild or relocate the establishments?"

For the first time his smile wavered. His gaze didn't though. "We're still determining that."

She tipped her head to the side, still looking right at him. "And in the meantime, there'll be no café. No garage, no gift shops, no spa? Just an empty parcel of land that you'll sell to whoever bids the most for it?"

A gasp echoed through the auditorium.

"We're not here to cause alarm, Miss Winter. I can assure you this will be good for the local population. Creating more jobs and a secure future." Damn he was smooth. Everybody relaxed back into their chairs.

"So it's not true that my family has sold the town to you, and you're planning to break it apart and sell it at a profit?" she asked him, her voice thick.

His eyes raked over her, dipping to her lips. There was a tick in his stupidly handsome jaw.

"You seem very emotional," Josh remarked lightly. "Kevin, perhaps you can take over the microphone, and I'll speak with Holly in private?"

She opened her mouth to say something, but the microphone was taken from her. She frowned at the usher, but he was already moving up the aisle to the next raised hand.

Josh Gerber had silenced her. She frowned, and looked over at her cousins.

"I'll be back," she said.

"Be careful," North said. "I don't like this." He glanced at Josh then back to her. "Do you want me to come punch him again?"

Holly tried not to laugh, "Yeah, well I don't much like *him*. And it's okay, I've got this." She grabbed her purse and coat and headed toward the exit. If Josh wanted a fight, he could have it.

As she made her way down the aisle, she heard Everley's murmured reply.

"Of course she likes him. She couldn't take her eyes off him."

7

Holly walked along the hallway toward him, her dark waves bouncing against her shoulders as she came closer. Her brows were pinched together, and he had to bite down a smile.

The cat had claws.

"You're angry," he murmured as she came to a stop in front of him. She was close enough for him to smell her fragrance. Flowery and sweet. She tipped her head to the side, and he couldn't help but follow the fine line of her jaw.

"I'm not angry. I'm disbelieving. And from somebody who's seen a lot of divorces, don't *ever* call a woman emotional. That's a free tip. No need to thank me." Holly's expression was grim.

Josh's lips twitched. She'd been pretty eight years ago, but now she'd grown into her beauty. She had this way of holding herself that made him want to touch her, to make her sigh, to see what it would be like to see the softer side of Holly Winter.

The side he knew for certain existed eight years ago.

He tipped his head to the side. "You have questions. Ask me them."

"Why wouldn't you answer them in front of the audience?" she asked him. "Don't they deserve to know the truth, too?"

"The truth that I'm trying to save this town?"

She blinked. "No you're not. You're trying to push everybody out to make a profit. I've looked up your company. I know what you do."

A weird thrill shot through him. "You Googled me."

She stared defiantly up at him. "Yes."

"That's interesting. I Googled you, too."

The thick lashes that shadowed her cheeks flew up. "What did you discover?"

"That you're a caped crusader without a cape. That you like to fight for the underdog, even if the underdog just wants to go home and have a good sleep." He gave her a half smile. "I also discovered something else." He stepped closer, his eyes on hers. "We're more alike than you think."

"I'm nothing like you." She spoke with a quiet firmness.

Josh's eyes flickered to her pretty mouth. "We both make money from destruction. The only difference is, your destruction involves people."

Her jaw tightened. "I'm paid for what I do because I'm good at it. I'm good at protecting women from men like you. Men who wield too much power. Who take without giving."

Josh held himself still, even though it felt like he'd been slapped in the face. "Is that what you think of me?"

She pulled her lip between her teeth, as though embarrassed by her outburst. "I don't think anything. I don't know you." The anger had melted from her voice.

"You seemed to know all about me a minute ago," he pointed out.

"All I know is that you're trying to destroy this town. For money."

He nodded slowly. "That's what you think. Okay."

She tensed visibly. "It's what I know."

His lips curled, though he felt no humor at all. "You think you know all about this place?"

"Of course I do. I grew up here."

He nodded. "And you're an accountant. Good with money, right?"

She didn't answer. Just looked at him with those deep chocolate eyes. A man could get lost in there if he wanted to.

"Maybe you're not as great of an accountant as you think," he said quietly. "Because if you were, you'd know this town is bankrupt. There's no money here. Your grandma kept it going for as long as she could, but the money's gone. The reason it's being sold is because your family has nothing left. Maybe if you were half as good with numbers as you think you are, you would have known this."

She shook her head. "That's not true."

He shrugged. "Go ask them. Your mom and uncles. Or go talk to the people running businesses here. Take a look at the houses people rent, hell, look at this theater." He gestured behind him. "It's falling apart. Sure, the cracks are covered with tinsel and flashing lights, but when they're gone, there's nothing left. Without my company and my money, this town will dwindle to nothing. So you might want to think about that before you start accusing me of selling out."

She blinked, her bottom lip trembling.

"I should go." For the first time she sounded uncertain.

He reached for her arm, feeling like a bastard. "Holly, I..."

She shook her head. "I'm sorry. I need to get out of here."

She turned on her heel, and flew down the hallway as quick as she'd came. But instead of being all fire and ice, she looked defeated.

When he turned to walk back to the main theater, he saw Elizabeth standing there.

"Everything okay?"

She nodded. "Kevin's answering the last question. Did you want to come on stage and make any closing remarks?"

He shook his head. "No, I don't. I think we're done here."

"I don't understand how we didn't know," Holly said. "Why didn't Grandma tell us the money had run out? We could have helped. I'm an accountant, I could have looked at places to get efficiencies." She looked up at North, who was leaning against his breakfast counter.

"She hid it from all of us." North blew out a mouthful of air. "I'm the one who was here the whole time. If anyone should've noticed, it should've been me."

"Why would you have noticed? On the surface nothing changed." Everley cradled her mug of coffee between her hands. "She just kept pumping in money so the town continued going fine."

"Until there was no more money left." Holly sighed, looking out of North's window to the valleys beyond. Slopes of Christmas trees stretched as far as the eye could see. North owned all the land and all the trees, along with his business partner, Amber Stone. Holly could see her in the distance, dealing with some customers. It was prime Christmas tree buying time – North should be out there working right now.

Instead he was in here, trying to work out with them how things went so wrong.

"Are you sure he was telling you the truth?" Everley asked Holly.

She nodded. "I talked to Dolores after the meeting was

over. She's hardly getting by, has been since visitor numbers went down a few years ago. Charlie Shaw's making a loss, but he's riding the wave until retirement. And the spa and bookshop have been looking at closure. They're kind of relieved that there's an end in sight."

"Why didn't they come to us?" North asked.

"They didn't want to worry Grandma while she was so ill. And then they didn't want to make a fuss after she died. And when they finally went to see our parents, they were assured that a plan was in operation to make everything better." Holly glanced down at North's beautifully tiled floor. "What they didn't say was that it involved the businesses getting bulldozed for a ski resort."

Gabe sighed loudly. He'd joined them after his conference call. "So what do we do next?"

"What can we do?" Everley asked. "It's over. There's no legal recourse, and even if there was, we couldn't make it work financially."

"We don't know that for sure." Gabe glanced at Holly. "You work with some lawyers. Can't they help with the legal side?"

"They're divorce lawyers. But I could ask them to look at the contract. Even if they can't help, they probably have contacts that do."

"Okay then." Gabe nodded.

"It's not even a long shot," Holly added, because she didn't want to give them false hope. "Even if we could get out of the contract, it would involve our parents paying Gerber Enterprises back the money. And we all know they won't do that."

"We could raise the money," Everley suggested.

"Not that much money, honey." North ruffled her hair.

"What if we paid in installments? Or got a loan of some kind?" Gabe asked.

"No bank's going to give a loan to a failing town." Holly

gave him a soft smile, to take away the sting. "And I can't see Gerber Enterprises letting us pay in installments."

"They might if a certain CEO was persuadable," Everley murmured.

North looked at her with interest. "What do you mean?"

"Didn't you see the way Josh was looking at Holly? And that whole caveman thing of meeting her at the back of the auditorium? He's got a thing for her. It's obvious." Everley folded her arms across her chest. "I bet Holly could persuade him to do anything."

"Dear God, no." North shook his head, a grimace pulling at his face. "That's not happening."

"Do I get consulted on this?" Holly asked.

"You should listen to him," Gabe said. "He's right. Don't go messing around with this guy, Holly. He's the enemy. And you're way too nice, you'll end up feeling sorry for him."

"No I won't." The last person she felt sorry for was Josh Gerber. What was it he called her? A caped crusader without a cape. Hah. He really was a handsome asshole.

North's phone started to buzz. He lifted it to his ear, his voice curt as he answered some questions. Ending the call quickly, he glanced over at Gabe. "Amber's getting overrun at the store. Want to come with and help for a couple of hours?"

"Sure." Gabe nodded. "Let me just get my boots."

North turned to Everley and Holly, who were finishing the coffee he'd made them. "I'll catch you two later. And I meant what I said, no messing around with this stuff. And no getting close to Josh Gerber. We'll do this thing properly, okay?"

"Sure." Holly nodded.

Everley waited for him to walk out of the door, and for Gabe to follow him, the two of them climbing onto snowmobiles and heading down toward the Christmas Tree Store.

"You're going to at least try, aren't you?" Everley asked, her brows lifting. "Get closer to Josh Gerber and help us find a way to stop him?"

"I can't think of anything else to do." Holly felt her skin warm at the thought of confronting Josh again.

Everley grinned. "That's my girl. And what North doesn't know won't hurt him."

"We must stop meeting like this." Josh's voice was a warm caress. It was just after six the next morning, and Holly was standing outside the Cold Fingers Café. Her breath was turning to vapor in the frosty air.

Josh was wearing a gray woolen coat that skimmed his broad chest. Why was it that he looked like he'd just stepped off the cover of GQ, while she felt like something the cat had dragged in?

"Are you still in town?" Holly asked him, her voice light. "I thought you would have scurried back home already."

"Why's that?" He tipped his head to the side.

"I assumed you'd prefer to watch the destruction from afar." Her eyes were sparkling. "Emotions and misery don't seem like your thing. I'm guessing you prefer cool, hard dollars."

She pushed the door open, and the bell rang as warm air rushed over her. The sound of Christmas music echoed from the speakers.

The windows of the café were covered with garland, with tiny fairy lights sparkled among the greenery. A tall Christmas tree was covered with decorations that customers had brought in and added to over the years, and on the far side the owner, Dolores, had lit the fire, so it would be ready for her early morning customers.

But the tables were all empty. She knew Frank would come in soon, but would there be more customers today?

Holly was all too aware that empty tables meant empty cash registers.

"Good morning. What can I get you?" Dolores beamed over the counter at them, not blinking an eyelid as Josh stood only a couple of inches away from Holly.

She could smell the deep notes of his cologne. What was it about the way he smelled? It made her muscles clench in a way that wasn't right this early in the morning.

"An Americano to go, please?"

Josh interrupted her. "I'll get this. And she'll drink it in here."

Okay, so he didn't smell *that* good. She opened her mouth to berate him, then remembered she was supposed to be getting closer to him.

"It's okay, I'll pay for my own," she said, passing a five dollar bill over to Dolores, before stalking to a table by the fire. She sat on a chair with her back to the counter, but that didn't stop her from hearing Josh's reply.

"Put the five in the tip jar. I've got this."

She swallowed down her annoyance.

She had no idea why he brought the snark out in her. She wasn't usually like this.

"I think you remember me." Josh slid her coffee in front of her, pulling out the chair opposite hers. He sat down, stretching out his long legs so his calves were almost brushing hers.

"What?"

"You definitely remember me from all those years ago. But I'm trying to figure out why you keep pretending you don't."

He had something in his right hand. He was turning it over in his palm.

"What's that?" she asked, pointing at it, grateful not to be talking about her sketchy memory any more.

He slid his hand into his pocket. "Nothing."

Yep, he was definitely aggravating. "If it's nothing, then show me," Holly said.

He smiled. "No."

"Then I don't remember you. At all."

He smiled as though he was enjoying himself. "Do you still like butterflies?"

She took a sip of her coffee. "What makes you ask?"

"I still think about your butterfly panties sometimes. I regret throwing them in the dumpster. I should have kept them."

A flush stole over her body, and it had nothing to do with the fire. "Why would you have kept my panties? That's a freaky thing to do."

His eyes met hers. "Because they'd be a memento. Of the best night of your life."

"Of *my* life?" Her brows lifted. "Are we talking about the night I don't remember?"

"You remember." He sounded so sure.

"Why would I remember? It had to be pretty banal since it's completely wiped out of my memory."

He leaned in, his voice sugary and low. "Because I made you come three times. And you begged for more."

She opened her mouth to say something, then closed it again. After taking a sip of her coffee, Holly decided on, "Maybe I was faking."

"Nope."

"You think you can tell when a woman is faking?" she asked him.

He moved his legs, his calves pressing against hers. "Is this when you go all Harry and Sally on me and fake an orgasm in the café? Because I have to tell you, I'd be up for that."

She eyed him carefully. "I don't think you could even induce a fake one right now."

"I'm wounded." He touched his chest with his palms.

He was enjoying this. And in a weird way, so was she. It felt good to duel with somebody who knew exactly how to fight back. And if he was the target of all her frustration right now? Well, he deserved it.

And she had a feeling he could take it.

"Why are you so insistent on me remembering that night?" She ran her finger over the rim of her coffee cup. "Have you been jonesing after me for, what, seven or eight years now?"

"Eight. And yes, every night I cry into my pillow and send a plea up to the stars that you'll finally come looking for me." He focused his gaze on hers. "I've thought about nothing but you for every moment of every day for the past eight years." The sarcasm in his voice was cutting. She bit down a laugh.

"And now you're going to destroy my town because it's the only way to get me out of your head?"

He grinned. "It's like you're reading my mind. I'm going to offer this place up as a sacrifice to the gods. Destroy it and along with my memories of you. It's the only way I can survive. But you're wrong about one thing. It's not your town, it's mine."

"Tomayto-tomahto." She tipped her head to the side, taking a sip of the steaming coffee. "You know I'm going to fight you, right?"

"I was pretty sure you would. But it's futile. I always win."

"Not always. You didn't win me."

"Who says?"

She swallowed hard. "I do."

He folded his arms over his chest. "You remember me. You know you do." His voice was soft. "I'm going to get you to admit it."

"I'll lie and say I do if you'll give me my town back." She lifted a brow.

"Not going to happen. I told you I always win."

"You won't win my memories." She inhaled slowly. She could feel the warm pressure of his calves against hers.

For a moment, her mind was full of that night. His warm lips against hers, the hard weight of his body as they tangled together – underwear on, because somehow that made it better. The warmth of his skin as he touched her again and again, with a teasing pressure that took her to the edge.

"Are you thinking about it now? Because I am."

"I'm thinking about how pissed you'll be when you lose everything you have." She flashed him a smile. "And how much I'm going to enjoy it. I might even take a photo of your face and have it framed."

"I'd be happy to pose any time. I assume you'll be putting it right next to your bed."

"I have enough nightmares already." She finished the last dregs of her coffee. "But thank you for the offer."

His eyes dipped to her lips. "You have nightmares?"

She leaned forward, her voice dropping. "Yes, I do." He leaned in too, as though he was trying to hear her. "I keep getting these images in my brain of some strange guy stealing my panties and climbing into my bed. It's disconcerting." She put her cup down and stood, pulling her coat on and sliding her hat over her tumbling curls. "Goodbye, Mr. Gerber. Have a safe trip home. Don't crash your car or anything."

He started to laugh. "You definitely remember."

"It's a shame you'll never know. When are you leaving town anyway?"

"Later today." He paused. "Probably."

She slid her gloves on. "Well, it's been a ball." She turned on her heel, waving goodbye to Dolores before glancing over her shoulder at him one more time.

His eyes were trained on her, that stupid smirk still playing at his lips.

Pulling at the door, she inhaled sharply, glad for the blast of ice cold air that snaked against her skin.

He was leaving today. That was a good thing. She was all big talk and bravado when she told Everley she'd have no problem getting close to him, because this confrontation felt dangerous.

Not because of Josh. But because of herself. She enjoyed it more than she should have. And nobody knew better than she did that it would all end in tears.

❧ 8 ❧

"What do you mean one of us should stay here?" Kevin's eyes widened. "I can't stay. I'll miss my son's Christmas Concert. My wife will kill me."

"I know." Josh nodded. "You should definitely go home. You can't miss that."

"And I need Elizabeth to stand in for me at a meeting. It's all day tomorrow. I can't find and brief somebody else in that short of time."

Josh put his hand on Kevin's arm. The man looked like he was going to have a tantrum. "It's okay, I have it covered. I'll stay. You two can leave."

Kevin blinked. "*You'll* stay?"

"That's what I said."

"But..." Kevin frowned, forming a thick monobrow above his disbelieving eyes. "Why would you stay here? You have an empire to run."

"Because I don't trust the Winter family to behave while we're gone. And this deal is too important to have them mess it up now. And anyway, I can still run the business from here. There's this little thing they invented called the internet. I can still attend meetings and send emails from the living room."

"But you hate Zoom. That's why we don't let people work from home."

"I also hate losing millions on deals that can easily be saved." Josh shrugged. "It's a few days. Maybe a week or two at the most. I can handle it."

Kevin glanced at the two overnight bags he and Elizabeth had put by the door. "You're sure."

"I'm sure."

"What about the car? If we take it you'll be without one."

Josh glanced out of the glass pane in the front door. "Willa has arranged for a car service to take you back." A black sedan turned into the driveway at that moment. "Here it is now." He loved it when a plan came together. "Now go, I have this handled. Enjoy your kid's concert. And Elizabeth, you did a great job here. I'm impressed."

She smiled shyly. "Thank you."

"Are you sure about this?" Kevin asked. "It's just... weird. And out of character."

"Thank you for your hard work."

Once the pair were out of the door and he'd heard the car pull away, Josh walked over to the table where he'd set up his office, letting out a sigh of relief. He'd asked Willa to extend the rental until Christmas. He was sure he didn't need all that time, but it was worth extending just in case.

It also gave him enough time to secure the deal and make sure the Winter family wasn't conspiring against him.

And enough time to figure out why Holly Winter insisted on pretending she couldn't remember him. It was grating at him, and he had no idea why. It was obvious she remembered him. She'd almost admitted to it at the café, after all.

I keep getting these images in my brain of some strange guy stealing my panties and climbing into my bed. It's disconcerting.

His lips curled at the memory of her soft, teasing voice and her wide, mock-disbelieving eyes. What was it about her? She did things to him just by opening those pretty lips.

She made him want things he had no business wanting. Things that made him feel more alive than he'd felt in years. About eight years, to be exact.

He opened his laptop and logged in, thanking the Gods of the World Wide Web that whoever owned this place had a booster installed in every room. Typing in his log in details, he wasn't surprised when a chat box appeared on his screen.

WILLA MARKS: Are you there, Joshua? Your grandfather keeps calling. Says he can't get through on your cell phone.

Willa was the only person at work who called him Joshua. It had taken him two years to stop her from calling him Mr. Gerber. He didn't have the heart to invest any more time in training her to call him Josh.

JOSH GERBER: Reception is patchy here. I'll call him when I get a chance.

Lies, all lies. He'd blocked his grandfather's number because he didn't have the energy to deal with the old man right now. He'd unblock it on the way home. When everything was back to normal, and Winterville was a forgotten project.

. . .

WILLA MARKS: Do you want me to check which provider has the best coverage? I can get you switched over in an instant.

His lips twitched at Willa's suggestion. *Busted.*

JOSH GERBER: No need. I won't be here long. If my grandfather calls again, tell him everything is under control.

WILLA MARKS: I already did. He doesn't believe me. But I'll try again. In the meantime, I've cancelled a few of your face to face meetings, and put the rearranged dates in your calendar. I've also changed the ones you asked me to teleconferences. There are a few urgent emails to check in your inbox – I've flagged them. And your grandma wants to know what you're doing for Christmas.

Working, probably. Or sleeping. Maybe both. His family didn't really celebrate Christmas. Or at least his grandfather didn't, which meant that nobody else should either.

He typed back quickly.

JOSH GERBER: I'll call her later.

WILLA MARKS: You're a good boy.

. . .

He grinned at her description. He was neither good, nor a boy, but he wasn't going to disabuse her of her impressions. Even if his reasons for staying here for the next few days were pretty bad.

He closed the chat and pulled up a browser window, typing quickly into the search bar.

Holly Winter

Yeah, he'd Googled her before. But now he could do it without Kevin or Elizabeth in the vicinity.

Leaning back in his chair, arms folded behind his head, he watched as the results loaded up. She was such an attractive woman. And a worthy opponent. His lips curled into a grin. Let the battle commence.

It was Everley's idea to hand out flyers to the townspeople, as well as to staple posters on every available surface in the town square. Holly smirked at the words written across the front. Winterville Against Redevelopment, WAR for short. It was stupid and pointless, but it made Everley happy.

Which was always a good thing. Because a happy Everley was always fun to be with, and she was exactly the kind of distraction Holly needed. Sure, her cousin was a little attention seeker when she was younger – the towns-folk used to call her Mini Candy – but she'd calmed down a little now.

"I can't wait for those assholes to find these," Everley said, standing back to admire her work. There were posters every-where, WAR standing out against the red brick buildings and windows. It looked strangely incongruous considering it was Christmas time.

"In that case, you should post them on Instagram, because they've already left."

"What?" Everley frowned. "When did that happen?"

"This morning. Charlie Shaw said one of those big black sedans came to pick them up. He saw it pass at about eleven."

"And Josh too?"

Holly shrugged. "I guess so." And she was glad, she really was. Sure, sparring with him this morning had been fun, but he was a distraction. She'd spent more time thinking about how to rile him up than how she was going to help save this town. Now that he was gone she could take a deep dive into the accounts and talk to her lawyer friend who she'd sent the contracts to. Figure out if there was a possible way to stop this deal from going through.

"Oh." Everley looked crestfallen. "I didn't think he would. I guess our plan of getting you close to him won't work."

"No." Thank God, because it was definitely a double edged sword. "Anyway, this is a good thing," Holly reminded her. "They won't be here to stop us from posting these things everywhere. Or to come to our meeting tomorrow." They'd asked everybody to come to the Jingle Bell Theater again, this time to set up their resistance.

"I really liked the idea of you being our inside man."

Holly tucked the fliers under her arm. "That was never going to happen. I know I was all pumped up about it, but let's face it, he just wants his money. I'll never persuade him otherwise."

"He likes you."

"He's aggravated by me," Holly corrected her.

"And you like him." Everley pointed out.

Holly laughed. "Now I really know you're going crazy. Did you hit your head on the printer when you made these fliers?

Leave the day dreaming to Alaska, we're the hard nosed women of the family."

"I'm still a hard nosed woman." Everley gave her a smile. "But I also think it's so sweet that he came back for you."

"He didn't come back for me. He came back to bulldoze our town square to the ground." Holly ignored the little thrill shooting through her at Everley's words. "And he left just as quickly as he arrived, so I don't think it had anything to do with me."

Everley's smile melted. "Maybe I was just hoping that one of us would have something nice happen."

Holly slid her gloved hand into her cousin's, squeezing it tightly. "We agreed romance died when we were twenty-one, remember?"

"And that neither of us were suited for marriage." Everley sighed. "I remember."

"So what's changed?"

"Nothing." Everley shook her head. "I'm just being silly. Maybe the thought of this place disappearing is making me sentimental."

"Maybe Josh coming back has reminded you of your own past," Holly suggested. "And the one who got away."

Their eyes connected, and Holly gave her a soft smile. She knew the ins and outs of Everley's past, the same way Everley knew hers. They both wore their scars on the inside.

And they made them stronger, not weaker

"Do you think this could work?" Everley asked, eyeing the fliers Holly was holding.

"Probably not." Holly sighed.

"We have to try though, don't we?"

"Yeah," Holly said. "We do."

Everley looked up, her eyes widening as she glanced over Holly's shoulder. A slow smile curled at her lips. "Maybe we've got them on the run more than we thought," she said, her voice low.

"What do you mean?"

"Look." Everley's smile widened, as Holly turned to follow the direction of her cousin's stare.

That's when she saw Josh Gerber, reading one of the fliers, his head tipped to the side. A breeze was lifting his thick, dark hair, as he lifted his phone to snap a photograph before pulling his phone to his ear.

"He didn't leave," Everley murmured. "Which means one of two things. Either he's more rattled by us than we thought."

"Or?" Holly looked at Josh again. He was walking off toward the café, his phone still to his ear, completely unaware they were watching him.

"Or he's stayed because of you." Everley clapped her hands. "Either way, I call that a win."

9

"I called to let you know that I'll be staying at the Regency for a few days, in case you need to call me," his grandma said.

Josh frowned. "Why are you in a hotel?" he asked his Grandma, still staring at the flier advertising a second town meeting. He'd leave it where it was, he'd already taken a photograph with his phone.

"Your grandfather is being difficult. I thought I'd give him a few days to huff and puff and get whatever it is out of his system."

"What kind of difficult?" His voice was low. A cold breeze was blowing through his hair.

"You know what he's like. He's throwing a fit because he can't get a hold of you and taking it out on everybody else. Thank heavens he can't drive himself to the airport otherwise he'd be halfway to you by now."

He squeezed his eyes shut. "I'll come home. You shouldn't have to deal with this."

"You'll do no such thing. That will only give him what he wants. Let him stew for a while, you're the one in charge.

Anyway, I could do with a lovely break. I have a facial booked in for this afternoon, and some of the girls are coming into the city to meet me for dinner this evening."

His grandma's friends were all in their early eighties, like his grandma herself. It made his lips twitch to hear her describe them as girls.

"Maybe you shouldn't go back."

"I'm eighty-three years old, sweetheart." His grandma sounded amused. "I'm not about to start a brand new life. And anyway, I love the stupid old man."

And wasn't that the kicker? It didn't matter how much of an asshole his grandfather was, he still had the devotion of a woman he didn't deserve. No matter how many times Josh had tried to get her to see a lawyer, or an apartment that was beautifully furnished, she wouldn't leave the man who sometimes got so angry he drove her out of her own home.

There was so much warmth in her voice. "Anyway, tell me about Winterville. Is it as pretty as it looks in the pictures?"

"I'm about to bulldoze it, Grandma."

"Stop it. No you aren't. You're about to make it better, the way you always do."

That was another thing about his grandma. It wasn't just his grandfather who basked in the glory of her devotion, Josh did too. She saw the good in everything, even when there was no good to be seen.

He had an inkling that if she was Satan's grandma, she'd go around telling people just how lovely it was that he kept everybody warm.

"Will you still be there for Christmas? It looks lovely at Christmas. You could eat dinner at the Winterville Inn. Do you know they gather around the tree and sing carols?"

Yeah, he knew. "I won't be here *that* long. And anyway, we don't celebrate Christmas."

"Yes we do. And anyway, you should have some fun. I'm

worried about you, darling. You're a workaholic like your grandfather. You need some time to relax."

He bristled at the comparison. "I'm relaxed. I'm not even wearing a tie. And I don't know how long it's going to take." Or how long he'd insist to himself he was only here for business, and not to make Holly Winter remember that one night they had together.

"Maybe you could go sledding," his grandma continued. "Are you going to decorate your rental house for the holidays? There's a Christmas tree farm nearby, it looks like so much fun."

"How much have you been studying this place?" Josh was trying not to laugh. He wouldn't be decorating anything.

"Your grandfather left some documents and brochures out. I took a look."

"Well, it's not like it used to be. The place has gotten a little downtrodden."

"That's because poor Candy Winter died. Did I tell you that I met her once? At a gala to raise money for childhood literacy. Oh my, the woman was a human dynamo. She managed to persuade Oscar Gentry to open his wallet, and everybody says the world will end when those demon moths escape."

Josh chuckled.

"Oh darling, I have to go. I just saw Mindy Latham walk past, and it looks like she's had some work done. I need to get all the details."

"Of course. Have a good break and I'll talk with you soon."

"Take care of yourself. And have *fun*. You might even like it."

He shook his head and ended the call, then sent a message to Willa, asking her to arrange a voice conference with his grandfather. It was one thing to avoid him, another if it caused his grandma pain.

He pushed open the door to the café. Dolores looked up and smiled as he walked in.

Why was she smiling at him? Surely she should be spitting in his coffee. He'd never understand the people around here.

"What can I get you?" she asked him.

He slid his phone into his pocket. "Is it okay that I'm here?" What was this sudden attack of conscience? She was a business woman, a customer was a customer. And yet he wanted her to say it was okay.

Dolores blinked, considering his question. "Of course it's okay," she said, reaching across the counter to pat his hand. The easy gesture made his throat feel tight. "You're a customer and every customer is a friend. And you look cold," she said, her voice full of warmth. "How about you go sit by the fire and I'll bring you over a coffee and pastry?"

"That sounds good." For heaven's sake, he was choking up, and he didn't like it one bit. He'd drink his coffee and eat the damn pastry then go back to his makeshift office in the rental home and concentrate on the plans for Winterville's future, and tomorrow's town meeting.

Josh rubbed his thumb against the stone in his pocket. Whether he liked it or not, he was a Gerber. And he didn't have a sentimental bone in his body. For the sake of his sanity, he was planning to keep it that way.

The next morning, Holly was staring at handwritten numbers, her finger skimming down the length of the paper until she hit the bottom. She'd like to say Dolores was the only business owner she knew that still kept handwritten books, but Holly knew for a fact that Charlie Shaw did the same for the Cold Start Garage. Maisie at the Spa would probably too, if her grandson hadn't set her up with a snazzy new laptop and accounting program he insisted she use.

"What's this entry?" she asked Dolores, pointing at a payment of two thousand dollars. It was quiet in the café – she was the first customer by far this morning. She'd arrived before Dolores had even unlocked the door.

Damn insomnia. At least by being here she wasn't thinking about a certain businessman with golden flecks in his eyes.

"That's my contribution to your grandma's medical bills." Dolores gave her the softest of smiles. "Your mom and uncles couldn't afford them, so we all agreed to help by paying more rent."

"They couldn't afford them." Holly's voice was monotone. "How much did your rent go up?"

Dolores looked surprised at the twisted expression on Holly's face. "We agreed to a thirty percent increase until the debt was paid off. Your poor family shouldn't have to pay for it all. Candy was always so good to us, so of course we wanted to give something back."

Candy always made sure she had kick ass medical insurance. It was something she'd instilled into Holly from a young age. "There are only three certainties in life," she'd say with a low drawl. "Birth, death, and hospital bills. You make sure you're ready for all three."

That hadn't stopped her mom and uncles from taking advantage of the goodwill of the community, though. Sure, their inheritance was less than they'd been expecting. And all three of them had expensive tastes. But to take from these good, good people then sell the town from under them?

It made her feel sick.

"You should stop paying them now," Holly told her. "And put that money aside for your retirement." Holly grabbed a piece of paper and scribbled a number. "If you could earn this much from the café would you continue working here?"

Dolores blinked at the number. "Of course I would. I'd like to hand things over to my son. You remember Reynolds, don't you? He separated from his wife last year and he can't work nights anymore now that he has shared custody of their children. He's taking work where he can, but it's no stability for those girls of his." She smiled softly at the thought of her granddaughters. "I hoped they'd all come live here with me. I'd take more time off and help look after them."

"Maybe things will change," Holly told her, swallowing when she looked at the numbers Dolores had scrawled down. "The fight isn't over yet. You're coming to the meeting tonight?"

"Yes I am." Dolores patted her hand. "I think it's very sweet that you and your cousins are trying to find a way to keep things as they are."

Holly didn't feel sweet. She felt helpless. "If you leave these books with me, I'll make some projections for you. And some suggestions on what you can do with your money if the sale goes through."

"You're a good girl." The bell above the door tinkled. "And now I'd better get to work. This town doesn't work without a good injection of caffeine and Christmas music."

The clip clop of Dolores' shoes echoed through the café as Holly leaned over the ledger, tapping on the calculator app on her phone and making swift notes on her pad. She was so absorbed in the calculations that she didn't realize somebody was behind her until the flier was slapped down on the table by a very big, masculine hand.

And then she smelled him. The familiar notes of woody spice made her spine tingle.

She turned, expecting him to have a furious expression on

his face. But instead there was a hint of a smile. Was it weird she felt almost disappointed about that?

"Good morning to you, too," she murmured.

"Coffee?"

"No thank you."

He hung his expensive gray wool coat on the hook beside the fireplace, then pulled out the chair opposite Holly's.

"Please sit down." She didn't bother to hide the sarcasm in her voice.

"Thanks." He smirked, stretching out his long legs and folding his arms across his crisp white shirt. "What are you doing?"

"I'm knitting a scarf."

He chuckled at her obvious lie. Holly looked up, exasperated. "Is there something I can help you with?"

"I was wondering if anybody can come to your show tonight." He pointed at the flier.

"Anybody, as in *you?*"

"Yep." His lips were still curled. Why did he have to be so damn happy? It made her feel crankier than ever.

"I thought you were leaving town."

Josh lifted his hands up, turning them over as though inspecting them. "Nope, still here."

"And why's that?" Her eyes rose to meet his. And no, there was no connection there. The electricity shooting through her body was probably static from the fire.

"Because I'm kind of liking it here in Winterville."

She tipped her head to the side, the ledger in front of her forgotten. "You are?"

"Yep. And now that I hear there's a show tonight, I'm glad I stayed."

Holly let out a frustrated sigh. "It's not a show, it's a protest meeting. A protest against your redevelopment."

"At my *own* theater."

"What?" Holly blinked.

"You're holding the protest meeting at the theater I own. In the town I own." He didn't look in the least perturbed by it, either. "So I guess I'm kind of interested in what happens next."

"You own the theater?"

"It's included in the sale. And your family signed the contract."

Why the hell hadn't she thought of that? Of course he owned it.

"But you haven't transferred the money yet." She was almost positive of that fact. Her mom and uncles were haunting this town like the ghosts of Christmas past. Once they got their grubby mitts on the cash they'd be out of here faster than a speeding bullet.

"It's in escrow. Due to complete by December twenty-sixth."

"Merry Christmas to us."

His lips twitched. "It's okay. I'm happy for you to hold your little meeting in my theater, as long as I get an invite." He had that thing in his hand again – whatever it was. She squinted her eyes to try to get a look, but all she saw was a flash of white. Noticing her scrutiny, he closed his fingers and shoved his hand into his pocket.

"Here you are," Dolores said, pushing a tray in front of him. "Now I know you said you didn't want anything to eat, but I know how much you like these danishes. I made them myself this morning."

"You know me too well," Josh told Dolores, who beamed widely.

"Enjoy." She glanced at Holly. "Are you sure you don't want a top up, sweetheart?"

"I'm good, thank you." Holly shook her head. As soon as

Dolores walked away, Josh took a huge bite of danish, the crumbles falling over the table.

"Hey," Holly said, dusting off the ledger. "Can you try not to eat like a caveman?"

Josh swallowed his bite with a mouthful of coffee and looked up at her, his warm eyes full of scrutiny. "You definitely remember that night with me."

"Are we back to this again?" Holly gave a mock sigh. "I'm so sorry your prowess wasn't enough to break through my psyche. I'm sure I had a really nice time though."

Josh looked at her through thick eyelashes. "Admit it." His voice was low. Cajoling.

"Show me what's in your pocket," Holly replied, lifting an eyebrow.

"You really want to see?"

Holly nodded. It was weird, but she did. She couldn't work out what the hell it was, and it was niggling at her.

"And if I show you, you'll admit you remember that night?"

She tipped her head to the side, as though she was considering it. "If you want me to lie to you."

"Then I'm not showing you anything." His eyes were warm. Almost sparkling. "Come to dinner with me tonight instead."

Holly blinked at his abrupt change in conversation. "What?"

"Let me take you out to dinner. Maybe we can come to some mutual arrangement. A quid-pro-quo." The way he said it, with a thick, graveled voice, made her feel like he wasn't talking about her memory or what was in his pocket at all. But something different and altogether dirtier.

And damn if her thighs didn't clench tight at the thought.

"I'm busy tonight."

"With the show?" He nodded. "Come afterward."

"I have to wash my hair."

He laughed, and it almost took her breath away. It made him look carefree and boyish and so damn attractive that she had to clamp her lips together as to not let out a sigh. "Before I leave this town, you'll tell me you remember."

"Why are you so desperate for me to remember a night that happened years ago?" Holly tipped her head to the side, trying to work him out.

"I'm not desperate for you to remember. I *know* you remember. I just want you to admit it."

"Why?" she persisted.

"Because I always play to win." There was an intensity to his voice. It sent a shiver down her spine.

"Is that why you're here?" she asked him. "Because you think this is a game?"

Josh's gaze caught hers. He said nothing, surveying her as though she was a mystery he wanted to solve. She felt her cheeks warming at his scrutiny. At the memory of the night she'd known exactly how well his body molded against hers.

She didn't want to admit that she remembered him. That she still could almost feel the warmth of his skin, the softness of his kisses, the deep rumble in his throat as he brought her to the edge of pain and pleasure.

Because if she admitted it, he'd see the truth in her eyes. That she'd hoped for more than one night. That for a year after he'd left she'd expected him to contact her. He'd left her a note, and she'd kept it folded neatly in her purse until it was clear he wasn't coming back and she'd set fire to the damn thing

"I stayed because you're trouble," he told her. "And I want to make sure this sale goes through without a hitch."

"So much trouble you think it's funny we're holding a protest meeting in the theater you own?"

He was smiling again, and damn if she didn't want to wipe it right off his face. With her lips. And her tongue.

And maybe her inner thighs.

Ugh. Why did he have to be so attractive?

He finished his danish, washing it down with the remainder of his coffee, his eyes still trained on hers. Her gaze didn't waver. It felt like some kind of challenge. Watch Josh Gerber eat his breakfast and pretend it didn't make her think of sex. See a flake of danish cling to his bottom lip and pretend she didn't want to lick it off him.

Notice the way his throat undulated as he swallowed the last of his coffee and don't think about how she'd love to kiss her way down his neck, then the dip of his throat, tearing open the buttons of his expensive shirt to expose his beautifully toned body.

"I'll see you tonight, Holly," he murmured. It felt like a promise.

"Yes you will." She pulled her bottom lip between her teeth, and his eyes flashed.

And as he walked out of the café she wondered how long she'd keep lying to him.

10

"You can't hold this meeting." Uncle Joe crossed his arms over his chest. His face was puce, his eyes looking like tiny white marbles beneath his thick monobrow. "The sale has gone through. It's over. You will all benefit, eventually. Hell, we could even talk about giving you a little now if that's what you're worried about."

Uncle Noel gave a low grunt, as though he wasn't on board with that at all.

Holly noticed her mom wasn't here. She didn't ask where she was, either. To be honest, she didn't care.

Not a bit.

"We *can* do this, and we *are* doing this." Everley lifted her chin and stared straight at her father. Uncle Joe's jaw began to twitch. "Grandma would want us to defend the town. It's her life's work. We owe it to her, and so do you."

"Your grandma didn't leave enough money to pay a month's worth of costs to keep this place running. We don't have a choice, we have to sell." Uncle Noel was quieter than Joe, but he still looked furious. His eyes were trained on North, who'd pulled himself up to his full six-foot-three height. There was an air of menace to her oldest cousin that made Holly shiver.

No wonder the women of Winterville threw themselves at him. North was the perfect mix of gentleman and thug.

People were starting to arrive at the theater. As they passed, they eyed the Winter family with interest, as though they couldn't understand why Joe and Noel were looking so furious. So far, they'd managed to at least keep a veneer of family unity when faced with the townsfolk, even if it was completely manufactured. But this confrontation was leaving people in no doubt that the older generation of Winters were completely at odds with Holly and her cousins.

It felt uncomfortable.

Beside her, she could feel Alaska trembling. Holly slid her hand into hers, squeezing it tight. Alaska clung on for dear life.

"We need to go in," Holly said, watching the crowd pouring into the theater. "We promised we'd start at seven. We don't want to hold them up."

"She's right. There's snow forecasted tonight." Gabe nodded. "Let's go."

"If you go in there, then that's it. Don't ask us for anything. We're done with you." Uncle Joe reached for Everley, but North stepped in between them, shielding her.

"They can't go in. They don't own the theater. We can stop them." Uncle Noel sounded almost excited, as though the idea had just occurred to him.

"Technically, you don't own it either," Holly pointed out. "And I have permission to use it." She looked Noel dead in the eye. He cowered back. She wasn't scared of him. Or Uncle Joe. She ate overconfident rich men for breakfast back in Chicago everyday. She could deal with them here. "Now come on, we have a town to talk to."

They used the stage door, walking through the familiar

hallways that used to be bustling with dancers and singers, while the air would be filled with the echoes of the orchestra tuning up. Halfway through the show, Candy would run in breathlessly, reliably late. The atmosphere would change then, to one of hushed reverence. Where Candy went, everybody looked.

And now she was gone. Holly was still holding Alaska's hand. It had taken everything they had to persuade her to come.

"Everybody's here," Everley whispered, peeking out through the curtain. Then a moment later, she let out a long whistle. "Wow."

"What?" North frowned.

"Josh Gerber is in the auditorium. He's sitting at the back, behind Dolores and Charlie." She ran the tip of her tongue over her bottom lip. "Now that's interesting."

North looked over her shoulder, then stepped back, shaking his head. "I'll get rid of him."

"No, don't," Holly said quickly. "I told him he could come."

"What?" Gabe gave Holly a strange look. "Why?"

"Because technically this is his theater, and he gave us permission to use it. We can't throw him out of his own theater. He could have us arrested or something."

Gabe and North exchanged glances. "I thought we weren't going to talk to him." North exhaled heavily.

"I bumped into him at the café, and he had a flier in his hands. I didn't seek him out."

"Wait a minute, I thought they were leaving town." Gabe pressed his lips together, confused.

"The other two did, but he didn't go," Everley said gleefully. "He stayed because he's got a thing for Holly."

"He doesn't." Holly rolled her eyes at her cousin. "But I think we might have him nervous. He said something about playing to win. Which means he's considering he could lose." She wasn't going to tell them about him also telling her he wanted to win with *her*. To get her to admit she remembered their night together. As aggravating as Josh Gerber was, he didn't deserve to be at the end of North's right hook.

"I don't like it." North shook his head. "He's up to something."

"That's why I think Holly should get closer to him," Everley persisted. "That way we'll find out exactly what he's thinking."

"No." Holly shook her head. "It's not worth it."

"My thoughts exactly." North gave her an approving smile. The rumble of conversation in the audience was getting louder and more impatient. "We should get out there."

"How are we going to do this?" Gabe asked. "We haven't got a fancy presentation."

"We're going to do what Candy would do," Everley said. Of all of them, she was the entertainer. The one who knew how to capture an audience. "We'll sit on the edge of the stage and make eye contact. We ask them for their ideas. For their help. Let them own it along with us."

North raised his eyebrows. "That's actually a great idea."

"No need to sound so surprised." Everley elbowed him in the ribs.

"I keep forgetting you're a grown up now," North muttered, rubbing his side. "Sorry."

Everley yanked the curtain open just enough to give them a gap to walk through. North was first, followed by Gabe, and Everley. Holly glanced at Alaska. "You okay?"

"I wish none of this had ever happened." Alaska's eyes were shining. "Grandma wouldn't have wanted us to all be arguing so much."

"I know she wouldn't. But she wouldn't have wanted to have all these people made jobless and homeless either."

Holly nodded at the townspeople. "Let's go see if there's something we can all do together."

Everley smiled at the crowd, giving them a little wave, then sat down on the edge of the stage, her legs dangling above the empty orchestra pit. North did the same, Gabe sitting beside him. Holly nodded for Alaska to sit next to Everley, and took her place at the end.

Then everybody started to applaud. North gave Everley a bewildered look, and she shrugged. "Just go with it," she whispered.

North started to speak, thanking everybody for coming, and telling them he wanted everybody to have their say. "We don't have any fancy microphones or audio visual equipment, so we'll have to do it the old fashioned way and shout."

Holly looked over the crowd, her mouth dry when her eyes locked with Josh's. Her stupid, betraying heart started to hammer against her ribcage when she saw how at ease he looked. He was dressed casually, his broad torso clad in what looked like a gray cashmere sweater. His hair was mussed in that 'some woman just ran her fingers through it' kind of way.

A half smile tugged at his lips as his eyes took her in, making her skin feel like it was vacationing in Hawaii while she was sitting here in Winterville. Why did he always have to look so good?

And why did her body react to him every single time they were together?

"Holly," Everley murmured behind Alaska's shoulder, inclining her head toward North. "He just asked you to introduce yourself."

North's brow was raised as he followed the direction of her stare right toward Josh Gerber. Then the two men were staring at each other and there was no heat at all there. Just a cold, icy dislike.

Ugh.

"Um, hi, everybody." Holly attempted a smile. "I think most of you know me. I'm Holly Winter. I spent most of my childhood here, and like you, I want to keep this town exactly the way that my grandma built it."

"She won the state math bee three times when she was a kid," Frank Richards shouted out. From the corner of her eye, she could see Josh grinning.

Please don't. She offered a prayer up to the heavens, but Frank stood up anyway.

"Hey Holly, what's fifty-five times seventy-six?"

Her heart dropped. "Four thousand one hundred and eighty." At least thirty people got their phones out and started tapping into them, no doubt checking her arithmetic. When they looked down at their screens they all let out a little 'ooh'.

"See? She's a math genius," Frank proclaimed. "Always has been."

Holly glanced pointedly at North. "Maybe we should move this along."

"Of course we should." He took a deep breath. "Okay, so let's get this meeting started. Who has a good idea on how to stop Winterville from getting demolished?"

Josh leaned back on the velvet-covered flip chair, his eyes trained on Holly. She was wearing a pair of jeans so tight she looked like she'd been poured into them, and a bright red sweater that matched her lipstick. Every time she moved, her hair caught the spotlights that were trained on the Winter cousins, illuminating her dark, tumbling waves.

And every few minutes her eyes would catch his and he felt a thrill rush through him.

Fact was, he couldn't remember the last time he'd had this

much fun. Sure, he was technically the enemy here, and everybody was being very careful not to refer to him by name. But it was like watching a movie. As though George Bailey had come to life and was desperately trying to save Bedford Falls before the big bad Mr. Potter turned it into Pottersville.

Which technically made him the asshole, but he'd forget about that small part.

"We should whip up some publicity," one of the younger people at the front shouted out. "Talk to the newspapers and the TV stations. They love human interest stories at this time of year."

Everley nodded, her expression serious. "That's a good idea. But they'd need a hook. What could it be?"

Josh leaned forward, tapping Dolores on the shoulder. "They could put on a show in the theater, like Candy used to. That would get some good write ups." His voice was low, because there was no way he wanted anybody to hear him. He wanted Dolores to take the idea and run with it.

She blinked. "Yeah, that would be a wonderful idea."

He nodded at the stage. "You should tell them."

Excitedly, she put her hand up. North beckoned her toward the stage, because there was no way he could hear her voice from the back. Dolores made her way up the aisle and stopped at the edge of the stage, where she whispered something into Everley's ear.

Everley blinked, then looked at Josh. He looked away, forming his expression to one of boredom.

If you'd asked him why he'd suggested it, he'd tell you it's because he was enjoying watching them fight against him. Sure, he didn't want bad publicity, but this could be a positive thing. Get some good attention to Winterville.

Anyway, they could get all the publicity they wanted and they still couldn't stop the redevelopment. This town and everything in it was his. Or it would be once the escrow closed.

And no, it had nothing to do with the way all five of them were excitedly whispering to each other. Nor the way Holly kept looking over at him.

And definitely nothing to do with the way all the blood rushed between his thighs whenever their eyes met.

He shifted uncomfortably in his seat, crossing his legs to hide the effect she had on him. Everley jumped to her feet, pulling Alaska and Holly with her, while Gabe and North watched on.

"Ladies and gentlemen," Everley called out to the auditorium, her eyes sparkling. "Dolores has had a wonderful idea. We're going to put on a show!"

❧ 11 ❧

"It was your idea, wasn't it?" Holly asked Josh. The meeting was over and the theater was empty, save for Everley and North who were still in the auditorium. Gabe and Alaska had headed back to the Inn, leaving Holly to lock up the front doors.

"What was my idea?" Josh had deliberately hung around until everybody had left. Not because he wanted to listen in but because he was so damn drawn to her it wasn't funny.

"To put on a show. Dolores said something to Everley about you suggesting it."

He shrugged. "I think I said something like 'I hope they don't put on a show, because it would be one more thing I don't want to deal with.'" It was amazing how casually the lies slid off his tongue. And how much he enjoyed Holly's disbelieving stare.

"Why would you suggest it?" she persisted.

He shrugged. "I just told you I didn't. I said I didn't want it to happen."

Holly sighed. "You're so damn aggravating, you know that?"

"Right back at you, memory loss girl." Without thinking, he slid his hand into his jeans pocket, his thumb rubbing across the smooth pebble he'd transferred in there. Too late, he realized Holly was staring down at his movements.

"Are you looking at my crotch?" he murmured.

Her cheeks pinked. "Of course I'm not." She dragged her eyes up to his. "I just want to know what's in your pocket."

He lifted a brow. He was trying so hard not to laugh.

"I didn't mean it like that, you ass."

Josh shrugged. "If you want to put your hands in my pockets, be my guest. You might like what you find there."

"I'm pretty sure I'd hate what I find there." Her eyes darkened, her lips parted. Her breath was steady but fast. "But thank you for the image. I'll be rinsing my brain with bleach later."

"Have you thought of going out to eat with me instead?" he asked her. "Because the offer still stands."

"I'd rather eat my own hand off, finger by finger."

This time he couldn't stop his laugh. She was delicious. Somewhere in his psyche he knew it was messed up to be this attracted to somebody who clearly loathed him.

But it felt so right, too.

"Holly," a low female voice called out. Holly glanced over his shoulder, her face turning ashen when she saw who was standing there.

"Mom?" Holly straightened her shoulders, as though she was going into battle. "I was wondering where you were. Uncle Noel and Uncle Joe looked lost without you."

"I need to speak to you," her mom said, her eyes narrowed as she stared at Holly. "In private."

Holly glanced at Josh. "I'm busy. I'm about to go to dinner with Josh."

He lifted a brow but said nothing.

"Oh, I didn't realize it was you, Mr. Gerber." Her mom's

voice softened. "How lovely to see you again. Can I steal my daughter for a moment? It won't take long."

Holly closed her eyes for a second, then opened them again. There was a look of resignation on her face. "Five minutes," she told her mom, then turned to Josh. "I'll call you when I'm done."

He could tell from the tone of her voice she intended to do no such thing. She didn't have his number for a start.

"I'll wait for you at the Inn," he told her. "For our dinner." Now she couldn't get out of it.

Unlocking the theater door, Holly walked back into the lobby, her mom following close behind. Josh glanced at the Inn, fully intending to wait for her there, even if she was almost certain not to turn up.

But then he realized the door was still open a crack. It was as though the universe was enticing him in. So he shoved his hands into his jeans pockets, his fingers grazing against the pebble again, and leaned nonchalantly back on the theater wall, trying to look as inconspicuous as possible.

"Why are you stopping the sale from going through? Do you hate me, is that the problem?"

Holly sighed. This wasn't the conversation she wanted to have tonight. Or any night, for that matter. She couldn't remember the last time she and her mom spent any time together.

It was so much easier to avoid her than to get hurt by her again.

"This isn't about you," Holly told her. "We're just trying to do something good."

"But I need that money, Holly. We all do." Her eyes were shining. Holly had forgotten how easily her mom cried.

"This is about more than money. It's about grandma and her legacy."

"Your grandma didn't leave a legacy. She left debts and problems and we're trying to solve them. Do you think I want to be here? You know I hate the cold." She shivered, pulling her collar tight around her neck. "But we have to sort this out, once and for all."

"Grandma wouldn't have wanted this." Holly's voice was low.

"And you'd know what she wanted, wouldn't you?" Her mom sounded hurt. "Because you and she were so close. I remember all the times she tried to take you away from me. I guess she's finally succeeded."

"She didn't take me away from you. You pushed me away all by yourself."

"Of course she did. Every Christmas all you wanted to do was be here with her. Every summer, too. It was all Grandma, Grandma, Grandma. And you know what? She loved it. Because it meant she was a better mother to you than I was."

"That's not true."

"She told me as much. When she came to Italy six years ago."

Holly's throat tightened. She didn't want to think about six years ago. Or Italy. Or the huge mistake she'd made. "Mom..."

"You jilted your fiancé on the day you were supposed to get married. And then you let my mom whisk you away and left me with the fallout."

"I knew you'd be angry with me. And you were." Holly's breath caught in her throat. What a mess this was. Getting engaged to a man she hardly knew was one of the worst mistakes of her life. And she bitterly regretted the way she handled it. Especially since he was the nephew of her mom's then husband.

But she'd been young and afraid and she'd let her grandma rescue her. And she knew that had hurt her mom.

She just didn't know how to make it right.

"You didn't have to call her," her mom said. "She loved it, do you know that? Loved that you needed her more than me. And now you're doing it again. Choosing her instead of your mother. When all I want is your support. I don't understand why you hate me so much."

Holly felt like she'd been slapped. "Mom, I don't hate you."

"Then let us complete the sale. Let me walk away from this place. I hated it when I was a child and I hate it now."

"But I love this town." And that was the truth. The difference between them.

Tears pooled in her mom's eyes. "Then I guess you've made your choice." She pulled open the door, a blast of icy air lifting her blonde hair. Stepping outside, she slammed the door behind her.

Holly's stomach clenched. She hated the way they always ended up in a fight. It had been this way ever since she could remember, even though Holly had always hoped things would change.

It wasn't her grandma's fault. It was Holly's and her mom's. And right now, there was no way to make things better.

Snow had started to fall by the time she'd composed herself. Holly locked the theater door behind her and looked up at the sky. It had that granite, heavy kind of look that promised more than just a dusting on the ground. When they were younger, North would get excited on nights like these, talking about the snow ball fights they'd have the next morning.

It was tradition to always have battles with the first layer of snow. Her heart clenched at the memory.

"Are you okay?"

She almost jumped out of her boots. Josh was leaning against the theater, sheltered by the overhang, his hands stuffed into his jeans pockets as he stared at her.

"What are you still doing here?"

He shrugged. "I thought you might need help."

A horrible thought occurred to her. "You didn't overhear my conversation with my mom, did you?" She felt suddenly exposed.

His brows knitted, his eyes scanning her face. It felt like he was weighing his answer. "What part?" he finally asked, confirming her worst fears.

He'd heard every word. Of course he had. The universe hated her. Why wouldn't it pile some more crap onto her day? A wave of emotion washed over her. She hated the way she and her mom never connected. And how every conversation they had ended in an argument. It was exhausting and emotional, and now Josh Gerber was staring at her with what looked like sympathy in his eyes.

And she couldn't take it. Not now.

"I need to go," she said, fresh tears stinging her eyes.

Josh reached for her arm. "Are you sure you're okay?" His voice was soft.

The lump in her throat grew into a fully fledged rock. His annoyance, she could take. His anger, too. But sympathy from this man who knew how to press all her buttons?

It might kill her.

Screwing her face up to stop the tears from flowing, she pulled her arm from his grasp. "I'm sorry... I have to..." She turned on her heel, stalking into the ice cold night.

"Holly, wait!"

Ignoring his shouts, she kept going, gritting her teeth

when her heavy-soled boots slid on the freshly fallen snow. She was heading toward the one place she knew she could hide and nobody would find her. Tears were flowing down her face, and she couldn't quite understand why. She was used to her relationship with her mom. It couldn't be that.

Maybe it was the mortification of Josh trying to be kind to her.

Her old cabin was at the bottom of the slope, beyond the large modernized ones that tourists used to fight over. It should have been demolished years ago. Maybe Candy had kept it for a night just like this one.

For Holly to be able to escape to.

She yanked open the door and stepped inside, the mustiness of the damp wood filling her nostrils. Where once a fire had burned, the grate was full of dust and soot. There were still two twin beds on either side of the room, and in between was a door to the basic bathroom that she used to shower in every day. Thank goodness the electricity was still wired up. The overhead light flickered to life as she flipped the switch.

They'd all had their own cabins when they were younger. North, Kris, and Gabe had shared two between them, and Alaska and Everley's cabin was a row down from Holly's. Candy had insisted that if they were working for her during their holidays and vacations then she would provide their accommodation.

And she'd loved this little place. It had been hers and hers alone. The beds covered with the butterfly designs she'd adored at the age of fifteen. She shook her head when she realized that beneath the dust they were still there. Smoothing her hand over the surface of the coverlet, she cleared enough of the fabric for her to sit down dust-free, and let out a long sigh, wiping the tears from her cheeks.

It was in this cabin that she'd brought Josh Gerber to on that fatal night. They'd curled up almost naked together beneath the covers, his lips and fingers taking her to places she didn't even know existed.

And then the next morning he'd been gone. Flown to London to start a new job, working for his grandfather's British business.

The truth was, she thought she'd meant more to him than a one night almost-stand. She'd waited months for him to contact her, to ask her to visit him or offer to visit her. But he hadn't done so much as friended her on Facebook.

And now he expected her to admit that she still thought of that night? No way, buddy. Better to pretend it hadn't happened at all.

She hated how much her body reacted to him every time they were close. The years had been more than kind to him. He'd been beautiful eight years ago, but now he was devastating. With those dark eyes and razor sharp jaw, he was impossible to ignore.

And she wanted to ignore him. She really did.

A loud knock at the door made her lift her head up. She'd stopped crying, thank goodness. She didn't want anybody to see her like that.

It was inevitable, when she opened the door, that it was Joshua Gerber III standing there on the stoop. As though the last eight years hadn't happened and he was back after that night. He'd changed his mind and come back for her.

Dear God, she needed to stop reading romance books in between cases.

She was twenty-eight years old. A successful, confident woman who didn't need a man to validate her. Taking a deep breath, she straightened her back and made her eyes meet his.

And yes, she might have clenched her thighs a little. But it was cold, dammit.

"I would have gotten here faster, but these boots weren't

made for running." He lifted his foot up, and she just about managed not to smile. "And I kind of forgot which cabin was yours."

"Have you been here before?" she asked innocently. The snow was falling heavier now, deadening their voices.

"Are we back to this again?" His voice was smooth. "Yes, I've been here before. You let me stay here when I had nowhere else to go." He dusted the snow from his hair. "Can I come in before I catch pneumonia?"

She stepped aside. "You know that's not true, right? Statistically you're more likely to get pneumonia during the winter, for sure. But there's no causal effect. It's just the season."

His lip twitched. "Thank you for that information. But I'd still prefer not to freeze my ass off." He looked around the cabin, his brows knitting. "Holy shit, this place looks exactly the same." Josh walked over to the bed, reaching out to trace a butterfly beneath the dust. "You have the same bedding. You always had a thing for butterflies."

She felt that rawness again. "I learned about the butterfly effect at science camp when I was twelve. I was obsessed by it for years."

He looked over his shoulder at her, his gaze as soft as a caress. "I remember. You had butterflies on *everything*."

She opened her mouth to reply, but nothing came out.

"Do you know how many times I got turned on to the thought of your butterfly thongs?" he asked. He walked toward her, his stare unwavering. She could feel the pit of her stomach start to twist and turn. She was frozen to the spot. She couldn't move if she wanted to.

She was a rabbit facing a devastatingly handsome, stalking fox.

"Why do you keep lying to me?" he whispered, reaching

out to trace his finger over her bottom lip. A pulse of desire rushed through her, making her tingle all over.

"Maybe you weren't as good as you thought."

He laughed. "Maybe I just need to remind you."

She tipped her head to the side. His finger had stilled on her lip, his eyes darkening as they held hers captive. "Maybe you do," she whispered, her muscles clenching at the thought.

A slow smile pulled at his lips, as though he could see the desire shining out of her. As though he knew her body was buzzing with electricity. He pulled his hand away, and she immediately missed his touch.

"Do you want me to kiss you, Holly?" His hooded eyes dipped to her lips as she moistened them with the tip of her tongue.

"I think *you* want to."

"You're right. I do."

Her heart was hammering against her chest now. "What's stopping you?"

"I want you to ask me."

"You want a lot." Her breath caught in her throat.

"Yeah, I do." He looked down at her body. Even wrapped in a thick coat, his stare made her shiver. "But we have a history. This time, I don't want you to forget it happened."

"Then maybe you need to put in some effort." She wasn't going to beg him. No way. "Or you could take a photograph."

He grinned. "That's the kind of thing that'll get me in the newspapers for all the wrong reasons. I want your consent, Holly." He stepped closer still. "Say yes."

Consent is sexy. She'd heard that before. But she'd never felt it until this moment. Until Josh Gerber was looking right into her eyes, his body so close to hers that their coats were touching. She had to incline her head to hold his gaze, enough to make her feel wobbly on her feet. Why did he have to smell so good? She was almost dizzy with the scent of him.

He cupped her cheek, running his thumb across her jaw. "Say yes," he said again, his touch setting her skin on fire.

Her body was screaming at her to answer. Her nipples were hard, and her thighs ached. Yet there was still something holding her back.

"You know what I remember about you?" he murmured, his thumb pressing against her lips. "How sweet you tasted. It was snowing, that first time I kissed you. I was dressed as Santa, you were an Elf. And I was trying to warm you up, but really I wanted to touch you all over. Do you still taste as sweet?"

"There's only one way to find out." He was seducing her with his words. Making her feel like she'd been somebody worth remembering. And it was so confusing, because they were enemies. Fighting each other for the future of this town.

But he was looking at her as if he'd given up fighting. Against her, against himself.

As though he wanted to make love, not war.

He dropped his head until his brow was pressed against hers. She could feel the heat of his skin, the dampness of his hair, the sweet warmth of his breath as it dusted against her skin.

And that's when she gave up the fight, too.

Letting out a lungful of air, she reached up, brushing her palm against his rough jaw. "Kiss me," she said, her body starting to shake.

And he did.

❧ 12 ❧

From a young age, Josh had learned that the things you wanted most were almost always a disappointment when they came. Gifts, holidays, going to a rare ball game with his grandfather – that turned out to be an opportunity for him to schmooze clients while pretending to be grandparent of the year.

He'd come to terms with that fact. Absorbed it into his being.

But kissing Holly Winter again was no disappointment at all.

Her lips were soft yet demanding, her arms tight as they wrapped around his neck, pulling her body against his. He slid his hands beneath her coat, exploring the hollow of her back, their mouths parting until his tongue tangled with hers.

She was everything he could remember. He ached for her. Without breaking their kiss, he slid his hand between them to unzip her coat, exposing her soft cashmere-covered chest to the air, before running his hands over her curves.

He loved the way her breath hitched at his touch. The

way she arched her back toward him, until her soft breasts brushed against his rough palm.

He walked her backward, toward the bed, turning them around so he was the one who fell on the dust-covered mattress, a cloud of gray puffed around them as she crawled her way onto his body.

His coat would be ruined by the dust, but he didn't give a damn. He was too busy kissing her to think about that. And she was kissing him back, and it was driving him crazy in the best of ways.

She tangled her hands in his hair as he slid his palms beneath her sweater, memorizing every curve and dip of her body.

His lips moved against hers, tasting every gasp and breath, feeling her fingers scrape against his scalp, marking him. She tasted of sweet desire, as her tongue tangled with his.

Pushing her sweater up to expose her snowy white skin, Josh propped himself up with his elbows until his lips touched her stomach, kissing his way up to her ribs. Her nipples were hard and prominent against the white lace of her bra. He sucked one through the fabric, making her moan out loud.

She'd been twenty-years-old the last time they'd been in this cabin together. And he'd been twenty-four. Still young enough to believe in life, in attraction, in a future that was bright. Not jaded by the world and all that lived in it.

Now he was older. More experienced. And desperate to give her everything she needed. He wanted to make her call out his name, to beg him to touch her, to slide inside her.

He wanted her to remember him, the way he remembered her.

He kissed her again, a slow, luxurious kiss that made her throat rumble with need. Her breath was slow and ragged, her body shaking against him. He wanted to make her feel so good she'd never forget him again.

He broke the kiss for a moment, and she frowned. Her eyes met his, and he could see himself reflected in them.

"Tell me you remember." His voice was gritty as hell.

Her chest hitched as he curved his hand around her bare waist, steadying her. There was a strange look in her melted chocolate eyes. As though she was almost afraid of him.

"I remember," she whispered.

"Thank fuck."

Then he was kissing her again, pushing the sweater over her head. She was scrambling at his coat, pushing it open before sliding her hands under his own sweater, letting out a strangled moan as she traced her fingers up his hard abdomen. The air surrounding them was ice cold, but the heat of her touch made him feel like she was burning from the inside out. He wrapped his arms around her body to block out the icy air, eyes hooded as he slid his hands over her bare back.

"You're so beautiful," he rasped. She was glorious beneath the harsh light of the cabin. Her breasts were full and high, her nipples dark and pointed through her bra, her waist slender before it flared out to her denim covered hips. He wanted to kiss every inch of her body until she was begging him for more. Wanted to tease her with his tongue until she never forgot him again.

Or never pretended to.

She tugged at the hem of his sweater, and he lifted himself up, holding his hands above his head to help her. She let out a tiny sigh, her eyes raking his chest, before everything went black as the sweater covered his eyes.

And then there was a knock on the door.

Not a gentle one, either. A loud, insistent rapping that made her body freeze against his.

"Hol, you in there?"

Her cousin. *North.* Holly yanked Josh's sweater back down, and he blinked, her horrified face coming into focus.

"You need to go," she whispered frantically, reaching for her own sweater. It was covered in dust.

"Where?" he frowned. From where he was laying, there was only one exit and Holly's big, burly cousin was standing right outside it. Subconsciously, Josh touched his jaw, remembering the way North had slammed his fist against it all those years ago.

Another knock.

Shit.

"Just a minute," Holly called out, her voice tight. "I'm in the bathroom."

Josh grimaced, because he was almost certain that bathroom hadn't been usable for at least five years.

"Let us in," a female called out. "It's freezing out here."

"That's Everley." Holly practically yanked Josh up from the bed, and frogmarched him to the bathroom, pushing the door open and him inside. He blinked as his boot sank into something that definitely didn't feel like tile.

Snow. It was snow. He looked up to see a hole the size of a dinner plate in the roof, snowflakes lazily dropping down into the dark room.

"Stay here," Holly whispered. "Don't move."

"It's freezing. The roof is gone."

"I'll get rid of them."

She slammed the bathroom door closed. The only light in the room came from the moon shining through the hole in the roof, reflecting in the snowflakes. Josh moved to the left, knocking the snow from his foot and sighed heavily as he heard the cabin door creak.

"Are you okay?" North asked. "We've been looking for you

everywhere. Dolores said she saw you hurrying away from the theater crying. Did something happen?"

"What's that on your hair?" Everley asked. "Ugh, that's dust. What the hell are you doing in here? This place is a deathtrap."

"I just need somewhere quiet to think," Holly told them. "Go back to the Inn. I'll be up in a minute."

"We're not leaving you here," North told her. "The storm's getting worse and you don't have the right kind of coat. Come up with us now. Alaska is making hot chocolate."

Holly let out a long breath. "Okay. I just need to get something from the bathroom."

"You used the bathroom?" Everley let out a retching sound. "You must have been desperate."

"Something like that," Holly said grimly.

A moment later, Josh heard footsteps on the floorboards, then the bathroom door flew open and Holly slid back inside.

"We must stop meeting like this." He gave her a crooked smile.

"This isn't funny. If North catches you in here he'll go apeshit."

He ran his finger along his bottom lip, remembering exactly what North going apeshit meant.

"You stay here while I leave with them," Holly continued. "Count to a hundred or something and by then we should be close to the Inn. Then you can make your escape."

"You're okay with me going out into the storm in these clothes?" he asked, only half joking.

"I'm more okay with that than with North seeing you here."

She had a good point. "Okay. Go with them. But we need to talk."

Holly blinked. "What about?"

"About what happened in here tonight. With us."

"But there is no us." Her brows pulled together. "I was all kinds of upset and you tried to cheer me up." A shaft of moonlight through the roof caught her profile, making her skin glow. He wanted to touch her all over again.

"I didn't kiss you to cheer you up," he told her, his voice low. "I kissed you because—"

"Holly, hurry up!" Everley shouted. "What the hell are you doing in there? Has the curse of the Inn's beef pie hit again?"

"Oh for god's sake." Holly shook her head, reaching for the door handle. "I need to go."

Biting down a grin, Josh reached for her wrist, circling it with soft fingers. "Come to mine for dinner tomorrow night."

"Now that really is a terrible idea." Holly's eyes met his. Damn, she was pretty. Why did her cousins have to chase her everywhere she went?

He nodded. "I know."

Holly's gaze flickered to his, as she exhaled softly. "I'll be there at seven."

1252 Wonderland Avenue. 7pm. I won't be cooking beef pie. – Josh

How did you get my number? – Holly

I have my sources. And a lot of friends in the CIA. – Josh

Seriously. How did you get it? – Holly

. . .

It's on the flier you posted all over town. All of Winterville must have your number by now. Remind me to talk to you about privacy and security when you're here. – Josh

Who said I'm still coming? – Holly

Aren't you? – Josh

I guess so. But I hate lying to my family. – Holly

Then tell them. Simple. – Josh

Do you have a death wish? Us finding your broken cadaver could solve a lot of problems, but you're too pretty to die young. – Holly

Holly Winter thinks I'm pretty. I can die happy now. – Josh.

Don't die. Dead men can't cook and you promised me dinner. – Holly.

It's okay. You can use me for my culinary prowess for as long as you want. - Josh

. . .

How was it he could sound dirty even when he used normal words? Holly closed her eyes briefly, taking a deep breath. She wasn't kidding when she told him this was a bad idea. And yet she couldn't help herself. She wanted to see him. Needed to, even.

Not just because that kiss last night made every single nerve ending in her body start to sing his name. Or because he promised to cook for her – and let's face it, she'd do just about anything for a good home cooked meal – but because she had questions. So many questions.

And he was the only one who could answer them.

"I need you to come up to the attic with me." Everley walked into the lobby where Holly was sipping a coffee. Piped Christmas music was softly filling the air, occasionally interrupted by the crack of a log from the blazing fireplace. Alaska was at the desk, leaning over the computer with her bottom lip between her teeth, and Everley had been in the office, making phone call after phone call.

"Why do we need to go up there? It's scary." Holly shivered, remembering the time Kris had lured them up there with the promise of moonshine and beer, before locking the door and leaving them in there for hours. Their grandma had discovered them when their shouts and banging had finally gotten her attention.

"Because I have an idea and I need to go through Grandma's old costumes." Everley sighed. "Do you know how many people would love to help but can't get away at such short notice?"

"I can imagine." They hadn't given themselves much time either. They planned to hold the concert on Christmas Eve, less than two weeks away.

"So I'm going to go on social media and beg for help. It's time to start taking this to the next level."

"Can't we wait for North? He's not scared of the attic."

"North's overrun with customers right now." Everley looked around the empty lobby. "At least somebody is. When did this place stop getting over booked?"

"When Grandma stopped putting on the show," Alaska said, looking up from her computer. "Things slowly dwindled. And I think quietly we were all grateful for that, because we wanted to spend time with her."

"Maybe you could go up to the attic with Everley?" Holly suggested to her cousin.

Alaska grimaced. "No way. I still have nightmares about the time Gabe dressed up as a bear and I was sent up to check out the noises. And anyway, I'm busy." She smiled smugly. "I can't leave the desk."

"Looks like it's just you and me, kid." Everley grabbed Holly's hand.

The Winterville Inn attic was as dark and foreboding as Holly remembered. The air felt deadened by the layers of snow on the roof, and the thick wooden floor Candy had installed when the Inn had been constructed. They walked to the corner of the room, lit only by a single bulb and looked around. It was full of old boxes and furniture that the Inn no longer needed. In the corner was a stuffed moose that stared balefully at them. And a layer of dust covered everything.

"I guess we go through the boxes," Holly said, bringing her attention back to the clutter around them. "Do you think anything in here is useable?"

"Candy always took good care of her costumes. I think she used to use those crates to hang them in." Everley pointed at a group of five upright crates, taller than them both. "Let's go with the first one."

Everley tugged at the lid, which was at the front of the crate, but it didn't move an inch. Her hands were covered with dark gray dust. "Ugh, I should have brought a crowbar."

Holly leaned down, running her hands over the wooden

crate. "There's a latch here," she said, hooking her finger over the metal on the side. The lid opened with a groan, but instead of costumes, it was stuffed with boxes full of old photographs and papers.

"Oh my god, she never got rid of anything, did she?" Holly pulled out a box, smiling as she looked at the old pictures laying inside. Candy with her Hollywood friends, laughing on set. Candy standing in front of what looked like a half-constructed Winterville Inn, a baby in her arms, along with two small boys staring up at her like she was a goddess.

"She really was beautiful," Everley murmured.

"You look just like her." Holly wasn't lying. Everybody agreed that Everley bore an uncanny resemblance to their grandma at the same age. With her blonde waves and high cheekbones she was a true beauty.

"Oh my god, is this us?" Everley asked, pulling out a color photograph. The six cousins were dressed up in little elf outfits. Holly laughed, because North had the stormiest expression on his face. He had to be eleven or twelve in that photograph, and was clearly unhappy to be dressed the same as his kid cousins and younger brothers.

"What's this?" Holly touched a wooden frame. She pulled it out and frowned, because it was Candy in full color, wearing a white dress and holding a beautiful bouquet of roses, smiling up at a man.

It was only when Holly looked at the date that she realized her mistake. It wasn't their grandma, it was Everley. Holly hastily tried to put it back into the box, but Everley grabbed it, a little sigh escaping from her lips.

"I didn't know she kept this," she said, her voice a little more than a whisper. "I thought I'd burned them all."

"Maybe she thought you might like to look back at this one day." Holly gave her cousin a sympathetic smile. Everley's marriage to Dylan Shaw was over almost as soon as it began.

Everybody said they were too young. So they'd run away to Vegas as soon as she was twenty-one, telling nobody until she came back to town with a thin gold band on her finger.

Everley's eyes shone as she ran her fingers over the photograph. "I loved him so much then."

Holly's throat felt tight. "I know you did. And he loved you. Look at the way he's smiling at you."

Dylan was wearing a dark gray suit and pale blue tie, his dark hair falling over his eyes. And the way he was staring at Everley made Holly's stomach turn to goo.

"I guess marriage and me didn't mix, huh?" Everley tried to smile, putting the photograph back in the box.

"Join the club." Holly's soft gaze met Everley's. "At least you went through with the ceremony."

"At least you didn't have to get an annulment," Everley countered, taking a deep breath. "Or face your ex's father whenever you're in town." She wrinkled her nose, but they both knew she loved Charlie like her own dad.

"When was the last time you saw Dylan?"

"I don't know." Everley frowned. "A few years ago. He doesn't come back often, thank goodness."

"Charlie said he's still working for Doctors Overseas."

A smile ghosted Everley's lips. "He always was trying to save the world."

Everley tried to put the box back into the crate, but it wouldn't go in. Sighing, she took some papers from the next box to make room. "Anyway, Dylan is old history. I'm more interested in the present day. And why you hid Josh Gerber in your cabin bathroom last night."

Holly lifted her head. "You knew he was there?"

Everley smiled smugly. "I do now." She lifted the papers to the side, idly flicking through them. "I even have a name for the two of you, if you're interested."

"I'm not."

"It's Jolly. See what I did there?" Everley told her. "Josh and Holly. It's perfect."

"To have a couple name, we'd need to be a couple," Holly pointed out.

"Yes you would. So what were you two doing in the cabin?"

"He heard my confrontation with my mom." Holly quickly filled Everley in, telling her about their conversation in the theater lobby. "I was upset and he followed me. And then we ended up on my old bed."

Everley gaped at her. "No way."

"Way," Holly said, grimacing.

"Did you...?"

"Nope."

"But you wanted to." It wasn't a question. Everley was grinning now. "Oh this is perfect. One of us might get our happily ever after. Jolly forever."

"You do realize you're twenty-nine years old, right?"

"I know. But when I'm here in Winterville I tend to regress to teenagedom. Sorry." Everley wrinkled her nose. "But seriously, do you like him?"

Holly swallowed hard. "I think so." At least, her body did. "But we can't seem to be in the same room without either wanting to hit each other, or ripping each other's clothes off."

Everley sighed. "Oh, that's perfect."

"Is it?" Holly wasn't so sure. "We're on two different sides. And I know we thought it would be a good idea for me to get close to him, but..." She shook her head. "Maybe tonight isn't a good idea."

"Tonight?" Everley's brows rose. "What's happening tonight?"

"He's asked me to dinner. He says we need to talk."

"Oh, when a guy says that he means he needs to rock your world. Talking is just an excuse. Although..."

"What?"

"We need to keep him on our side. I need his cooperation to use the theater for the show on Christmas Eve. If you two are special friends, he won't interfere."

"Special friends?"

Everley wiggled her eyebrows.

"I'm not sleeping with Josh Gerber just to get him to agree to your show."

"Of course you're not," Everley smiled. "You'll sleep with him because he's a gorgeously sexy man who sets your lady parts on fire. The theater is just an added bonus." She looked down at the papers in her hand. "Hey, are these the original deeds to the town?"

Holly leaned over her. The papers were old and yellowed. They were handwritten in ink, text covering at least ten pages. "These should have gone with the other documents as part of the sale."

"Maybe our parents didn't know they were here." Everley looked at the papers again. "Do you understand a word of this?"

"Some. They're the rules for who can live in the town and the usage of the land. But I'm not a lawyer, I don't really understand them. I guess I could send them to my lawyer friend and get her to look them over."

"Do that." Everley handed Holly the pile of papers and replaced the box they'd removed, somehow managing to shove the crate shut. "But first we need to find me a costume and fast, because you can't go to dinner with hair like that."

"Hair like what?" Holly touched the back of her head, and grimaced at the frizz she could feel there. "Oh."

"You need to go wash it," Everley told her. "You'll thank me for it later."

❧ 13 ❧

Josh was wearing casual clothes again. Jeans and a black shirt, unbuttoned at the neck so she could see a tantalizing hint of his chest, and a smattering of hair that made her mouth feel dry.

"Come in." He gave her a smile. "Let me take your coat."

Holly unhooked her scarf and unzipped her padded parka, handing it to him. His eyes raked over her, taking in the gray wool dress that hugged her curves, and the sheer stockings that did nothing to keep out the cold.

"Did you drive?" he asked

"I did." She lifted a brow. "I figure if it snows I'll be safer driving than walking home."

"You could stay here." It sounded like a throwaway comment, but it made her body react anyway.

"I think I'll chance it with the roads."

He led her into his kitchen, and she took a seat at his breakfast bar. Damn, it smelled good in here. "What are you cooking?" she asked, as he opened the refrigerator, pouring them both a long glass of water.

"Boeuf en daube." He passed her the glass, taking a long,

cool sip from his own. "With winter greens and sautéed potatoes."

Holly blinked. "From scratch?"

"Yep."

"So you can cook?"

"You sound surprised about that," he murmured, propping his chin on his hand and smiling at her.

"I guess I thought you'd be too busy taking over the world to learn life basics. Most guys I know prefer takeout."

"I'm thirty-two years old. It'd be a sad life if I only ate takeout." He blinked, his thick lashes sweeping down. Did he have to be so damn handsome? "Anyway, I like to cook when I get the chance."

She tipped her head to the side. "Do you cook for women a lot?"

Josh looked down, smiling. "No."

"So you don't invite them around and seduce them with the smell of boeuf en daube?" Holly raised an eyebrow. "Shame, because it'd definitely work."

"I don't invite women to my home as a rule." His eyes flickered to hers.

"Why not?"

"Because it gives them the wrong idea." He sounded guarded.

She leaned forward, her gaze still captured by his. "What kind of wrong idea?"

"That I'd make a good boyfriend." There was a lightness to his voice. "I hate to disappoint people."

"You invited me to your home," she pointed out, looking around the modern, white kitchen.

"Technically, this isn't my home." He took another sip of water.

Holly shifted in her seat, taking in his smooth masculinity. He had an ease to him that invited people in.

She wondered how many women had gotten the wrong idea about him despite his efforts.

"You like to hide behind technicalities a lot," she observed, her voice casual.

"I do?" He blinked again, a half smile ghosting his lips.

"The theater is technically yours, yet you let us have our meeting there anyway. This house is technically yours while you rent it, yet inviting me here isn't like inviting me to your home."

"I didn't say that." He put his glass down, running his finger over the rim.

"So you're not hiding?"

"Oh, I think we're both hiding, Holly. We just choose different things to hide behind."

"You think I'm hiding?" She tipped her head to the side.

"I think you're afraid of being too open." He turned his smile up a notch, as if to take the sting from his words.

"Maybe I've learned from past mistakes."

The oven timer beeped. Josh walked over and opened it to check the food, then closed it again. "Another five minutes," he murmured. "Would you like some more water? Or a glass of wine?"

"Water's fine." She looked down at her half-empty glass. "But a top up would be lovely."

He pulled the bottle from his refrigerator, this time walking around the breakfast bar to top her up. As soon as he was close she felt her body react to him. Her nerve ends danced beneath her skin as she breathed in his warm, deep cologne.

"Why did you lie about not remembering me?" he asked her.

Holly swallowed. She wasn't certain she knew the answer herself. But she was so glad she'd stopped playing that game.

Her body had felt lighter since she'd admitted the truth to him in her old cabin.

"I guess I didn't want you to think I'd been pining after you all these years." As soon as the words escaped she knew they were true. And she didn't like how vulnerable they made her feel.

Josh chuckled. "I'm pretty sure you weren't sitting by the telephone for eight years waiting for my call. After all, you almost got married."

"You heard my mom say that." Of course he did. Another truth she didn't want to admit.

"Yeah, but I knew before."

She did a double take. With her on the stool and him standing, the height difference between them was exaggerated. "When did you know?"

He shrugged.

"I answered your question," she pointed out. "Maybe you could answer mine."

"Quid pro quo." He nodded, his eyes not leaving her face. "I guess we could play that game. But only if you promise to be open and honest."

"Like Clarice and Hannibal," she murmured.

"Which one are you?" His eyes sparkled as he looked at her.

"I'm not sure yet."

He raised a brow. "I call shotgun on eating you first."

She shook her head, amused. "You like playing games, don't you?"

His smile was devastating. "Yes I do. And I think you do, too."

"Okay then." She nodded. "It's on. Answer my question."

His gaze caught hers. "I knew about your engagement when it happened. But I didn't realize you didn't go through with it until recently."

What? He knew about it all those years ago? She opened her mouth to ask another, but he held up his hand.

"My turn," he murmured. "Why didn't you marry him?"

"Because I realized I wasn't in love with him." She let out a low breath. She hated thinking about that time in her life. It felt like she'd been a different person, living a different kind of life. "My turn."

"Go ahead." He was enjoying this.

"Why didn't you contact me again after you left Winterville?" she asked him.

He grimaced, as though embarrassed. "I flew straight to England and it was a shit show of a project that meant working eighteen hour days for a year. And I had it in my mind that if I couldn't be a good boyfriend, then I should just leave you alone until I was more available."

"An occasional email would have been nice," she murmured.

"I know. I was an idiot. A young, self obsessed idiot who thought that he had something to prove. And I was willing to give up everything to prove it."

"Even me."

Their eyes connected. "I'm sorry." He shook his head. "And if it makes you feel any better, you dodged a bullet with me. I'm still work obsessed. I still spend too many hours in the office. I'm not boyfriend material."

It was like he was warning her off. "Another technicality," she said.

He put his hand on the breakfast bar, next to hers. All he had to do was reach out and they'd be touching.

"What do you mean?" he asked, his smile bemused.

"It's something else to hide behind. You tell people you're not boyfriend material because you're afraid."

"Afraid of what?" His voice was thick.

"Afraid of intimacy. Of being vulnerable. Of playing the game and losing."

He looked at her for a minute, his eyes considering her words. His lips were soft, his jaw hard, and she felt a fresh flood of warmth envelop her body.

"What makes you think I'm afraid of that?" he asked.

"Because I'm afraid of those things, too."

He moved his hand, weaving his fingers into hers. "I've forgotten whose turn it is to ask questions," he said, three tiny lines forming above his brow.

"Maybe we're out of questions." She squeezed his hand, amazed at how excited she was just from the slightest of touches.

"I don't think I'll ever be out of questions with you." With his free hand, he reached out, cupping her face, and stooped until their brows were touching. "If we do this, somebody's going to get hurt. Maybe both of us."

"I know." Her chest clenched.

"And if we don't do this..." He ran his tongue over his lip. "It'll hurt, too."

She tipped her head to the side. "That's what we like to call a no-win situation."

He smiled, shaking his head. "I don't like those."

"Nor do I," Holly said. Their faces were so close she could see flecks of green in his blue-gray eyes, forming a halo around his darkening pupils. "Maybe we can call it a no-lose situation."

"Potayto-potahto." He moved closer to her, until his hips were between her thighs. Her heart was hammering against her chest, the need to touch him flooding her body. Her head was in line with his chest, and she could see the outline of his muscles through the thin fabric of his shirt.

"Holly." His voice was a breath. She felt the warmth of it on her face. A wave of dizziness washed over her, and she reached out to steady herself, her palms pressing into his sides, feeling the warmth of his taut skin through his shirt.

He exhaled more heavily this time. It sounded strangled. He stepped closer, still, and she could feel the hard ridge of his excitement pressing against her.

Then he kissed her. Softly, at first. A maddening brush of his mouth that made her ache for more. With a slow moan, she parted her lips, inviting him in. He slid his tongue against hers, making her body pulse and contract. Her thighs tightened around his hips as though to cage him in. He was delicious and talented, filling her with desire, as his hands cupped her face gently and his mouth took hers again and again.

When they finally parted, they were breathless. He looked down at her, his gaze soft.

"Stay tonight," he asked.

She nodded. She wasn't going to fight anymore. She was out of reasons to push him away.

A slow smile pulled at his lips as he moved toward her again, his gaze intense. But then the oven timer went off again, and he stopped, his eyes crinkling as he laughed.

"Saved by the bell," he said, tracing his finger on her lips before walking around the breakfast bar to the oven. "I hope you're hungry."

Yes she was. In every way.

❧ 14 ❧

Electricity hung in the air as they ate at the small table overlooking the mountains. Sure, they were chatting casually, but every now and then their eyes would catch and he'd feel the pleasure of her stare through his body, making him ache with need.

She looked beautiful in the soft lamplight, her wool dress hugging her curves in all the right places, her long dark hair falling in tumbling waves down her back. But what captured his attention was the way she held herself, so strong and proud. She had a confidence to her that was innately sexy.

He loved that she'd opened up to him. Her vulnerability only made him want her more.

Since she'd decided to stay, he opened a bottle of wine. Holly lifted her glass to her lips, closing her eyes as the cool, crisp Sauvignon Blanc slipped down her throat.

"You know the first time we met, I wasn't old enough to drink," she said, putting her glass back on the table.

Josh winced. "You make me sound like a cradle robber. You were twenty, I was twenty-four." Though truthfully at the time, he'd thought she was older. Even then, her cool beauty had captured him.

She smiled softly, looking down at her plate. "So when did you learn to cook?"

"A few years ago. I got so sick of takeout and ready made meals. I started with those food boxes that companies send out, then graduated to my own recipes."

"Maybe you could teach me." She wrinkled her nose. "I'm still at the takeout stage."

"It's a challenge when you work all day. By the time I get home, I'm usually exhausted and starving. I bet you are, too. It's easier just to pick up your phone and order." He shrugged. "But I find it relaxing, standing in the kitchen and making dinner. A way to decompress from the day."

"You can decompress with me any time."

He laughed at the innuendo of her words. "I'll bear that in mind."

She rolled her eyes. "I meant cook for me. I love home cooked food. When we're in the middle of a case I usually end up eating at the office. Somebody calls for pizza or Chinese and we wolf it down while staring at our computers. I'm shocked I'm not the size of a house."

He ran his gaze over her perfect curves. "If you're anything like me, it's feast or famine. There are days when I don't have time to eat at all."

She lifted her fork to her mouth, letting out a soft moan as she ate a piece of the succulent beef. "If you cooked for me every day, I'd eat constantly."

Damn if that didn't make his chest pound. Not just the moan, but the idea of cooking for her. What the hell was wrong with him?

"Explain your job to me," he said, trying to push that weird thought away. "I get the forensic accountant part, but how did you end up working for a divorce lawyer?"

She didn't seem surprised that he knew all about her job. "I started out working for an accounting firm. I was moved to their forensic team almost right away. I have this weird knack of being able to look at a sheet full of numbers and immediately hone in on the number that looks wrong."

"*Wrong?*" he asked, his brows knitting.

"When somebody shows me accounts that have an error, it's like the wrong number is red and flashing in my eyes. I can scan a spreadsheet with ease and see it. Then I investigate where that number originated and follow the trail. Usually I find out what the person or company is hiding."

"Like one of those spot the difference pictures?"

She smiled. "Exactly like that. Numbers have patterns. When they don't follow it, it's jarring."

There was something so appealing about the way her face lit up. She loved her work and it showed.

"So you were working for an accounting firm," he prompted. It was weird how he wanted to know so much more about her.

"And I was called in to consult on a divorce case. The guy was hiding three million dollars and it was my job to track it down. He'd created a whole chain of shell companies in an attempt to cover up what he was doing. It took a long time to track it all down. But eventually I did and the judge made him pay."

"You sound pleased about that."

"There's usually such a power imbalance to most of the divorce cases I work on. I like working for the underdog. Helping people escape bad marriages with a hope for the future. And yeah, there's a little schadenfreude in sticking it to the bad guys." She shrugged.

"Would you feel the same if it was a woman hiding the money and the man being the underdog?"

Holly nodded. "Yeah, I do. Right now, the imbalance is firmly in one direction, but things are changing all the time. Human nature is human nature. Rich women are just as likely to hide their money from the courts as rich men. I've worked on a few cases like that."

"You're a modern day Robin Hood."

She laughed. "I've been called worse. Someone once described me as a crusader without a cape."

He grimaced. "Sorry. I was an asshole."

Her eyes softened. "It's probably a good description. I like helping people break out of relationships that hurt them."

He thought about his grandma. About all the times he'd tried to persuade her to leave his grandfather. How much more confident would she be with somebody like Holly on her side?

"How about you?" Holly asked, looking at him over the rim of her wine glass. "Do you enjoy what you do?"

"Sometimes." He half-smiled, his gaze holding hers. "I like making money."

She leaned forward. "But there has to be more to your life than money."

"It's a family business. There's never been any question that I'd end up running it. That's what I was brought up to do."

"Is it what you *want* to do?" she persisted, as though she didn't understand his answer.

His stomach tensed. "It's not about want. It's about duty. You of all people must understand that."

Her smile was tentative. "We're all products of our upbringing. And I guess that's why we're both here. Fighting against each other to keep what our family created."

He didn't like that they were on opposite sides. "What if we didn't talk about that?"

She frowned. "About what?"

"About the whole fiasco involving this town. What if we don't mention it at all? I don't tell you what I'm doing, you don't volunteer what you and your family are up to?"

Holly tipped her head to the side. "Don't you want to know?"

No, he didn't. He didn't want to be her enemy. He wanted to be her friend. Her lover. He wanted to make her smile, not cry.

"I just want to escape from it with you."

Until he said it, Josh didn't realize how much he wanted that escape. Needed it. Needed her to push it all away until it was only the two of them and nothing else.

His body ached for her in a way he didn't understand. But he was giving into it nonetheless.

A blush stained her cheeks as her eyes locked with his. "I want that, too." She put her silverware on the plate, her chest rising and falling with her breath. "It sounds like heaven."

"Have you finished?" He glanced down at her plate.

Holly nodded.

"Then come here," he said, his voice thick and low.

Her breath hitched. "I should clean up."

"Leave it. I'll do it later."

She bit her bottom lip and stood, and he reached for her hand, pulling her toward him until she was straddling his muscled legs. He inhaled sharply, the sweet smell of her perfume invading his senses.

He was as hard as a rock, aching with need for her. She was staring at him with those wide, melted chocolate eyes, and he felt like the king of the damn world. "I want to make you feel so good you forget your name," he told her. "And call out mine instead."

Her eyes grew wider still. She shifted on his lap, the movement making his cock thick with pleasure.

"I want to taste you until you arch your back off my bed. I want to be covered in you." He ran his finger over her lips, and she exhaled softly. Her face was flushed, her chest high. He could feel her thighs clenching his. "I still remember how sweet you taste."

She ran her hands up his chest, her palms brushing his nipples, and he had to bite his lip not to let out a groan.

"You're full of promises," she murmured. "But will you deliver?"

They shared a smile. "If I don't," he said, standing, and lifting her into his arms. "You can sue me."

"I always play to win."

Josh had said that to her in the Cold Fingers Café, when she'd refused to admit she remembered him. And now, as he stared down at her, his eyes heavy-lidded, his full lips parted, Holly wondered if he knew that he'd already won.

There was an intensity to him that took her breath away. After their kisses got hot and heavy, he'd threaded his fingers through hers, wordlessly taking her to his bedroom and kicking the door shut.

His bed was a California King that dominated the room, the thick mattress barely giving as he lay her down on it, her dark hair fanning out around her like a halo. He stood at the foot of it, his burning eyes raking down her body, his jaw set tight as he slowly slid his hands along her stockinged legs from her calves to her thighs.

Her chest hitched as he reached the seam of her stockings, his fingers sliding onto her bare, soft skin. His thumbs pressed into the sensitive flesh of her inner thighs, the ridge in his jeans thickening as he ghosted them over her satin panties.

Hooking his hands beneath her thighs, he hitched her legs up, pulling her toward the end of the bed. Dropping to his knees, so his gaze was in line with her body, he pulled her stockings down one by one, throwing them to the floor before returning to touch her once more. His hands were firm and sure as they slid back up her legs, his mouth soft as he pressed open kisses against her thighs. Holly had to grip the bedcovers to stop herself from arching her back, closing her eyes as he pressed his nose against her damp panties.

"You smell like I've died and gone to heaven." His voice was rough.

"Don't die yet."

He chuckled and hooked his thumbs into her panties, dragging them down before pushing her legs further apart, lifting them over his shoulders to give him better access to her aching core.

She should have known he'd be good at this. But it still came as a shock when he found the sweetest of spots with the tip of his tongue, sending shockwaves of pleasure through her body. He softly licked her again and again. It was too much and not enough. A maddening pleasure that made her want more.

Then he pushed his face against her, sucking her between his lips, the vibration of his moan making her clench hard. Damn, he was really good at this.

"Watch me."

She propped herself up on her elbows, his dirty gaze catching hers, and he pulled at her again. She was still wearing her dress – and Josh was fully clothed. The carnality of his touch and his tongue was overwhelming.

She was twenty-eight years old. She'd had boyfriends, a fiancé. She wasn't inexperienced, for goodness sake. But she'd never seen a man so intent on giving pleasure. He slid a finger inside her, then another, hooking them to hit the spot that made her back lift off the bed.

With his free hand, he pushed her back down, his hand firmly on her stomach as he sucked and licked until vibrant colors appeared behind her tightly closed lids. Her breath was stilted and fast, her heart hammering against her chest, and the pleasure... she wasn't sure she could take much more.

"I'm going to..."

His eyes softened, as though he was smiling against her. Then he slid a third finger in, the pressure making her eyes widen before it tipped her over the edge. She trembled around him, the power of her orgasm making every muscle in her body tense. He slowly slid his fingers in and out, coaxing every last piece of pleasure, before pulling them away and sliding them between his lips.

"Take your dress off," he said. He watched, fully clothed, as she pulled it over her head. "And the bra."

She did as instructed, unhooking it and throwing it to the floor. His eyes flashed, a smile tugging at his lips. "You're beautiful."

"And you're overdressed."

His smile widened. He took his time undressing, unbuttoning his shirt to reveal a broad, muscled chest with a slight covering of hair. Holly swallowed hard, her gaze dropping as he unbuckled his belt and unbuttoned his jeans, taking his time as though he was completely in control of the situation.

All that was left were his dark shorts, the thick outline of his desire jutting against the black fabric. She could see his plush tip pushing at the waistband, and she swallowed hard, because damn, he was bigger than she'd remembered.

With his shorts still on, he grabbed a condom from his wallet, then climbed onto the bed, caging her in with his arms. He fingered a loose tendril of hair that had fallen against her cheek, his expression almost tender as he pressed his lips to the dip at the bottom of her neck.

"Are you okay?" he murmured. His lips glistened from her.

"More than okay." She reached up, sliding her fingers into his hair. Their eyes met, and her chest contracted.

He was so damn beautiful she wanted to cry.

Instead, she slid her hand down between them, dipping inside his shorts to circle her palm around him. Josh let out a low groan, closing his eyes as she slowly moved her fist, her thumb circling the moistness at the tip of his hardness.

"If you keep doing that I'm going to mess up my shorts."

She laughed at his warning. "Maybe that's what I want."

Josh shook his head. "No you don't. You want me inside you."

Her breath caught, because he was right. She did.

There was an emptiness inside her. A void that only he could fill. She wanted to feel the thickness of him as he made her his. To feel the warm tautness of his chest against the soft swell of her breasts.

Holly tugged impatiently at his shorts. Josh moved so she could pull them over his muscled thighs, her fingers grazing against the soft hair that covered his calves. Then he was naked, too, looming over her in all his glory, and she felt her chest tighten again.

What was wrong with her? She felt like she was on the edge of tears. She blinked them away as he slowly brushed his lips against hers.

"Are you sure you're okay?"

She nodded. "I need you inside me." She ran her finger along the ridge of him and the sound of his moan grounded her.

The rip of the condom packet echoed through the silence. He slid it on, then held himself at the base, sliding himself against her slick warmth, lining himself up with the part of her that needed him the most.

She held her breath, as he kissed her again. His lips warm and hungry. Dropping his brow against hers, he slowly pushed himself inside her until he'd filled her to the hilt. For a moment he held himself still, allowing her to become accustomed to the pressure, and she looked at him through half-open eyes.

His jaw was tight, his eyes burning. He took her calves in his hands and pushed her legs up, so her knees were hitting her chest, her calves grazing his shoulders. She was open to him. Vulnerable and oh-so-needy. His throat undulated as he swallowed. Then he rocked his hips until he almost pulled out, before he pushed back into her, building the rhythm between them.

She could feel it again. The pleasure built inside her, stroke by stroke, coiling and hissing until another release was inevitable.

Josh pressed his lips to hers, his tongue caressing and sliding, his skin heavy and slick as he rocked them both to oblivion.

"If you forget me after this, I'm quitting sex for good."

She laughed against his mouth, then gasped because damn, he knew how to angle his body. She grasped onto his shoulders, her body arching to meet his, her toes curling with anticipation of the release his body promised.

"I knew you would feel like this. So tight. So good." His rhythm increased, his jaw tightened, and his fingers dug into her hips as he held her. "Should have done this before. Should never have left."

Tears stung at her eyes again. Her throat felt so tight it was getting hard to breathe. "Josh..."

"Say my name again." His voice was as rough as his movements. His body was slick with perspiration.

"Make me feel good, Josh."

Without missing a beat, he pushed his hand between their bodies, his fingers coaxing pleasure as he began to throb inside her. When it came, the wave was almost unbearable. It lifted her up so high that all she could do was cling to him, crying out his name as she convulsed around his thick, hard length.

Then he was joining her in pleasure. His groan low and thick, his hips stilling as he pulsed hard and hot. "Holly." He kissed her roughly, releasing his hold on her so she could collapse bonelessly against the mattress.

For a moment they lay there, his hard weight intensifying the ache, his slow kisses, making her feel so wanted it almost hurt.

"I need to pull out," he warned her. Holly nodded, still trying to regain the power of speech. Securing the condom with his fingers, he pulled his hips back, and the sudden loss of fullness made Holly sigh.

She was already missing him and he was still here.

"Don't move," he told her. "I'm just heading to the bathroom then I'll be back."

"I don't think I could move if I wanted to."

He laughed and walked away, and yes, she ogled his perfect ass, because perfection deserved to be admired. A minute later, he was back with a warm washcloth and a towel, telling Holly to stay still as he cleaned her up, his movements gentle against her sensitive skin.

"Would you like a drink?" he asked her.

"Water would be good."

He gave her a smile, as though pleased with her answer. "Anything else? A sandwich? Some chips?"

She grinned. "I think you already filled me up."

Josh chuckled and grabbed his shorts, pulling them on

and walking out of the bedroom. Holly lay back on the bed, staring up at the white ceiling, her breathing still stilted.

He was an attentive lover. She'd expected that. But she hadn't expected the sweet softness afterward. It made her feel warm and wanted, and so damn confused.

And despite the aching between her legs, and the sheen of perspiration covering her body, she wanted more. So much more.

🕸 15 🕷

"Closing a deal like this shouldn't take so long. Why aren't you home yet?" His grandfather sounded less tetchy than usual. Maybe a few days without his wife had mollified him. "Do you need me to come out there and sort things out?"

Josh shook his head, a small smile playing at his lips. Even a telephone conversation with his grandfather wasn't dampening his mood today. Not after a night with Holly Winter.

She was still in his bed, fast asleep. He didn't have the heart to wake her up. Not after they'd spent most of the night with him inside her. She needed the rest, from the way she was snoring.

He reminded himself to tease her about that.

"It's all under control," Josh said into the headset Willa had ordered for him. He was scanning today's *Wall Street Journal* as they spoke, lifting a steaming mug of coffee to his lips.

"So when are you coming home?"

"When I'm ready."

His grandfather grunted. "I don't like it. You need to be in the office. The staff will start slacking off if you aren't there. You know what it's like, Christmas begins earlier every year. I bet they think every day is a party when you're not there."

"I trust my team. They work hard. And anyway, with all the technology I have it's like I'm in the office."

"It's not the same," his grandfather grumbled. "Do you have a date for your return?"

The bedroom door opened and Holly walked out. She was wearing his t-shirt, her long, bare legs making his body respond. Her dark waves were coiled into a messy bun on the top of her head. When their eyes met he gave her a long slow smile, pointing to his headset to let her know he was on a call.

She nodded and walked toward him, grabbing his half-drunk cup of coffee and lifting it to her lips, taking a long sip. The intimacy of the action made his smile widen.

Then she hooked her leg over his, straddling him, her hands still cradling the cup.

"I don't know when I'm coming home yet." Josh held his breath as he hardened at her closeness. "Probably after Christmas. Once everything is finalized."

He'd made that decision last night. He couldn't leave. Not yet.

"After Christmas?" Grandpa shouted. Holly bit down a smile, then leaned forward to press her lips against Josh's throat. He shifted her slightly, the tumescence of his need almost painful.

"I want everything finalized. The escrow goes through on the twenty-sixth. After that nothing can go wrong."

"Wanna bet?" Holly mouthed. He grinned at the challenge in her raised brows.

"But what about Christmas? It's a time for family," his grandfather protested.

"We never celebrate Christmas. It's not a big deal." He

was getting bored of this conversation. He wanted to end it and bury his face between Holly's thighs. Then he wanted her to ride him in this chair until neither of them could walk.

And after that he probably needed to do some work.

"I still don't understand it. This isn't like you, Josh. Surely there's nothing you have to do there that you couldn't do remotely from the office."

Josh ran his hand up Holly's bare thigh, biting down a smile as she closed her eyes in appreciation. "There are a few things that are difficult to do remotely."

"Like what?"

Like Holly Winter.

She was kissing his neck again, leaving a trail of warmth along his skin as she caught his earlobe between her teeth.

This woman was going to be the death of him.

"I need to go," he said, his voice strangled as she rolled her hips against him. "I have another call to make."

"But we haven't finished," his grandfather protested. "Who's going to tell your grandma you won't be home for Christmas?"

"Goodbye, Grandpa," he murmured as Holly lifted the headset, placing it on the desk. He had the presence of mind to end the call before she looped her arms around his neck and pressed her chest to his, kissing him softly and warmly until his grandfather and work were all but forgotten.

Yep, he was definitely staying here for a while. He had things he needed to do in person, including making Holly moan his name as he took her to heaven with his mouth.

Everything else could wait.

"I really have to go," Holly murmured. It was almost eleven o'clock in the morning, and he'd gotten nothing done. Apart from making love to Holly twice, including on his desk. The floor around it was currently surrounded by the files and papers he'd swept away to lay her body down on there.

"Stay here. You can lay on my bed and wait for me while I make some calls." He was only half-joking. He really didn't want her to leave. Not least because he wasn't sure she'd come back again.

"You have work to do." Holly smiled. "And so do I. And our work is diametrically opposed." She was wearing last night's dress, her hair brushed and pulled into a high ponytail, her skin glowing from the long, hot shower they'd taken together.

"How about we call a truce and spend the next few days in bed. The result will be the same, but the waiting will be so much more pleasurable."

Holly lifted a brow, looking amused. "You're only trying to win again."

"Being in bed with you for the next few days would definitely be a win," he murmured threading his fingers through hers.

She pressed her lips to his. "How about you agree to give up on redeveloping the town? Then I won't have to fight you."

"Where would be the fun in that?" He smiled sadly. "No can do."

"That's a shame." Her eyes were still sparkling. "Anyway, I need to go back to the Inn and change. Plus my cousins are probably wondering where I am."

"What are you going to tell them?"

She tipped her head to the side. "That I've been trying a new angle on you."

He laughed at her innuendo, sliding his hands down to her hips. "Come back tonight. Bring a bag. I want you in my bed again." It was crazy how much he wanted it. Wanted *her*.

She stared at him for a moment, her gaze open. "We really shouldn't." She sounded hesitant.

"I know we shouldn't. But we want to, don't we?"

She pulled her bottom lip between her teeth. Damn, she was adorable. "What if I'm too sore?" she whispered.

"Then I'll hold you all night against my manly chest and read you romantic poetry."

Holly laughed. "You had me at manly chest. What time should I be here?"

"Whenever you're ready. I have meetings until seven, but I can always stare hotly at you until they're done."

She nodded. "Okay, but I'll bring the food tonight. It's my turn."

"Works for me."

His laptop let out a shrill ring, reminding him that he was supposed to be in a video conference. "I have to get that."

"I know. And I have to go." She pressed her lips to his. "I'll see you later."

He brushed a stray lock of hair behind her ear and kissed the smooth skin of her throat. "You will."

He watched her walk out of the house, her hips swinging as she made it to her rental car. Once she was safely inside and driving away, he turned to his laptop, lifting his headset and accepting the call, the boardroom of Gerber Enterprises flickering to life on his screen.

"Apologies for my lateness," he said, though he wasn't sorry at all. "Where are we at?"

Elizabeth and Kevin turned to the screen, their spines straightening as they saw he'd connected.

"I got your email," Kevin said. "Are you sure you want to pay for a relocation company? It's not in the agreement, and it's going to cost a lot of money."

"I'm certain." The idea had come to him this morning. He couldn't stop the sale at this point – and he didn't want to –

but he could make things easier for the people of Winterville who'd have to leave in order for the resort to be built. Bringing in a team of corporate relocators would help them find new homes and new jobs. At a cost to Gerber Enterprises.

"Okay, we'll get onto that," Kevin agreed. "You're the boss."

Yes he was. And right now he was okay with that.

It had taken twenty minutes in a second shower of steaming hot water, followed by an intense session with a mirror and the contents of her cosmetic bag for Holly to finally look presentable. Sure, she still had shadows beneath the layers of concealer, and every time she walked her inner thigh muscles took her back to Josh's bed, but at least she'd made it out of the Inn.

The snow had stopped sometime overnight, and the roads were freshly plowed, but the roofs and lawns of the town were blanketed in a fresh layer of white that glistened in the winter sun.

Her first priority was coffee. She pushed open the door to the Cold Fingers Café, and Dolores gave her a great big smile.

"The usual?" Dolores asked.

"Yes please." Holly opened her purse to find her wallet.

"You can put that away. Your coffee is paid for."

"It is?" Holly looked up, her brows knitting. "Did I over pay last time?"

"No." Dolores' grin hadn't moved an inch. "Mr. Gerber asked me to put all your coffees and pastries on his tab. So this is on him."

Holly pressed her lips together. "In that case, you need to

put all *his* purchases on my tab." She pulled her card out and passed it to Dolores. "I'm good for it."

Dolores chuckled. "What the hell is going on with you two? It's like that movie..." Her brow creased. "What's it called? The one with Tom Hanks and that pretty girl who was married to Jerry Lee Lewis."

Holly blinked. "I have no idea."

"She means Meg Ryan," a voice called from across the café. Everley was sitting in front of the fireplace, a laptop in front of her.

"*Sleepless in Seattle?*" Holly asked, unsure.

"Nope. It was the one where they hated each other."

"*You've Got Mail,*" Frank shouted out. Holly bit down a laugh. How long had he been watching romcoms?

"Yep. That's it." Dolores crossed her arms. "They hated each other but loved each other really."

Holly's cheeks flamed. But she said nothing. Love was a strong word. Lust felt better right now.

Dolores passed Holly her Americano, along with a pastry she insisted was on the house, and Holly walked over to where Everley was sitting, a half-eaten danish on a plate in front of her.

"Comfort eating?" Holly asked, sinking into an easy chair.

"Nope. It's the first thing I've had all day. Did you hear about my Instagram post?"

"No. I didn't even know you posted it." Holly grabbed her phone, opening up the app.

"That's because I did it last night while you were canoodling with the enemy." Everley grinned, pulling out her phone and opening up Instagram. She passed it to Holly. "And we'll come back to that, because I need *all* the details. But first I need to finish making this list. Because Gray Hartson has offered to come sing at our show. And now everybody wants a ticket. I have no idea how we're going to fit all of them."

Holly looked at the screen, watching her cousin's video appeal for help. She was dressed in one of Candy's old costumes, her hair coiled into a topknot like Candy used to wear. She blinked at the number of likes and comments.

Everley had gone viral. And the biggest name in rock had replied. Gray had been a friend of their grandma's. He and his family lived in a small town a few hours away. He was being so sweet to offer to sing on Christmas Eve.

There were so many comments from people begging for tickets, offering to pay astronomical sums to be there. It took her a full five minutes to scroll through them all.

Then she saw a name that made her look at her cousin. "Dylan Shaw commented. I didn't know he had Instagram."

"I guess the internet's made it to wherever he is." Everley swallowed. "Should I block him?"

"Do you want to?" Holly asked her, passing back the phone. Everley's eyes were shiny. Other people might not have noticed, but it was clear she was panicking over her ex-husband's comment.

"I don't know. I don't want to think about him, I guess." Everley picked up her danish and stuffed it between her lips. "Okay, so now I'm comfort eating."

Holly laughed. "At least his comment is nice."

You look more beautiful than ever.

Everley swallowed her pastry, chasing it with a mouthful of coffee. "It's weird though, isn't it? All the ghosts of our past coming out of the woodwork."

"Your paths were bound to cross again. His dad still lives here."

Everley really did look upset. Holly decided to change the subject.

"So, what can I do to help with the show?" Holly asked.

"Can you do the accounting?" Everley looked up at her. "I'd be so grateful."

"Of course I will. You don't need to ask. I'll do whatever you need me to. I know how overwhelming this must be." Holly gave her cousin a soft smile. "And you're going to sing, aren't you?"

Everley looked uncertain. "I don't know. Everyone will be there for Gray Hartson... I might be out of place."

"You've worked in shows for years. Spent all that time on Broadway and in touring productions. You *have* to sing," Holly urged her. "You'll be representing us all. And Candy."

"What are you talking about?" Gabe asked, throwing himself into a spare chair next to Holly.

"I'm telling Everley she has to sing in the concert," Holly told her cousin.

"Of course she does. That goes without saying." Gabe gave Everley a warm smile. "You'll be amazing."

"Who'll be amazing?" North asked. "Oh, Holly, there's a message for you at the Inn. Alaska took it."

"A message?" Holly asked. "Do you know who from?"

North shrugged. "Ask Alaska. Anyway, what are you all talking about?"

"I'm telling Everley she has to sing at the concert."

North smiled at his cousin. "Yep, she definitely has to sing." He winked at Everley. "You can do the finale. Sing *Every Day Feels Like Christmas*." Candy's signature song. It would bring down the house. "Maybe Gray can sing with you."

"I'll think about it." Everley sighed. "We don't have much time. Thank God Kris has the website and ticket sales under control." He was doing it remotely from England.

"And I've spoken to an A/V company one of my friends owns," Gabe said. "They're willing to provide all the sound and light equipment for free. They'll even throw in some technicians."

Everley smiled. "That's fantastic. People are so kind."

"Candy's name is known everywhere," North said. "She was such a generous person, and people like to give back."

"Yeah, they do."

The café door chimed, and Josh walked up to the counter. His eyes swept over to where she was sitting, but his expression didn't change. He leaned forward to say something to Dolores, but Holly was too far away to hear him. Whatever Dolores said in return, it made him give a small smile then look over at Holly again.

Their eyes met and her stomach gave a little lurch. Dolores passed him a cup of coffee and he lifted it up, raising an eyebrow at Holly.

She bit down a smile. Dolores must have told him she'd paid for it. She wanted to give the air a fist bump because this was so much fun. Instead, she lifted her own cup up, as though to toast him.

"What are you doing?" Gabe murmured, looking from Holly to Josh and back again.

"Just reminding him we're still here," Holly murmured. She really needed to take more care, because there was no way she was admitting to Gabe or North that she'd spent most of last night beneath Josh Gerber's very delightful body.

"You should ignore him. He's not worth our attention." North shook his head. "Why is he still here anyway?"

Everley folded down her laptop. "Beats me." She bit down a smile, glancing slyly at Holly. "Anyway, I need to get back to the Inn and talk to Alaska about something. And you need to pick up your message," she said to Holly. "Want to join me?"

"Sure." Holly drained her coffee and glanced at their boy cousins. "I'll see you guys later."

"We should have a family meeting tonight. We have a lot to go through," North said. "How about we get takeout at mine?"

Tonight? She'd already promised to go to Josh's. Everley must have noticed Holly's expression fall, because she quickly demurred.

"I can't make it tonight," Everley said, her lips curling. "I have to... um... do some womanly things."

"Womanly things?" North grimaced.

Gabe chuckled. "What kind of womanly things?"

Everley leaned forward, her expression serious. "You don't want to know," she whispered. "It'll ruin the mystique."

North wrinkled his nose. "Ev, your mystique was ruined the day you walked into the lobby of the Inn and stripped down to your Care Bear undies."

"I was four years old," Everley protested. "And I wanted everybody to love the Care Bears as much as I did."

Holly coughed down a chuckle.

"Don't you laugh." Everley shook her head at Holly. "Remember your butterfly panties? They caused way more problems than my Care Bear ones."

North's jaw twitched. "Yeah, the less said about those, the better."

"Can we stop talking about my panties and get out of here?" Holly said, helping Everley pack up her laptop. She wanted to get out of here before North remembered why he hated Josh so much.

Those damn butterfly panties. She wished they'd never existed.

Although, it still sent a shiver down her spine that Josh ended up walking around with them in his pocket all those years ago.

"Yep, we've gotta go. We have things to talk about." Everley side-eyed Holly. "Very, very womanly things."

"Get out of here with your womanly things," Gabe said, shaking his head. "You're ruining my masculine vibe."

❧ 16 ❧

Everley leaned on the Winterville Inn reception desk, grinning at her sister. "Okay, so long story short, Gray Hartson has agreed to headline the concert. I'm going to sing the final song. And Holly and Josh Gerber have been banging the brains out of each other."

Alaska looked up from her computer, her eyes catching Holly's. "I knew there was something between you two."

It had taken the entire walk from the café to the Winterville Inn for Holly to fill her cousin in. She'd only given her the barest of details, but clearly Everley was filling in the gaps herself.

"It's so dreamy," Everley said, her expression soft. "Two houses, both alike in dignity."

"Can you quit with the Romeo and Juliet quotes?" Holly said, shaking her head. "We're not exactly mortal enemies."

"But you *are* on two different sides," Alaska pointed out. Her long blonde waves were coiled up into a bun. "How are you going to deal with that?"

"I don't know," Holly said honestly. "We haven't talked about his plans for Winterville."

"They were too busy doing other things to talk," Everley said, giving them both a wicked grin.

"Don't you have a concert to arrange?" Holly asked her, shaking her head. Everley never failed to make her grin. "And I hear you have a message for me?" she said to Alaska.

"Yep. Your friend Natalie called. Your phone is off and your voicemail is full. I tried it as well and got the same result." Alaska rooted beneath the counter, then brought up a complimentary slip.

Natalie would like you to call her ASAP.

Holly pulled her phone from her purse. Sure enough, the screen was blank. The battery must have died while she was at Josh's last night. She hadn't even thought to check. "That's my lawyer friend. I sent her those deeds we found." She grimaced at her phone again. "I'll go upstairs and charge it," she said, taking the slip from Alaska. "Thanks, honey."

"No need to go upstairs, we have chargers here." Alaska pulled up a box full of plugs and cords. "You can't begin to imagine how many people either lose theirs or forget them. They're the new toothbrushes."

"I'm going to head into the business suite," Everley said, hugging Holly tight. "I'm guessing you won't be here for dinner tonight."

"Not tonight," Holly nodded. "But that's okay, because you have *womanly* things to deal with."

Alaska frowned. "What kind of womanly things?"

Everley rolled her eyes. "Nothing. I was digging Holly out of the mess she's made."

Holly left her cousin to fill Alaska in, and wandered over to a sofa next to an outlet, sliding the charger into her phone. A moment later her screen lit up, then a barrage of notifications filled it. Three missed phone calls from Natalie, notifications from Instagram – including Everley's latest video, and a billion messages and texts filled her eyes.

Of course she clicked on the ones from a certain Josh Gerber.

You're so damn beautiful. – J

That one was sent right after eleven. She couldn't have left his house long before he'd sent it. She smiled at the thought of him sending it as he sat in a video meeting. The next was sent twenty minutes later.

What time are you coming tonight? I need you here early. – J

She loved how impatient he was to see her. She felt exactly the same.

I just ran up to grab something from my room and the bed still smells of sex. Is it wrong that I like it? – J

No, not wrong at all. She swallowed hard, the memory of his body on hers making her skin feel hot.

What the hell, Winter? – J

But thank you for the coffee. – J

. . .

Although now I'm thinking of ordering coffee for the whole town and putting it on your tab. Just to see your face. – J

By the way, you still look beautiful. – J

She laughed, remembering his face when Dolores must have told him his coffee was already paid for. She slid her fingers across the phone screen, her smile still curling her lips.

You looked pretty good yourself. – H

Everley had disappeared from reception, no doubt pulling her hair out in the business suite. Alaska was talking to one of the few guests, leaning over one of the free paper maps they supplied, drawing out directions.

Thank god. I was starting to think I had the wrong number. Wanna come over and play? – J

I'm busy! And sore. I also realized I forgot to ask you a question last night. – H

What question? – J

What's the thing you keep in your pocket? – J

. . .

Come over here and find out. – J

Good try. I have work to do. Some asshole is trying to demolish my grandma's town. – H

He sounds like a bastard. Want me to beat him up? – J

It's okay. I'm looking forward to doing it myself. But thanks for the offer. <3 – H

I love the way you tell me you're going to beat me up then send a heart. It makes me feel all warm inside. By the way, that thing in my pocket? It's missing you. – J

Shut up, I'm busy. I have phone calls to make. I'll see you tonight. – H

My pocket and I look forward to it. Xx – J

With a stupid grin still on her face, she closed her message app and pulled up her contacts. A moment later, her friend Natalie answered, her warm voice echoing through the phone.

"Hey stranger. I've been trying to get a hold of you all day."

"Sorry about that." Holly grimaced. "I forgot to charge my phone."

Natalie sighed. "Oh my. You really have switched off from the world. I can't imagine not having my phone fully charged twenty-four-seven. Nancy would personally hunt me down no matter the time of day or night."

"I was distracted. And how is Nancy?" Nancy was Natalie's boss. A kick ass divorce attorney that made grown men cry. Holly adored her.

"Busy as always. We have a new case brewing, but we won't start work on it until the new year. You'll be back by then, right?"

Holly swallowed. "Yeah, I guess I will." Strange how she didn't want to think about that.

"But that's not why I'm calling. I got those papers you scanned. And I got one of my property lawyer friends to take a look. He says he's found something interesting, and potentially game changing, but he wants to run it by another lawyer first."

"What kind of thing?" Holly asked, her brows knitting.

"Something that might help you save your grandma's town. But he doesn't want to get your hopes up until he's confirmed it. He should have more news tomorrow if you'll be around? He's suggested a video conference at seven."

"Seven tomorrow night?" Holly remembered their family meeting. "Yeah, that would work. Will you be there?"

"Um, yeah. I kind of promised to go out for dinner with him afterward." Natalie sounded almost embarrassed.

"Oh God, don't you want to go?" Holly wrinkled her nose. "Sorry about that."

"Oh no, I *definitely* want to go. Ryan's hot as hell. I'm just embarrassed because I kind of used your problem to get closer to him."

Holly laughed. "In that case, I approve. And I'll get to see exactly how hot he is tomorrow, right?"

"Yeah you will. And I really hope he has some good news for you. I can't believe those assholes bought up your grandma's town just to demolish it."

Holly pulled her lip between her teeth. She really was sleeping with the enemy, wasn't she? Maybe if things were different, she'd confide in Natalie and tell her about Josh. But Natalie was hundreds of miles away, and this situation was way too difficult to discuss over the phone.

Even Everley and Alaska knowing made her feel uncomfortable. She wasn't sure she could cope with Natalie's judgement, too.

"Listen, I have to go. Nancy's working a late one and I need to get our order in for Barracuda. I'll send you the Zoom link tomorrow, okay?"

"Sounds good," Holly agreed. "I'll make sure my cousins are there. We all have an interest in this."

"That's fine. Talk to you tomorrow, Hol."

"Laters." She ended the call, wondering what the hell Natalie's friend had uncovered. Letting out a lungful of air, she slid her phone back into her purse and waved to Alaska, who waved back. She needed to get ready for her evening with Josh.

The enemy.

Why was her life suddenly so complicated?

Josh fell back on the mattress, pulling her with him so her body covered his. "Jesus, I'm broken."

Holly laughed against his chest. "That makes two of us." They'd been in bed since she'd arrived at his place, save for an emergency break to inhale some food. He was too irresistible for his own good.

"You're an addiction, you know that?" Josh brushed a tendril of hair from her brow. "I keep trying to concentrate on work, but all I can think about is you."

Her heart thrilled at his words. "Maybe that's my plan. Distract you while we steal the town back from you."

The corner of his lips quirked. "What a way to lose money." He ran his fingertip down the line of her spine, making her shiver. "You want a drink?"

"No."

"A shower?"

"In a bit. I don't think I can walk right now. There are no nerve endings left in my legs."

Josh laughed, running his soft lips over her brow. How easy life would be if they could always stay here. Not think about work or family or fighting over this town. He was holding her again, his thick biceps pressed against her upper arms, and she couldn't remember the last time she felt this good.

Or this safe.

Which was wrong, because she wasn't safe. And wasn't that confusing? Her body was saying one thing, and her heart the other.

"I'm pretty sure I'll never walk again. I'm too old to go three times in one night."

"You didn't feel old to me." She kissed his chest, and he stirred beneath her. "Feels like part of you wants to go again."

He winced. "Ignore it. It's like one of those ghost limbs. You think you can feel it, but it's really not there."

Holly laughed, and the movement made him even harder against her. "It's definitely there."

"Let's talk about something else. See if we can get him to go away." Josh lifted her chin so he could kiss her. She sighed against his lips, kissing him back, feeling her body slowly coming back to life.

"How about I ask you that question again?" Holly suggested, a sparkle in her eye. Maybe she'd finally get an answer.

"Okay. Shoot."

She pulled her bottom lip between her teeth, eyeing him carefully. "What's the thing you keep in your pocket that you don't want me to know about?"

Josh grinned. "I thought we were ignoring him?"

Holly narrowed her eyes. "You know what I'm talking about."

"It's stupid." He ran his tongue along his bottom lip. "But you can look if you want. It's in my pants pocket. Right side."

"Really?"

"Yeah. Go on." He nodded, watching with interest as she clambered naked over him, and reached for the pants she'd stripped off of him earlier. Sure enough, there was a lump in the pocket. She reached in, her fingers touching a smooth, cool surface.

"A pebble?" She frowned, lifting it out and inspecting it. It was about an inch and a half long, made of smooth, white stone.

"Turn it over."

She glanced at him and then back at her hand, turning it in her palm. On the other side she could see paint, faded to almost nothingness. She pulled it closer, her brows knitting as she tried to work out what it was.

"It's a butterfly," Josh said softly. "Or at least it was when I got it."

She tipped her hand, looking closer at it. Sure enough, the outline looked like it had wings, though they were very worn away. "When did you get it?"

"I found it in London, a few days after I arrived there."

"A few days after you left here?"

He nodded. Her heart felt funny. Like it was trying to knock its way out of her chest. "Why did you get it?"

"Why do you think?" He was looking at her carefully. Like he was almost afraid of her reaction.

"I don't know what to think," she admitted. "When you left, I assumed you forgot all about me."

"When I left, you were all I could think about. Then one morning on my way to work I walked past a pile of stones. They were all painted with different designs. In front of them was a sign saying to help yourself. So I picked the butterfly."

"But why did you keep it?"

"I don't know. I liked the way it felt in my hand, I guess. And the butterfly was pretty when you could actually see it. The years have worn it away."

Holly rubbed her thumb over the surface of the pebble. It was smooth and cool. "If you thought about me when you left for London, why didn't you contact me?" For that first year she'd practically lived by her phone. Checked her social networks constantly for a friend request that never came.

"I wish I had. At first I thought I could forget about you, but that was easier said than done. Then when I got back to Cincinnati the following year, I decided to go for it. Call you and see if you'd meet me."

"But you didn't call?" She turned on her side, her brow furrowed.

"No. I saw your engagement announcement online." A regretful smile flitted across his face. "And realized I was too late."

She closed her eyes, squeezing them tight. "Would you have come to me if you hadn't seen the announcement?"

"I would've at least contacted you. But I figured you'd moved on. And that was a good thing, because I truly believe

I would have made you unhappy. Workaholics have that tendency."

"I didn't get married," she reminded him.

"I know that now. But I didn't then. I forced myself to stop looking online about you. It didn't help."

"I was angry at you for not contacting me when you said you would."

He slowly nodded. "I get that."

"And when my mom introduced me to her step-nephew, and he made it clear he was attracted to me, I guess I thought maybe it was my chance to move on."

"Holly, I didn't expect you to wait for me. I only have myself to blame for all this. Everything that happened is old history. We're here now. That's all that matters."

But for how long? She wanted to ask, but she was afraid of the reply. Because this time they had together was strictly limited. In a few weeks, the deal would be complete and he'd walk away from Winterville – and from her. Again.

And she wouldn't pine over him. Not this time. For the simple fact that he'd have taken away her family's home. When it was just the two of them in here it was easy to forget that.

Only one of them could win. Which would mean neither of them winning in the end. That made her heart hurt. Because she'd never felt like this before about a man. Not even the one she was supposed to marry.

"Are you okay?" Josh asked her.

Holly nodded. "Yeah. Just taking a trip down the 'what if' highway."

He smiled gently. "That's a crap highway to take. Goes nowhere." He reached for her hand, taking the pebble from it and putting it carefully on his bedside table, before he pulled her against him. "We should get some sleep. It's some crazy hour in the morning."

"That's because you insist on using my body for your pleasure." She smiled against his chest.

He kissed the top of her head. "All the more reason to sleep while you can." He pulled the covers over them, tucking her against him. The warmth of his embrace felt like a balm to her soul.

"Good night, Josh," she murmured, her eyelids heavy. She nestled into the crook of his arms.

"Sweet dreams," he said, as she felt her muscles loosen and her eyes close. Her breathing slowed and regulated as he gently stroked her hair.

Through the thick haze of her sleepiness, she thought she heard him speaking, but it sounded so far away.

"What if I fell for you?" It was just a murmur. "Could it ever work out?"

She wanted to say yes, but sleep stole her words away.

✢ 17 ✢

Holly had the worst case of morning-after breath. Josh was thankfully still asleep, with one hand behind his head, the other down at his side. The sheets were tangled around his waist, revealing his perfectly sculpted chest, the early morning sun making his skin look warm and inviting.

He was breathtaking, but he definitely didn't need to be anywhere near her breath right now. Tiptoeing to the bathroom, she brushed her teeth thoroughly before pulling on his t-shirt and padding toward the kitchen to grab a glass of water.

Josh's makeshift office was set up in the corner. His laptop was closed, his papers neatly collected in a pile.

Unlike him, she'd always been a messy worker. The only order she had in her life were numbers. If he laid his eyes on her office, he'd probably have a fit.

Before she could reach for a glass, the silence of the room was interrupted by the shrill ring of his phone. Not wanting it to wake him up – because, let's face it, he was way too pretty when he was asleep – she reached for his phone and pressed the end call button.

Except her finger slid, and she accepted the call.

Dammit!

"Joshua?" a female voice asked.

Holly blinked as the screen flickered to life. It was a video call? Double damn. An older woman appeared on the screen, her face perfectly made up, her silver-blonde hair beautifully styled around her broad brow.

"Sweetie, are you there? I can only see the ceiling."

Holly froze. What the hell should she do? End the call and wake Josh up? She squeezed her eyes shut, trying to imagine *that* conversation.

"Honey? Can you hear me?" Then a mutter, "Maybe I'm not doing this right."

Exhaling heavily, Holly pulled the phone toward her, simultaneously smoothing down her hair with her other hand.

"Um, hey. Josh isn't available at the moment. Can I take a message?"

The woman didn't bat a lash. "I'm Josh's grandma. You're new. And I see you're wearing his t-shirt."

He could hear talking. And *laughter*. Josh rolled over on the bed, frowning when he saw Holly wasn't there. But it was definitely her voice he could hear. Maybe she was on the phone with one of her cousins. He grabbed his shorts and looked around for his t-shirt, wondering where the hell he'd thrown it last night.

Ah well. He'd find it later. Right now he needed a glass of water.

The voices got louder as he walked down the hallway to the kitchen. Holly laughed again, and it made him smile. Damn, he was an idiot for that woman.

"Every woman should have her own bank account," Holly

was saying. "And her own credit card. You should get one today. Seriously. Not because you have anything to hide, but because you're a strong, independent woman."

"I'm too old to change my ways."

"You don't look a day over fifty."

His grandma laughed. Wait! *His grandma?* With a sense of foreboding, Josh pushed open the door to the living area.

Holly was leaning on the breakfast bar, his t-shirt barely covering her sweet behind. She was holding his phone, grinning into the screen, her face propped up on her palm.

"I knew I liked you," his grandma said.

"If you like me, get a bank account," Holly replied to her. "You can do it over the internet. I'll send you some links."

Josh cleared his throat. "Good morning."

Holly looked over at him, her eyes wide.

"Is that you, Joshua?" his grandma asked.

He frowned at Holly. "Um, yeah, Grandma, it's me."

Holly lifted an eyebrow at the screen. "I won't put him on the screen, he's practically naked."

Jesus Christ.

His grandma laughed. "It's nothing I haven't seen before."

Holly held his phone and walked toward him, a grin on her face. Thank god the screen was facing her and not him.

"I wouldn't be practically naked if somebody hadn't stolen my t-shirt," he pointed out.

Holly was close enough for him to grab the hem of his t-shirt. He folded it in his fist, giving it a yank.

"Actually, he does want to talk to you," Holly said, turning the phone around and shoving it toward him. "There he is."

"Oh! He really is naked."

"I'm wearing shorts," he reassured his grandma, taking the phone from Holly's hand as he shot her a dark glare.

Holly smiled wickedly, grabbing the t-shirt and pulling it

over her head. "There you go, Josh. You can have it back now."

She was standing naked in front of him. Her long dark waves tumbled wildly over her shoulders, the tips grazing the swell of her breasts. Her nipples were hard and dark, her skin almost glowing beneath the kitchen lamp.

She'd never looked more beautiful. He swallowed hard, his fingers curling around the t-shirt.

"Grandma, I have to go." His eyes stayed on Holly's. Her lips were parted, tiny breaths escaping from them.

"You can't. I called you to talk about when you're coming back."

"I'm going to get dressed," Holly mouthed. She brushed past him, and he turned the phone just in time so his grandma couldn't see the naked woman walking through his kitchen.

He was a gentleman, dammit. Even if Holly was trying to lure him over to the dark side.

"I don't know when I'll be back yet." He watched as she walked through the door, her plump behind swaying. His mouth felt so dry he could light matches with it.

"Will it be before Christmas, do you think?"

"I have no idea." Right now he couldn't think past the next few minutes.

"Is Holly still there?"

He slowly brought his eyes back to the phone. "No, she's gone to another room." His bedroom. With his bed. Where she was probably laying naked right now.

"I like her, Joshua. I like her a lot. You should ask her to marry you."

Dear God, give him strength. "Grandma, I have to go."

"Of course you do, sweetie. Call me back later when your other brain is working."

He rolled his eyes and ended the call, stalking back to the bedroom, his t-shirt coiled in his hand like a weapon.

He was annoyed. And turned on. Not to mention ready to show Holly exactly who was boss.

From the way she smiled sexily up at him from his bed when he exploded into the bedroom, she was ready to find out, too.

"How did you end up talking to my grandma anyway?" Josh rubbed a towel over his hair as he walked into the kitchen. He was late for his first meeting of the day, but right now he didn't care.

Holly was making coffee. Which wasn't difficult, since it involved loading capsules into the machine and pressing a button. But he still liked watching her do it. Like they were a normal couple, getting ready for the day together.

Holly grabbed a cup and slid it beneath the spout. "I thought I should talk to her and ask her when she'd be available for our wedding," she said, her voice giving nothing away. "Since we've had sex and all." She tipped her head to the side, her gaze catching his. "You are going to make an honest woman of me, aren't you?"

"I don't think anybody could do that."

"Yeah, well I was hoping for some kind of heirloom engagement ring or something. I figure your grandma was the one to hit up."

He leaned on the counter, taking the cup she passed him. "How did you really end up talking to her?"

"Your phone rang and I thought I'd rejected the call, but I accepted it by mistake. I kind of panicked." She wrinkled her nose. "Sorry."

"It doesn't matter. And by the way, she already asked when we're getting married."

"Does she ask that about every woman you date?"

There was something in her voice – an inflection – that sounded almost vulnerable.

"Do you want to know about my dating history?" he asked her. "Because I'm an open book."

She pressed the machine again, this time filling her own espresso cup, before lifting it, steaming, to her lips.

"I just want to make sure nobody else has that heirloom ring. It's all mine."

"If you come over here you can ask me anything." He sat down on his office chair, spinning it around to look at her. Holly put her empty cup down on the counter and slowly walked around it. Even dressed, she turned him on like nobody else could. Her jeans were tight, nipping in at the waist, where her cashmere sweater hugged her perfect curves. He patted his legs, and she sat down on them, facing him so her thighs were straddling his.

And he wanted her all over again.

"You ask, I'll answer." He kissed her neck with soft lips.

"Don't you have a meeting to get to?" she asked him, her brow arching.

"I'm the boss. They'll wait." He grabbed his phone and quickly typed something on the screen. "In fact, it's canceled. So go ahead. Ask me what you want."

"Have you ever been engaged?" Her voice was tight.

"No." He slid his hand down her side, his fingers caressing the sliver of skin between her sweater and her jeans.

She inhaled sharply. "Have you ever lived with a woman?"

"Apart from my mother and grandma?"

"Yes."

He trailed his lips up her throat. "Yes."

She tipped her head back to give him better access. "For how long?"

"Six months." He grazed his teeth along her sweet jaw.

"Why did it end?"

"Because I'm an asshole who forgets birthdays."

"You forgot her birthday?" she asked, shocked.

"Yep." He pressed his lips to the corner of her mouth. She tasted of warm coffee. Bittersweet.

"Don't you have an assistant for that?"

"She forgot, too."

"You should have fired her."

"I gave her a raise. The relationship would never have worked long term. It's all good." He curled his hands around her waist, pulling her closer, until her breasts were pressed against his hard chest.

"Is she the only woman you've lived with?"

"Yep. Until now."

"I don't live with you. I'm just staying over." She ran her fingers over his hair. He closed his eyes as she raked his scalp with her nails.

"I didn't mean this. I meant the future." He slid his hands beneath her sweater, drawing circles on her taut stomach.

"Do we have a future?" She gasped as he traced her breasts. "You said it yourself, only one of us can win. Which means the other's going to lose, and whoever loses is going to hate the winner."

He looked up at her through his lashes. "You'll hate me?"

"I meant you'll hate me, since I'll be the one winning." Her eyes widened as he rubbed the pad of his thumb over her nipple.

"I could never hate you." His smile was soft. He buried his face in her neck, breathing her in. She smelled of his shower gel. He liked that a lot.

"Did you know your grandma doesn't have her own bank

account?" Holly gasped as he grazed his teeth across her neck.

"Mmm." He didn't want to talk about his grandma right now.

"She should. I told her that. It doesn't matter how much you trust your spouse, you should always trust yourself more." The last few words came out strangled, as he traced his fingers up her inner thighs. "Don't you think?"

"I'll give her your email address. You can tell her about it in more detail."

Holly smiled. "Too late. She's already given me hers. I'm sending her a few different accounts to choose from."

Josh blinked, his fingers stilling. "She's going to open one?"

Holly shrugged. "That's what she said."

He swallowed a laugh, because in one video call Holly had managed what he'd been trying to get his grandma to do for years. "Okay. Can we stop talking about her now?"

"What do you want to talk about instead?" Holly ran the tip of her tongue over her lip, their eyes catching.

"I figure we should stop talking." His voice was low. He cupped the warmth of her with his palm. "And start doing."

"Oh no, buddy. Not again." She shook her head. "I'm broken, remember. Any more action down there and I'll be raw."

"I have a very soft tongue." He gave her a crooked smile. He needed to taste her again. "And you'll get to rest tonight. Since you won't come over and stay with me."

"I told you, I have a family thing."

"I'll wait for you."

"You need a break as much as I do. You said it was like somebody had set you on fire down there."

He circled his thumb softly against her, through the

smooth fabric. Her lips parted as her dark, needy eyes met his. "Joshua..."

"I only get called that when somebody's telling me off."

"I am telling you off," Holly insisted. "If we do this again, I'll probably die." Her legs parted as he slid his hand along her waistband. "Dear God, what are you doing to me?"

He chuckled. "The same thing you're doing to me. I just want to taste you. That's all. I promise I won't hurt you."

"Okay." Her eyes flashed as they met his. He dipped his fingers inside the waistband of her jeans, beneath her panties, swallowing hard when he felt how slick she was. The next moment he was dragging her jeans down, lifting her onto his desk and burying himself between her sweet, taut thighs.

With the gentlest of touches and kisses, he swallowed down her pleasure, feeling his own desire rush over him as she begged for more, his teasing almost-licks sending her into a frenzy.

Sure, she wouldn't be here with him tonight, but he'd make sure she wouldn't be thinking about anybody else.

And for the rest of the day, he'd remember exactly how good she tasted.

❧ 18 ❧

"Oh. My. God." Everley leaned over the laptop she'd set up on North's breakfast bar. "We've sold out already."

"Of the VIP tickets?" Alaska asked, peering over her shoulder.

"No. All the tickets. Every last one of them." She looked pale. "Kris only put them on sale an hour ago. I don't believe this."

Holly grinned at her. "Believe it. Gray's a superstar, and everybody wants to show their love for Candy. You should be proud of yourself."

"I'm more scared that I'm making a huge mistake," Everley whispered. "What if I can't pull this off and end up looking like an idiot in front of all those people? Not to mention Gray damn Hartson. My name will be mud."

"You're not going to make a fool of yourself." North gave her a reassuring smile. "The show's going to be amazing, and so are you. We've got your back, kiddo."

"We've already started dividing the work up between us," Holly assured her. "North and Gabe are going to help Alaska with the staging. I've already spoken to Kris and I'm going to take over the admin side so he can concentrate on the technology side. And you just need to work on the show itself." Holly hugged her. "Stop worrying. You'll do a great job."

Gabe looked at the sales numbers. "Our fighting fund is going to be big."

Holly's laptop was open next to Everley's, and it started to buzz, letting her know that Natalie had started their video call.

"Are you all ready?" she checked with her cousins. They nodded and she clicked to accept the call.

They crowded around her, staring at the screen as it flickered to life. Damn, her reflection looked exhausted. She had enough bags under her eyes to stock Target.

"Hey!" Natalie said, grinning. She was sitting at a boardroom table next to a handsome, brown haired man in a suit. Holly bit down a grin at the fact that their shoulders were touching. "This is Ryan Simpson. Ryan, the one in the center with brown hair is my friend, Holly."

"Hi Holly," Ryan said, his smile genuine. "I've heard a lot about you."

Natalie was blushing, and Holly bit down a smile.

Holly introduced her cousins, and they all exchanged pleasantries. Natalie shifted in her seat. Were her legs brushing Ryan's underneath the table?

"So, we should probably get into it," Ryan said, his gaze shifting to Natalie. "We have a table booked for eight."

"Of course." Holly nodded. "Natalie said you might have found something we can use."

"Yeah." Ryan glanced at the printouts in his hands. "These are copies of the original deeds for Winterville," he said. The casualness had gone from his voice, he was all business now. "There are a few interesting clauses in there, but I wanted to check that they'd been recorded with the county. Which they had, but the original paper records hadn't been transferred to the computerized ones. Which means the purchasers have no idea of the stipulations."

Holly blinked. "What kind of clauses and stipulations?"

"There's one that I think could help your case. In the original deeds, your grandma had it written that any tenant would have the opportunity to buy their property at market value if they gave written notice."

"I don't understand," Everley said, frowning. "What does that mean?"

"It means that according to the deeds, anybody who owns a business in town could buy the building as long as they have the money, and the new purchasers couldn't do anything about it."

Holly exchanged glances with North. He got it, she could tell by looking in his eyes.

"But they'd have to buy it at market value?" North said.

"Yes. And with cash. That's also in the deeds."

North shook his head. "Then it won't help us. The shops here don't have that sort of money hanging around."

"What about the proceeds from the concert?" Alaska asked.

"Still not enough." North shook his head.

"This is where Ryan is a genius," Natalie said, shooting him a smile. "Because you don't need to buy *every* building in Winterville. Just a few strategic ones. Buy those, and they won't be able to create a ski resort because the businesses will be in the way."

Holly's mouth dropped open. "That *is* genius."

"Do you know how much that would be?" North asked.

"I don't know the local market well enough to say. You'd need to have them properly appraised," Ryan told him. "But if you're strategic about it, it's definitely do-able. Especially if you have these funds your cousin was talking about."

"We do." Everley nodded, her eyes wide. "We'll have the money real soon."

"So all we have to do is tell Gerber Enterprises that we want to buy the businesses?"

"Yes, but there are a few things you need to consider." Ryan glanced down at his notes. "First of all, Gerber Enterprises could claim they didn't know about the clause. And they don't, because the papers were buried. I had to use considerable charm with the recorder's office to have them found."

"What else?" North asked, his expression animated. He was excited, Holly could tell.

"You only have two weeks to complete your transaction after notifying the company. Which means you want to have the money liquid and available."

"When will it be here?" North asked Everley.

"It gets released the day after the concert. Except that's Christmas Day, so we'll have to wait for the twenty-sixth."

North sighed. "Damn, that's forever away."

"No, that's a good thing," Ryan said, smiling. "You can notify them *on* Christmas Day and that starts the countdown. If their offices are closed for the holidays, it gives them less time to try to stop you legally. Once the two weeks are up and you've paid them, they have no choice but to transfer the rights to the current tenants."

"But we'll need to keep things quiet until then, right?" Everley said. "Otherwise they might try and overturn the clause?"

"Exactly." Ryan nodded. "If you can work out what buildings will cause the most problems by being bought, I can draft up the contracts and letters, and have them ready for you to issue on Christmas Day. Everybody concerned, including the tenants, need to keep quiet, that's all."

"Didn't I tell you he's amazing?" Natalie said, grinning.

"Gerber Enterprises can't find out," North said, glancing at Holly.

"Of course they won't," Everley said quickly. "We're not stupid. And we can all keep a secret, right?"

Her cousins turned to look at Holly. She had no idea what North and Gabe knew about her relationship with Josh, but Everley and Alaska knew where she'd been disappearing to these past few nights.

"Right, Holly?" Everley repeated.

"Right." Her stomach did a little flip flop.

"Thank you," North said to Ryan and Natalie. "Seriously, we're all really grateful for what you've done."

"I'll send Holly an email with all the details," Ryan said. "First thing in the morning. Because now this beautiful lady and I are going out for dinner." Natalie grinned and waved at them, saying goodbye as she clicked to end the call.

"Oh my God!" Everley cried out, when the screen went black. "We're going to save Winterville. Can you believe it?" She hugged Holly. "This is all thanks to you."

"This calls for champagne," Gabe agreed, walking over to North's wine refrigerator, and pulling out a bottle. "We have a lot to celebrate."

North was grinning. Alaska was hugging Everley. And Gabe was winking at Holly.

She smiled back, because this really was a good thing. It was everything they'd wanted.

They'd be able to save their grandma's town, and the homes of all the people who lived in it.

It was what she wanted, right?

"Are you okay?" Everley asked her later that night, as they accompanied Holly back to the Inn. Alaska had walked over to talk with the night receptionist, leaving them waiting at the elevator for a lift to arrive.

"I'm good. Why do you ask?" Holly gave her a tight smile.

"Because you were really quiet tonight. And you hardly drank any champagne. Unlike Gabe." She wrinkled her nose. "Who knew he was such a lightweight? I swear he could barely walk by the time we left."

"I'm just tired." Holly gave her a reassuring smile. "Nothing a good night's sleep won't cure." It wasn't a lie, either. Spending her nights with Josh Gerber was anything but restful.

Crazy. Sexy. Emotionally perfect. But definitely not restful.

"Are you worried about what's going to happen with Josh?"

The elevator arrived and three guests walked out. Everley and Holly walked inside, and Everley pressed the button for Holly's floor.

"Are you walking me to my room?" Holly tried not to grin.

"Kinda. Alaska will be forever, so at least I get to talk with you while I wait for her. So why have you got a long face?"

Holly leaned against the rail. "I just don't like keeping secrets. It feels wrong."

The doors closed, and Everley shot her a speculative look. "You really like him, don't you?"

"He's a good man. I guess it would be easier if he wasn't."

"I mean *like him*, like him." Everley lifted an eyebrow. "You're falling for him."

It wasn't a question, but Holly still found herself trying to find the right answer. "I think I could easily fall for him if I let myself," she finally said.

"Will you let yourself?" The elevator arrived at her floor, and Holly walked out with Everley close behind.

Would she? The thought of it made her want to panic. "I just want to enjoy it for what it is."

"But you wish you didn't have to hide this thing from him."

"Something like that."

"I think you're worrying over nothing." They'd reached Holly's door, and Everley leaned against the wall while Holly found her key.

"You do?" Holly frowned.

"Yeah. Josh is a businessman. He'll know this is purely business." Everley shrugged. "Put it this way, do you expect him to tell you all his plans for demolishing this place?"

Holly shook her head. "No."

"Has he told you anything about what will happen once the escrow goes through?" Everley persisted.

"No he hasn't. We don't talk about the sale very much." They were too busy doing other things.

"Then he wouldn't and shouldn't expect you to share anything about this with him either. Let's face it, he knows that you're opposed to the purchase, just like the rest of us. He doesn't need to know the details."

"I guess..." Holly slowly nodded. Everley was making sense.

"I haven't seen you this happy in years," Everley said, as Holly pressed her key against the reader. "Stop overthinking this. And for god's sake don't sabotage it. You deserve this, Hol. You deserve to be happy."

Her heart clenched. "So do you."

Everley's smile was tight. "I'm not talking about me. Josh will understand. He will. I've seen how he looks at you. Just try to enjoy this time you have together, and stop sweating this." She bumped her shoulder against Holly's. "And if you're still feeling guilty, just do something extra nice for him."

"Like what?"

Everley winked. "I'm pretty sure you can think of something. Now I'm going to move Alaska along. It's been a long day and tomorrow will be even longer."

"Let me know if I can do anything to help."

"You're already doing enough. Taking over the admin is a huge help." Everley kissed her cheek. "Good night, Holly."

"'Night, Everley."

She couldn't sleep. Which was laughable, because her whole body ached as though she'd competed in two Ironman Triathlons in a row. Instead, she was staring at the patterns in the plaster of the Winterville Inn ceiling, wondering why her stomach was still tied in knots.

Because you're not a liar. Or at least, she wasn't a good one. And she'd never wanted to be. She prided herself on honesty and integrity. That's what made her job all the more delicious.

A glance at her phone told her it was just after midnight. There was a message from Josh on there wishing her sweet dreams. She tapped out a quick reply.

Are you awake? – H

A moment later, Josh's reply appeared on the screen.

I'm just getting ready for bed. Are you okay? – J

. . .

Instead of replying, she hit the call button. He answered before she could even exhale.

"Hey." His voice was warm and soft. It sent a shiver down her spine. "Are you missing me already?"

Her shoulders relaxed. "A little," she confessed. "But my lady parts aren't. They just sent me a thank you note for giving them the night off."

Josh laughed. "How was your night?"

"It was good." She pulled her bottom lip between her teeth. "Can I ask you something?"

"Sure."

"Do you have a plan for what happens to Winterville right after the escrow goes through?"

Josh paused, as though considering her words. "Yeah, we do. But I figure you wouldn't want to know about that."

"I don't think I do." Damn, this was confusing. "Would you in my position?"

"No."

"Okay then." She exhaled heavily.

"And I couldn't tell you even if I wanted to. It would be commercial suicide. If something went wrong because I opened my mouth I'd have to explain that to our investors and employees." He paused for a moment. "You understand that, don't you?"

More than he knew. "Yeah, I understand."

"Are we still good? Because this isn't personal. It's not about you and me. That's completely separate."

Just like Everley said. "We're still good," she said softly.

"I'm glad." His voice was warm. "Because I don't want to spend another night without you. My bed is way too big."

She smiled. For the first time all night, it felt genuine. "I can't sleep without you, either," she confessed.

"You want me to come over?"

Her smile widened. "No. Because then we definitely won't

get any rest. Maybe just talk to me for a while. Your voice might bore me to sleep."

He laughed again. Damn, he was sexy, even over the phone. "Have you checked your purse today?"

"Yeah." She tipped her head to the side. Why was he talking about her purse.

"How about in the pocket at the front?"

"I don't use that pocket."

"Look in it," he urged.

She switched him over to speaker and climbed out of bed, grabbing her purse. Sliding her free hand into the pocket, she felt the cool, smooth surface of a pebble.

Josh's pebble.

It felt heavy in her hand. "I found it," she said softly.

"I'm surprised you didn't find it before. It's been there all day."

The corner of her lips curled up. "Why did you put it in there?"

"I don't know." He sounded almost shy. "Maybe since I can't be with you tonight, I wanted a little part of me with you instead."

That was so sweet it made her heart ache. She'd never have believed him to be the kind of man who kept something so sentimental for all these years. Or who'd anticipate that she'd need that sentimental something to make her feel safe while all alone in her bed. It warmed her insides.

Is this what it was like to fall for somebody? She felt off balance, like she'd just stepped off a rollercoaster and was swaying to one side. It would be so easy to fall in love with Josh Gerber if she let herself.

And so easy to get hurt by him. He was confusing and beautiful and so different to anybody she'd met before. Not the heartless businessman she'd written him off as that first day at the Inn.

"I'll look after it," she promised. "And give it back to you tomorrow."

"It's weird, because I keep shoving my hand in my pocket and being surprised it isn't there."

"Do you always keep it in your pocket?"

"Yeah."

"For all these years?"

He laughed. "You think I'm crazy, right?"

"Not at all. Some guys have a security blanket, you have a security pebble. It's quite sweet."

"Ugh. The curse of quite sweet. No guy wants to be called that."

"What do you want to be called?"

"A sex god."

It was her turn to laugh. She lay back on the bed, phone in one hand, the pebble in the other. And it was weird, but she *did* feel better holding it in her hand. "Maybe you can be both. A sex god with a pebble fetish." Her voice was heavy. She was starting to feel sleepy now.

"I'll take that."

"You do that." She yawned.

"Are you tired now?" he asked gently.

"Getting there."

"Want me to keep talking?"

"Yes please."

He started telling her a story about a phone call he'd had with one of his investors, whose wife had gone out for the day, leaving him with three children under the age of four. He hadn't even gotten to the punch line before her eyes had fluttered closed and her breath had evened out. Hearing his low, warm voice was enough to make her feel content.

Secure.

And a little bit in love with the one man she shouldn't fall for.

❄ 19 ❄

Holly rolled over in bed, her eyes blinking open. A slow smile pulled at her lips when she saw him looking at her.

"What time is it?" she asked him.

"Early. Just after six."

She stretched her arms. "I promised I'd meet Everley at the theater this morning. She wants to check out all the angles from the stage."

"How's she holding up?" he asked. "There's only a week until the show."

"I know. She's pretty manic, but then Everley's always manic. She doesn't know how to rest. She's like our grandma."

"Whereas you could stay in bed all day," he teased.

"I could if it was with you."

He ran his tongue over his lip. "Did I tell you I got a ticket to the show? Two, actually. I was wondering if you'd go with me."

Holly blinked. "You want us to go to the show together?"

He shrugged. "Maybe it's what the town needs. Two

opposing sides coming together for Christmas. Goodwill to all men and all that."

"You seem to know a lot about Christmas for a guy who doesn't celebrate."

"I'm agnostic, not a heathen." He brushed his lips across hers. "So what do you say? Will you come with me to the show?"

"I might need to be backstage for some of it," Holly said. "But you can come backstage, too. I'll clear it with Everley." A little vee formed between her brows. "I'm surprised you got a ticket. They sold out within an hour. You must have been pressing refresh every five seconds."

He smiled. "I bought a resale."

"You're still giving funds to the enemy, though."

His eyes caught hers. "I figure my money isn't going to make a difference one way or the other. And anyway, I wanted to be with you."

She was smiling again. And it made his body feel warm. He couldn't remember the last time he'd felt this content. It wasn't just the sex, although that was good enough. It was being with her. Watching her when she didn't know he was looking. Knowing the sharp sound of her inhales when he kissed her neck or caught her by the waist as she walked past him.

Yes, there were issues between them. Like the fate of this town. But when it was over, they'd work things out. He'd find a way to make everybody happy. And to make her smile again.

"So you're definitely going to be here for Christmas?" she asked.

"Yeah." He nodded. "I guess I am."

"What are you going to do on Christmas Day?" There was a strange look on her face.

"Work, I guess. The same thing I always do."

"You should come to the Inn for dinner. The chef is cooking up a storm. Maybe you'll even enjoy it."

"Are you asking me to join you and your family for Christmas dinner?" His chest felt weirdly congested.

She swallowed. "I guess I am. But only if you want to."

He kissed her softly. "I'd like that very much."

"We need to do something about this place, too. You haven't even got a tree."

"You want me to decorate?" He was bemused. "Even though I don't celebrate?"

She shook her head. "Not if you don't want to. I just wanted to do something nice. Show you how we do things. But I get that you're not big on Christmas, and that's fine, too."

There was a lump in his throat. She was trying to do something nice for him and it touched him. "I do want to," he said, his voice thick. "Maybe we could decorate it together."

"Do you have any meetings this afternoon?" she asked him, tipping her head to the side.

"Only a couple. And nothing that can't be moved. Why?"

"I thought we could go to the Christmas tree farm and choose our own. It's more fun that way."

"To *North's* Christmas tree farm? Is that a good idea?"

Her gaze was soft. "Probably not. But I want to do it anyway."

"People will see us together. Talk about us." He wasn't sure why he was giving her this warning. The fact was, he wanted people to see them together. He wanted people to know about them.

"I can live with it if you can." He tucked a lock of hair behind her ear, trailing his finger across her cheek.

Her face lit up. "What time can you be ready?"

"I have a meeting until lunchtime. How about we meet at the coffee shop at one?"

"Cold Fingers Café at one." She nodded, lifting her head to kiss him again, her soft tongue running along the seam of his lips. "Be there or be square."

Her cousin was so talented, it made Holly's heart ache to watch her. Everley was a human dynamo, running through stage directions with the crew, playing the backtrack to each song that would be sung at the show, putting cut out pieces of cardboard where each singer would be standing.

And then she sang the final song, her sweet, clear voice echoing through the empty auditorium. Gabe was sitting on the other side of the venue to Holly, and Alaska was in the middle, checking the acoustics on the left side, while Holly checked them on the right, taking notes during each song so they could give feedback to Everley afterward.

It was amazing how much she sounded like their grandma. It made Holly feel wistful and full of memories. Candy Winter had always dominated the stage in the Jingle Bell Theater. People had traveled from all over the country – all over the globe, even – to attend one of her many Christmas shows each year.

As she'd gotten older, she'd cut down her appearances, though she was always available to sing the finale, much to the pleasure of the crowds.

And now Everley was singing Candy's signature song, in a voice that sounded so much like their grandma it brought tears to Holly's eyes. This had to succeed. They were going to save this town and all these bittersweet memories of her grandma.

Everley hit the final note, holding it as it reverberated

throughout the theater. When she finished, a smile tugged at her lips. Holly, Alaska, and Gabe jumped to their feet and applauded wildly.

Everley walked down the aisle, slumping into a chair next to Holly. "Tell me it was okay."

"It was more than okay. It was amazing. *You* were amazing."

Everley's lips curled. "It's going to work, isn't it? We're going to save this place."

Holly nodded, her chest tight. "Yes we are."

Gabe and Alaska sat down on Everley's other side. "That's only the beginning though, right?" Gabe asked, running his hand along his jaw.

"What do you mean?" Everley frowned.

"I mean once we've saved it from redevelopment then we need to make it profitable. Otherwise it's only a matter of time before the place goes bankrupt. Gerber Enterprises will still own most of the land and property, right? They'll still want a return on their investment."

"Maybe they'll sell it back to us," Alaska said. "Or lease it."

"Maybe they'll back out of the sale and our parents will own it again." Gabe raised an eyebrow. "Though the thought of that makes my blood turn cold. They'll only try to sell it again."

"We'll make it work," Everley said. "Okay, so everything got a little neglected after grandma got ill. But we can start building it up again. Getting the tourists back here. The publicity from next week will help."

"We're going to need a business plan," Holly said.

"I won't be able to stay around," Gabe murmured. "I have to get back to training. And Kris won't be here either."

"And I'm great at putting on a show, but terrible with numbers." Everley grimaced.

Alaska lifted her eyebrows but said nothing. She knew her sister well.

The next moment, all three of them were looking at Holly.

She lifted her hands up. "No way. I have my career. My own apartment. I can't stay here and run Winterville."

"Couldn't you take a break?" Alaska asked, her voice quiet. "Just until we get the place back on track."

"I'm not a businessperson. I'm an accountant. They're two different things. North could do it. He's great at bossing everybody around." Holly was starting to panic. They were all staring at her like she had all the answers.

Gabe chuckled. "Yeah, but he's got his *own* business to run. He'd be able to help, but he's always so busy down there."

"And I'm busy, too," Holly pointed out.

"You told me you could choose your own cases and hours." Gabe tipped his head toward her. "Just a few months would help."

"And it would be so amazing to have you here with us," Everley said, smiling hopefully at her.

"We haven't even stopped the redevelopment yet," Holly said. "There's no point in making any plans until we do."

It was a lie. Of course they should be making plans. Josh would in their position. He had a whole new resort designed, after all.

And they just had a concert and an ancient clause in the town deeds with no plans for the future.

"That wasn't a no," Gabe said, grinning.

"It wasn't a yes, either." Holly tucked a lock of hair behind her ear. She wished she could talk to Josh about this. He'd listen and advise, the way he did when she overheard him on video calls. He never got heated or riled. His answers were always measured and considered.

He was exactly the kind of person she wanted on her side. And the one person who couldn't be.

"Let me think about it," she murmured.

Everley let out a whoop and kissed her cheek. "Take all the time you need." Then she grinned. "It's going to be amazing having you living here. It really is."

"Your usual?" Dolores asked as Josh walked into the Cold Fingers Café. *His usual.* Josh smiled at the sound of that.

"Yes, please. And an Americano with room."

"Maybe a pastry, too?" Dolores lifted a brow. "Holly likes those."

He didn't ask how she knew he was meeting Holly. Dolores wasn't stupid.

"Yeah, that would be great."

"And would you like me to put it on your tab or Holly's?" Her eyes sparkled. "Because strictly speaking, if you're ordering it goes on Holly's, and if she's ordering it goes on yours."

"Put it on mine." His voice was firm.

"Good choice." Dolores winked at him, then turned to the coffee machine, grabbing two cups.

Josh's phone started to ring. He pulled it out, frowning when he saw his grandfather's name lighting up the screen. He diverted the call to voicemail, then turned his phone off for good measure. If he was going to be playing hooky from work, he'd do it in style.

"Hi." Holly walked in, the cold breeze lifting the ends of her hair beneath her wool hat. Her cheeks were pink, and her lips swollen. "Sorry I'm late."

She hesitated for a moment, then rolled to her toes and pressed her lips to his cheek.

And damn if his heart didn't pound against his ribs.

"Two coffees and a pastry." Dolores passed them over the counter, and gave Holly a strange look. "He insisted I put them on his tab. I tried to resist, but the man's irresistible."

Holly's eyes met his again. "So I hear." Her lips twitched, and he smiled at her.

"Are you ready?" he asked her, inclining his head at the door.

"Yeah, let's go."

She was quiet as they walked to his car, sipping at her coffee as he clicked the key fob to open the locks. He held the door open for her and she climbed in. When he walked to the other side, he pulled the driver's door closed before he turned to her, a questioning look in his eye.

"Are you okay? You're really quiet."

"It's been a long morning." She gave him a small smile. "And my ears are still ringing from the music."

"Are you worried about us doing this? Because we don't have to. I can live without a Christmas tree."

She let out a long breath, then sat up straight. "No, I'm not worried about doing this. I promised you a Christmas tree and we're getting it. It's going to be fun. I just need to decompress a bit."

"I know a good way to do that," he murmured.

Holly laughed. "Yeah, and we'll end up in bed and treeless."

"Sounds pretty good to me."

She relaxed against the seat. "Nope, we're getting a tree. Come on, let's go."

He turned on the engine, driving out of the town square and onto the main road out of Winterville. He'd been to the Christmas Tree Farm once before – eight years ago, when Holly was showing him around the town.

"Remember when we came down here on the snowmobile?" Holly asked, clearly thinking of the same thing.

"I thought you were going to kill me. You drove like a maniac."

She smiled. "You were the worst passenger. You held onto me like a leech."

"That wasn't because I was scared," he told her, his lips curling. "It's because I wanted to feel beneath your coat."

As they rounded the curve in the road, the farm came into view. The landscape was covered with fir trees, large and small, stretched as far as the eye could see. He pulled into the almost full parking lot, in front of the expansive shop where most people picked up their trees, and switched off the engine.

"So, picking a tree is really an individual thing," Holly said, sliding her hand into his once they'd both climbed out of the SUV. He loved how she always had to be touching him. He felt the same way. "Amber's mom used to say that you don't pick the tree, the tree picks you."

"Amber?"

"She's North's business partner. Her mom used to run the farm until she died. Amber couldn't handle it alone, so she sold fifty percent to North. He's always loved this place, so it was a match made in heaven."

"I think I remember Amber's mom. Didn't she try to chase me off the farm?" His brows knitted as he tried to remember his last visit all those years ago. He'd been too distracted by Holly to recall it in detail.

"That's right." Holly grinned. "How could I forget that. Luckily Amber is much more chilled. She's like one of the family. We all love her."

As soon as they walked through the door, the smell of pine trees hit them. A sweet note mingled with the low mustiness, giving it an almost addictive quality. It reminded him of the aroma of turpentine on a freshly varnished floor.

"Hey!" A pretty brunette walked over to Holly and hugged her. "I didn't know you were coming today. North didn't mention it."

"I didn't tell him." Holly looked around the shop, her fingers still intertwined with Josh's. "Where is he anyway?"

"Guess." Amber rolled her eyes and looked at the far end of the shop. There was a huge picture window, overlooking the farm beyond. At least ten women were standing there, noses almost pressed against the glass.

"Chopping logs?" When trees fell or were unsuitable for sale, North would chop them for firewood. It was a lucrative side business for them.

"Yep." Amber's gaze swept to Josh's. "Can you believe it? He's just swinging an axe and it attracts all this attention. I'm just glad it's winter. It's so much worse in summer when he takes his shirt off."

One of the women watching him let out a long, low sigh. Amber shook her head. "There aren't enough good looking guys in Winterville. Speaking of which, we haven't been formally introduced, though I saw you at the town meeting." She looked down at Holly's hand, still enveloped in Josh's.

"This is Josh Gerber." Holly smiled at him and he melted a little. "Josh, this is Amber Stone. She's one of the few people who keep my cousin's head on his shoulders."

"It's a losing battle," Amber said dryly, as one of the ogling women rapped on the window and called out North's name. "The man practically has his own fan club." She glanced at Josh again. "I figure he doesn't know you're both here together."

"Not yet. But I'm guessing he'll figure it out." Holly gave Amber a tight smile. "We want to choose a tree for Josh's house."

"Of course." Amber walked over to the desk by the entrance, grabbing a pad, pencil, and yellow tie. "Do you know what kind of tree you're looking for?" she asked Josh.

"I have no idea." He glanced at Holly. "I haven't chosen a tree before."

Amber didn't flinch. "How big is your living room?"

"It's about three hundred square feet," he said.

"And the height of the room?" Amber jotted something down.

"Ten feet."

"Great. You can pretty much fit any kind of tree. The important thing is to decide what kind of shape you want, what color. And the sharpness of the needles, too. Holly knows most of this stuff, she'll steer you right." She handed the pad and ribbon to Holly. "You know the drill. Choose your tree, write down the row number, then tie a ribbon around it. We'll get it cut and bagged up for you."

"Do most people choose their own?" Josh asked.

"Not as many as they used to. We get a lot of online orders now, and sell a lot of ready-bagged trees. People just don't have as much time as they used to. Plus there's our trade supply. That makes up at least fifty percent of our business. North's done an amazing job at building that side of the company up."

A customer interrupted them. "Ma'am, I'm looking for a six foot tree. It needs to be hypoallergenic. Do you have anything?"

Amber smiled at the customer standing behind her. "You okay to go ahead and choose your tree?" she asked Holly.

"Sure, you go ahead and serve. We've got this."

They walked out of the shop and into the farm itself. There was a cold breeze blowing, lifting the branches of the trees that laid out before them, dancing through their branches and scattering their covers of snow.

Josh seemed pleased that she'd invited him here. Maybe it was a big step for them both. They were publicly acknowledging that they had a little something going on.

It made her feel warm and anxious in equal measure.

Warm, because she wanted to make him happy. Wanted to see that smile pulling at his lips more often.

And anxious? Because she was getting a little addicted to Josh Gerber.

She pushed her hand into her jeans pocket. His pebble was there. She hadn't given it back to him yet, and he hadn't asked. She kind of liked carrying a piece of him around with her.

"Holly." North looked up at her, the axe still in his hands, the blade resting on the half-cut trunk. "What are you doing here?"

"Hey." She smiled. "We're hunting for a tree for Josh."

North's eyes swept over them both, then landed on Josh. "Uhuh."

Holly squeezed Josh's hand. "Any tips on where we should look? I was thinking of a Douglas Fir, they always smell the best."

"You'll be spending most of your time cleaning up the needles," North said, his fingers still curled around the axe handle. There was a tic in his jaw, but his expression betrayed nothing. "We got some white firs over in the far field that are looking good. Smell good, too, if you treat them right."

His gaze slid to Josh then back to her. He remained silent.

She gave North a smile. "Thank you, we'll go check them out."

The two of them stared at each other for a moment, then Josh nodded, and North nodded back. A little thrill rushed through her – was North accepting the fact she was here with Josh?

Was it really that easy?

"You go ahead," she said to Josh, leaning up to kiss his cheek. "I just want to talk to North for a second."

Josh held her gaze. "Sure."

His boots pressed down in the snow as he walked in the direction North had indicated. North watched him leave, then brought his attention to Holly.

"So *that's* happening, huh?"

"I thought you'd be angry."

"Is that why you ambushed me with it here? To make sure I behaved?"

"Something like that. And Josh really does need a tree. His house is so empty." She pulled her lip between her teeth. "Thank you for not making a scene."

"It's a mess, Hol. You know that, right?"

"It's complicated, that's for sure." She nodded. "But it'll be less complicated once Christmas is over. At least I'll be able to be completely honest with him then." And she couldn't wait. Sure, they agreed not to talk about business and Winterville, but it still made her feel uneasy to keep secrets. And by then he would have notice.

"You think he'll be okay with what we're doing?"

"I have no idea. But it's business, right?"

North nodded. "Right." His eyes flickered in Josh's direction again. "The man's got it bad for you."

"Shut up." Her cheeks flamed.

"I'm not kidding. The way he looks at you says it all."

Holly pulled her lip between her teeth. "Do you think I'm crazy?"

"I think you like complex things. You like solving problems. And if anybody can solve this one, you can."

"I really thought you'd react badly." She bit down a smile, looking away. "You've never liked him."

"You know me better than that. I'm not such a hot head anymore. I worry about you. I want you to be happy. But you're a grown ass woman, Hol. What you decide to do with your life is up to you." He pressed his lips together. "And as for Josh, well I guess I don't know him yet, do I?"

He swung the axe again, and somebody banged their fist on the window, where they were ogling him from the shop.

"I told Amber to paint over that damn glass," he muttered.

"You could chop the wood elsewhere," Holly suggested. "Where you don't have an audience."

"Tried that. They just find me. And then they get hypothermia to boot. At least this way they keep warm and I don't have to worry about getting sued."

"Shut up," Holly said, grinning. "You love it." They all did. North and Gabe, even Kris. The three of them had attracted female attention since they'd been teenagers. Now they were in their thirties, and their appeal to the women of Winterville hadn't lessened any.

North rolled his eyes. "Go get your Christmas tree."

"I'm going." She blew him a kiss. "Thank you. I mean it."

"Yeah well. Just don't get hurt, that's all I ask."

"Not planning on it." She turned and headed after Josh, putting her smaller boots into the tracks he'd left, allowing her to catch up with him, feeling lighter than she had in days.

For somebody that didn't celebrate Christmas, Josh seemed to know a heck of a lot about it. After they'd picked out their tree – an eight foot white fir with a perfect conical shape and mid green needles that smelled citrusy and fresh when you touched them – they'd headed back into Winterville where he insisted on stopping at the Christmas All Year Round shop for decorations.

They'd spent half an hour debating the merits of angels versus stars on the top of the tree. In the end he'd chosen a star, a beautifully simple white design that looked like it was worth way more than the forty dollars he paid for it. They'd waited patiently while his lights and ornaments were packed up, then headed back down to the tree farm where North had cut and packaged their tree.

And now they were back at Josh's house, the log fire sparking and hissing, the stereo streaming a playlist that Josh had chosen – fittingly with Candy singing most of the songs.

She showed him how to fit the lights on first, followed by the decorations – simple ones, just like the star, that highlighted his elegant taste. Shiny silver ornaments mixed with white leaping reindeer and fake hibiscus leaves, along with a thick satin ribbon that they'd wound through the branches, reflecting the tiny lights in a way that was almost magical.

"Now you have to put the topper on," Holly said, passing him the big white star. "And make a wish."

"A wish?" His forehead furrowed. "Isn't that for blowing out candles?"

"It works for Christmas tree toppers, too."

"Let's do it together." He passed her the star, his fingers still curled around it, and she tried to reach to the top. And failed miserably.

"I'm too short."

"I'm not." He left her holding the star and slid his hands down her sides, tightening them around her waist. The next moment he was lifting her, until the top of the tree was an arm's reach away. She laughed as she slid the topper on, then he brought her down and pulled her close.

"Do you do this every year?" he asked her.

"Decorate a tree?" She shook her head. "Not every year. This year I wasn't planning on being in my apartment so I didn't bother."

"But you did it when you were a kid, right?"

"Yeah. Candy used to let us decorate together if we were all here at the right time."

"What about your mom? Did you decorate with her?"

Holly's throat tightened. She shook her head. "Not often. She didn't like the way I put all the decorations in one place when I was younger, so she'd do it while I was asleep. And as I got older, she was busy in her relationships. Sometimes she didn't bother decorating at all."

He pressed his lips to her brow. "I'm sorry," he murmured.

"It's okay. For the past few years I've helped decorate the trees at the women's shelter where I volunteer, and that's always been so much fun. All the kids get completely overexcited and local companies donate so many decorations and toys. I still get my Christmas fix, just in different ways."

"Is that why you volunteer? To give those kids a better life?"

She blinked. Nobody had ever asked her that before. "The shelter approached me because so many of their clients needed financial help. A lot of them had never dealt with money before, most of them weren't allowed to. Financial abuse can be as bad as other types of abuse. Another way to exert control."

"That's why every woman should have their own bank account," he murmured. "Like you told my grandma."

"Exactly. A shrink would probably tell me that my choice of job is directly influenced by how my mom lived her life. Flitting from husband to husband, always looking for somebody to take care of her. And when they weren't around, she'd come running home to her mom for help. She never took responsibility for herself." Or for Holly. And yeah, that *still* stung. "I like being able to help those who don't have power over their lives. I love watching them become empowered, become strong.

"Is that why you didn't get married?" he asked her. "Because you were afraid of being disempowered."

She let out a long breath. This conversation was well overdue, she knew that. If she was brave enough to take Josh to North's shop, she could be brave enough for this. Even if she didn't come out of it smelling of roses.

"I was young and stupid and made bad decisions," she told him. "My mom had recently remarried, and I'd just graduated from college. For the first time in my life, she actually wanted to spend time with me. She invited me to her new husband's house in Sicily for the summer. We'd swim together, go out for drinks, it was like she was a good friend for the first time in my life. And then I met Marco."

"Your fiancé." Josh's jaw was tight.

"He was my mom's husband's nephew. He worked for him.

We started double dating. I loved that my mom was giving me so much attention. She'd climb into my bed at night and we'd whisper and giggle about our men. And she'd have all these wonderful ideas about how we'd spend the rest of our lives in Sicily with them. It was like being part of her inner circle, when before she'd barely noticed me."

"So you agreed to marry him."

Holly bit her lip. "Yeah. And it was a mistake from the start. But it made everybody so happy. Especially Mom. I guess for her it was a vindication of the way she lived her life. She kept saying that she'd found her daughter again. And I lapped it up."

Josh sat on the sofa, pulling her onto his lap. She nestled into him, feeling his arms wrap around her.

"As the wedding approached, I started realizing what a mistake it was. I hardly knew this guy. I had no job, no prospects of getting one, and I was homesick as hell. Then I called my grandma and she told me I was making a mistake."

"Sounds like she was right."

Holly nodded, her face pressed into his neck. Damn, he smelled good. "Grandma flew over and my mom took it personally. Told her to butt out, that I was her daughter. That Candy had made more than enough mistakes with her own children, and she didn't need to stick her nose in here. So Grandma arranged for a private jet to pick her up from the airport. Told me there was a place on there for me if I wanted it. And that no matter what I did, she'd always love me and be there to take care of me."

"You left him."

"It didn't feel like I was leaving Marco. I barely knew him. It was my mom I was leaving. And she was so angry, so hurt. She wouldn't speak to me after."

Josh brushed his hand over Holly's hair, pulling her closer. "It wasn't your fault."

"I could have handled it so much better." She sighed. "Things between me and my mom were never great, but I made everything so much worse. I don't think we'll ever have the kind of mother and daughter relationship other people have."

"Would you like that?" he asked her.

She pulled her lip between her teeth, considering her answer. "I guess I'd like to be cordial with her. And not argue every time we see one another. But I don't know how to get to that point."

"For what it's worth," he said softly, his eyes catching hers. "I've never met a stronger woman than you. If anybody can make it work, it's you."

Her heart did a little flip flop. "Thank you."

A half smile pulled at his lips. His eyes were hooded, desire sparking in the depths behind them. "Do you want to know what I wished for?" he asked, brushing his lips across her collarbone.

"What?" She tipped her head back to give him better access. Her ass pressed against his legs, and she could feel him stirring beneath her.

"You, naked beneath my tree for Christmas."

Holly mock-winced. "Sounds painful. All those needles."

He chuckled. "That's why we went with the white fir. It'll smell good when they're sticking out of your ass."

She curled her arms around his neck. "Stop seducing me with your wanton promises."

"Then stop wiggling your behind on my groin."

"Never." She captured his lips, arching her back as he slid his hands down her spine.

"That's another thing I wished for," he whispered against her mouth. "Don't ever stop."

❧ 21 ❧

Josh re-read the email, his lips curling down as he typed out his reply. It was only three days until Christmas Eve. He thought he'd be done with crap like this until the new year. Shaking his head, he deleted it and picked up his phone because some things were better done in person.

"I know why you're calling," Willa said, as soon as they connected. "And it's not my fault. Oren's insisting on this meeting. And I really don't think you can do it by video call."

Oren Stiles was one of their biggest investors. When he said jump, you leapt like your life depended on it. It didn't stop Josh from feeling pissed, though.

"Did he say what it's about?"

"The Shalvis takeover. There's some resistance from the board and they're riling up the shareholders."

Josh rubbed his temple. This wasn't exactly urgent. "I thought that was all sorted. What does Crystal say?" Surely his head of investments could handle it.

"She thinks it's a storm in a teacup. But you know Oren, he wants to know that everything is going right. And sometimes only the CEO can console him. When I said it might be better meeting after Christmas, he started muttering about your grandfather. Said he'd be seeing him at some party and maybe he could intervene."

The last thing Josh needed was his grandfather intervening in anything. "Okay, book him in for me. I'll drive home tomorrow. Is there anything else I need to know?"

"Not at the moment." Willa paused. "Although if you're coming home, do I need to contact your housekeeper? And there's the Christmas party on the twenty fourth – will you be coming to that?"

"No I won't. I'll meet with Oren then drive back to Winterville on Christmas Eve."

"Are there problems still?" Willa sounded sympathetic. "I swear that purchase is more trouble than it's worth."

"Nothing I can't handle. I'm hoping everything will be finished by Christmas Day." Or at least the purchase side would. "Actually, while I'm back in Cincinnati, can you arrange for me to meet with Kevin and Elizabeth? And get one of our lawyers there. I want to talk them through something."

"Sure. I'll do that. I'll schedule them all in on the twenty-third. That way you can leave Cincinnati on Christmas Eve morning, save you from driving in the dark."

Josh bit down a grin, because once upon a time he'd driven through the mountains in the dark and almost totaled his car.

That's how he ended up here the first time.

This time he'd be coming back deliberately. Because he wanted to spend Christmas with the woman he couldn't get out of his mind. The one who made this place feel more like home than anywhere he'd lived before.

"Hey," Holly said, walking into the kitchen as he ended his call. She was fastening an earring. "I need to head out, I promised Everley I'd help her in the theater. Do you want to meet in the café later?"

"That sounds good." He flashed her a smile. "I need to head back to Cincinnati tomorrow."

Her face fell with disappointment.

"It's just for two nights. Don't worry, I'll be back on Christmas Eve. I promised to take you to the show."

"I remember." Her voice was soft. "Is everything okay? With work, I mean."

"It's all good. Nothing I can't handle." He kissed the tip of her nose.

"I'm not sure I can handle you gone. The last time we spent a night apart I couldn't sleep."

He smiled at her consternation. "You did sleep," he reminded her. "I talked until you snored."

"I didn't snore."

"You definitely did. It was kind of cute. If foghorns can be cute."

She shook her head. "I've changed my mind, I can definitely handle you gone. I'm going to starfish in bed and watch Chris Hemsworth movies."

"That's my girl." He kissed her again, this time wrapping his hands around her waist. "I'd ask you to come with me, but I'm going to be constantly working. You'd spend twelve hours in a car for the round trip, and then the rest of the time waiting around for me."

"I'd be your beck and call girl."

"*Pretty Woman*," he murmured. "Nice." He pressed his lips to her neck, feeling the heat of her pulse. "Anyway, when I take you home I'd like to show you around in style. Introduce you properly to my grandma."

Holly looked up at him, her eyes shining. "You want me to meet her?"

"Why wouldn't I? Isn't that generally what happens? You fall for somebody then take them home to meet your family."

A smile crept across her lips. "You've fallen for me?"

"Isn't that what I just said?"

"You did. But I wanted to double check. You could have said you're appalled by me and I misheard."

"I'm definitely appalled by you," he whispered in her ear. "Especially after that thing you did to me last night."

She laughed and pulled away. "That wasn't appalling. *That* was amazing."

"It was both appalling and amazing. And I'll be thinking about it while I'm away. Then when I'm back, we'll talk about us. How we're going to manage this thing with you in Chicago and me in Cincinnati."

Holly pulled her lip between her teeth. A flicker of something passed over her eyes. "Yeah," she said softly. "Let's do that." He could hear the thump of her heart against her ribcage.

"Uh oh," she said, stepping back. "I recognize that look, Gerber."

"What look?" He frowned.

"That sexy as hell, I'm going to get to tear Holly's clothes off and make her forget her name look."

"That's a look? Do other people have that look?"

She laughed. "Just you."

"I'm glad to hear it."

Holly's phone started to ring. She pulled it out of her purse and grimaced. "Oh shit, that's Everley. I was supposed to be at the theater five minutes ago." Holly rolled onto her tiptoes and pressed her soft lips to his. "Let's do something nice tonight. Something to get us through the days apart."

"Sounds good." He kissed her back, his hands caressing her hips. "Good luck at the theater. I'll see you at the café at one?"

"One's perfect. See you later."

"How's Josh's tree settling in?" North asked, as he walked into the theater. Holly and Everley were backstage, working through the admin tasks she'd asked Holly to take over.

"It's perfect," Holly said, smiling up at him. "You grow the prettiest trees."

"That's what I like to hear." He kissed both his cousins on the cheek, then put down the papers he'd been carrying. "So I've been talking with your friend, Ryan. I've approached the three businesses in town that we think would be most likely to stop redevelopment from working. They've all agreed to put an offer in on their buildings."

"Of course they have." Everley grinned. "They want this as much as we do."

"They've also agreed that they'll enter into a new loan repayment agreement with us. At favorable terms. We're going to set up a foundation." North glanced at Holly. "Any money that's left over will go into the foundation to pay for the running of this place. I really think we can make it work."

"That's good." Holly nodded.

"It's great," Everley said, clapping her hands together. "We can definitely make it work. We're like the dream team."

"Something like that." North rolled his eyes. "Anyway, I'm going to get these all scanned and sent to Ryan so we're ready to send them over on Christmas."

"And I need to head to the coffee shop," Holly said.

"You meeting Josh?" Everley gave her a wide smile.

"Yep."

North grunted but said nothing. He was getting good at that. And she was glad, because despite all this wrangling, Josh had told her he wanted to talk about their future.

And it warmed her inside.

As she walked out of the theater, Holly looked up at the sky. It was the palest of blues with fluffy clouds that reminded her of the ones she used to draw as a child. It hadn't snowed for more than two days – some kind of record for Winterville, though she'd heard some of the townsfolk muttering that they were due for a storm. As long as it didn't come before Christmas, and ruin Everley's show, she'd be happy.

The café was bustling when she walked inside. Frank waved at her from his usual table, and opposite him Charlie was grumbling about a delivery he was waiting on. She could see Josh sitting by the fire at what had become their table, two mugs in front of him, an unfolded *Wall Street Journal* in his hands.

"He insisted on paying for them again," Dolores said, looking up at Holly. "It's not my fault."

"Of course it isn't." They were over the tit-for-tat by now. "Everything okay?"

Dolores was one of the three businesses who would be buying their buildings. But she didn't let on.

"Everything's dandy. My son and his family arrive tomorrow for the holidays. He even managed to get tickets for the show."

"That's fabulous news." Though Everley would have found him some if he hadn't, the same way she had for all the townsfolk who wanted to attend.

"It's nice to see you having a little fun for a change, too," Dolores said, her gaze sliding over to Josh, who still hadn't noticed her arrive. That *Wall Street Journal* article he was reading must be riveting.

"Thanks." Holly smiled. "It *is* fun."

"And maybe something a little more than fun, too?" Dolores persisted. "That man has goo goo eyes for you."

Strange how many people said that. Every time Holly

looked at him it was like she fell a little more for him. Her biggest worry was that it was too hard too fast. And that it was impossible for him to feel the same way that she did about him.

And yeah, that scared her a little.

Okay, a lot.

But she didn't want to think about that now. She was too busy ogling the handsome CEO by the fireplace.

It was only when she sat down in front of him that he actually pulled the paper from his face. A big smile pulled at his lips, and he leaned forward to take her hand. "Hey."

"Hey." She squeezed his hand and grabbed her bag. "I have something for you."

"What is it?"

She curled her fingers around the pebble and passed it back to him. "I want you to take this with you to Cincinnati. So there's a little bit of me in your bag. It worked for me."

He picked up the pebble, looking at it as he turned it in his hand. "Thank you."

"Am I interrupting something?"

Holly blinked at the familiar voice. Her mom was standing by the table, her blonde hair elegantly coiled at the base of her neck. As usual, her face was impeccably made up, her clothes expensively styled.

"Mom." Holly tried to bring herself to smile. They hadn't spoken since the night at the theater. And it still hurt.

"Holly." She nodded, then smiled at Josh. "And Mr. Gerber. So the rumors I've been hearing are true."

"What rumors are those?" Holly asked. Josh nudged her foot with his beneath the table. When she looked at him, his eyes were full of warmth.

They grounded her.

"That you have a new boyfriend." Her mom's eyes flashed with interest. "I guess it's true."

Holly tried to think of something to say, but she felt frozen. As though keeping her mouth shut was the best way not to end up in an argument.

Josh was gazing at her, a question in his eyes.

"Um, yeah, it's true."

"That's wonderful. In that case, you should both come over to my place on Christmas Eve. I'm having a little cocktail party. The last one we'll be having in Winterville, I guess." Her laugh was a tinkle. "Garrick will be shaking from four p.m."

"I'll be at the theater. I promised Everley I'd help with the show," Holly said.

"I'm sure you can drop in first. It's our last holiday here, Holly. I'd like to see my daughter for some of it."

She could feel the argument brewing. It made her chest hurt.

"We'll be there at four," Josh said.

Holly blinked at him. He shrugged, then gave her a soft smile.

Her mom clapped her hands together. "Wonderful. I'll see you both then." Her mom kissed Holly's cheek, then smiled at Josh. "So handsome," she whispered, then turned around and walked out of the café.

"What was that about?" Holly asked, frowning. "I don't want to see her on Christmas Eve." She couldn't bear to argue on that day. It was too special.

"Why don't you want to go?" he asked her.

"Because it'll end in tears. It always does."

His expression softened. "I'm sorry. If you don't want to go, then we won't. I should've kept my mouth shut."

Holly sighed. "It's not your fault. It's me. I'm being a big kid by avoiding her."

"It's understandable." His voice was low. "But you said

yourself that you wanted things to improve between you. How can that happen if you keep avoiding her?"

"I don't know." Holly shook her head. "I guess it can't."

"So do you want to go?"

She exhaled heavily. "Okay, we'll go for an hour. But you can drive because I'm going to need all the cocktails."

"Of course I'll drive. I'm a better driver." He grinned. She loved that he knew how to lighten her mood just by joking with her. It was a beautiful thing.

"Says the guy who crashed into town all those years ago."

"One crash in fifteen years of driving, Holly." He folded his arms over his chest, as though that was the end of the discussion.

"I've had no crashes since I was sixteen."

"That's because you drive like a snail."

"I do not. I'm just careful."

"A careful snail." He lifted his cup to his lips, smirking.

She knew what he was doing. Taking her mind off her mom, and every other thing that seemed to be pulling at her brain. And it was working, because she was grinning madly at this man with the sexy eyes and dark hair that tumbled over his forehead.

Her CEO in shining armor.

"When are you leaving again?" she asked him archly.

He lifted an eyebrow. "First thing in the morning."

"Remind me to do that appalling thing to you again tonight. I want you aching while you're driving all that way."

His lip curled. "You see, that's the difference between us. You think that's a threat, I think that's a promise."

"Maybe it's a bit of both."

"Maybe." He stood, and kissed her on the brow. Funny how she was used to these public displays of affection now. She'd expected the whole town to be gossiping about them.

For there to be pages of comments on the Winterville Facebook Page.

Or at least for people to look at them when Josh Gerber kissed her thoroughly.

Instead, everybody was minding their own business, dammit.

"I'll see you at the house later," he said.

"You will. I'll bring dinner." She'd already spoken to the chef at the Inn. He'd agreed to make her dinner to go.

"Make sure you drive carefully."

She nodded, her expression serious. "Like a snail."

He laughed and headed for the exit.

❧ 22 ❧

The sound of music woke him up. Not the movie with Julie Andrews, but the crooning of a low voice singing about roasting chestnuts. Josh sat up in bed, frowning when he saw that Holly wasn't laying next to him, before he reached over to grab his shorts.

They'd spent the night talking and eating, then he'd taken her to bed for some thorough loving. And at the end, he'd felt a little lost, knowing that tomorrow night he'd be sleeping alone. Sure, he'd be back as soon as he could, but it was like he was leaving Narnia and the magic was going to disappear behind him.

Everybody back home would expect him to be the same person. But he wasn't sure who that guy was anymore.

He'd disappeared with their kiss in the cabin. Been over-written with his first slide inside her. Obliterated when he realized he was falling in love with Holly Winter.

Slipping his hands through his t-shirt – one that Holly clearly hadn't 'borrowed' – he walked into the living room, trying to find the source of the sound.

Another wave of Christmas music washed over him. The crooner was telling him that Santa was on his way. His brows creased as he looked around the room, his eyes alighting on the Christmas tree they'd decorated together.

The lights were sparkling, their tiny bulbs reflected in the shiny ornaments and decorations they'd liberally strung onto the branches. But that wasn't what caught his gaze.

It was Holly, laying naked beneath the tree, a bow tied around her waist, and a soft smile pulling at her lips.

"I thought I'd give you an early gift," she said, her voice throaty.

"Don't move," he told her. "I want to commit this view to memory."

She really was beautiful. Her skin was porcelain, her curves rising and dipping in all the right places. Her nipples were pink and hard, her dark hair splayed out in a cloud around her. She bit her lip and shivered.

"Are you cold?"

"Freezing. I didn't realize it'd take you this long to wake up."

He bit down a laugh. "How long have you been laying there?"

"Long enough for my nipples to feel like they're about to drop off."

He walked toward her, his gaze catching hers. Dipping at the knee, he ran his hands over her bare stomach, closing his eyes at how soft her skin felt.

"Can I open this?" he asked, his fingers trailing along the bow.

"You can." Her lips curled. "Merry Early Christmas."

"I have no idea how I'm going to top this gift," he murmured, pulling at the bow. The thick red ribbon parted, leaving her completely naked.

He ran a finger down her abdomen, touching the scant hair covering her core. Holly swallowed hard, letting out a soft sigh as he slid his finger along where she needed it most.

"I have to leave in an hour," he said, to himself as much as to her. How the hell could he walk away from this?

"I know. So get started, Santa."

This was turning out to be the longest day *ever*. Holly glanced at her watch, grimacing when she saw it was only one in the afternoon. She'd spent the morning with Everley, who'd been patient enough to listen to her mooning about Josh, before sending her off to the coffee shop so she could work in peace.

Then she'd spent an hour with Dolores, who was asking her about the plan to save Winterville now that Josh was gone. As one of the three strategic businesses buying their buildings, she was excited about being able to keep her café. She was even more excited when Holly showed her how she could save money on her supplies, start charging a few cents more for each cup, and how it would make the difference between being in the red and the black.

But now the lunchtime rush had taken Dolores' attention away, and Holly felt lost again. She stopped at Frank's table, gamely answering his math questions for five minutes, but even he'd gotten bored and had started working on his third crossword of the day.

There was nothing left to do except head to the Christmas Tree Farm and annoy North.

Today he was working in the shop. Though most of their customers had already bought their trees by this point in December, there was still a steady flow of people coming in. A couple of women were carefully looking at the Christmas garland, discussing the merits of holly versus ivy, while sending hot looks over at North as he leaned on the counter.

"Hey stranger," he smiled at Holly as she walked inside.

She leaned on the counter and smiled at the two women. They were frowning because she was blocking their view. "I see your fan club is here again."

"Shut up." He shook his head. "They're just really keen on the garland."

"How long have they been here?"

North sighed and shrugged. "About twenty hours."

She started to giggle, because the expression on his face told her how awkward he found this female attention. It was his own fault. In his younger days, he'd been a little too free with the ladies of Winterville. Now he had to pay the price.

"Where's Amber?" she asked. North's business partner usually ran interference for him, but she was conspicuously absent.

"She's delivering trees and garland to the theater. You probably passed her on the way. I said I'd cover the shop while she and Alaska decorated." He looked like he was regretting that offer.

"Hey, two of my favorite people." Gabe walked in, a grin on his face. He leaned down to press his lips against Holly's cheek. "I brought you some lunch," he said, passing a brown bag to North.

The women behind them started to talk in low tones. There was only one thing better than a Winter man; and that was *two* Winter men. Gabe had broken his own share of hearts while he was a young man. And now that he was a successful snowboarder, he got even more attention.

And unlike North, he seemed to revel in it. "Hello, ladies," he said, shooting the two of them a grin. "Are you looking forward to Christmas?"

They were about to hyperventilate at any minute. When Gabe gave a person his attention, there was no telling what would happen.

"Stop encouraging them," North said through gritted teeth. "Can you two just get out of here? You're ruining my mood."

"I didn't say anything." Holly held her hands up.

"Yeah, but you're all jittery. And I know why and I don't want to talk about it." North lifted an eyebrow.

"Why is she jittery?" Gabe asked, his brows knitting.

"Because her boyfriend's gone until Christmas Eve."

Gabe's lips formed a big 'oh'.

"I'm not jittery. I'm just bored. Everley doesn't need help, and you don't either. Even Dolores told me I needed to go out and get some fresh air." Holly wrinkled her nose. She never got bored. But now she couldn't remember how she kept herself occupied before Josh came into her life. It was stupid, she knew it.

"I have a ton of paperwork you can do if you're looking for something to occupy yourself with," North said, inclining his head at the office behind him. Holly looked at the stacks of bills and invoices on the desk and grimaced.

"No thanks."

"I'm going cross country skiing in a minute. Why don't you join me?" Gabe suggested.

"I haven't skied in years."

"It's like riding a bike. All you gotta do is shuffle your legs." Gabe shrugged as though it really was that simple. "Come on, we've hardly spent any time together and I'll have to leave for training in a few weeks. We've got Everley's old gear at North's house. She won't mind you borrowing it."

Holly nodded. "I'll give it a try." It had to be better than overstaying her welcome here.

Holly had skied a lot in her youth, but she'd always gotten frustrated that she couldn't keep up with her boy cousins. But right now the distraction was exactly what she needed. She smiled as she and Gabe sat outside North's lodge and clipped on their skis.

She was wearing ski pants and a sports top – necessary to soak up the perspiration – along with a light winter coat that would keep the wind out but stop her from getting overheated.

Because one thing was for sure, cross country skiing took a lot more energy than propelling yourself downhill.

Gabe took it easy on her at first, leading her along the simple trails that were used for hiking in the summer. There were no specific cross country routes in the backwoods of Winterville, just like there were no ski slopes or snowboarding hills. Candy had wanted to keep the town simple, and dedicated to all things festive. So they'd always been allowed to ski where ever it was safe, among the trees and around the mountain, where very few people went in the winter.

Holly kept her knees and ankles loose, letting out soft breaths as she thrusted herself forward with each leg sweep, her thigh muscles protesting at the effort they were putting in. She was moving in a herringbone pattern, the same way she would skate on ice, her body sweeping from side to side as she followed her cousin ahead.

"We've got a little downhill coming up," Gabe shouted, grinning at her as he looked over his shoulder. "You remember how to do that, right?"

"I put my skis in your tracks and hope I don't die?" She was panting now. How unfit was she? Even those long nights of exertion with Josh hadn't prepared her for this.

Gabe grinned, easily skiing down the slope, even though

he was cutting through virgin snow. He held his poles up, and angled his body forward, the only sound the rush of his blades against the track.

She took a deep breath. She never did like downhill skiing. Hated the way it made her feel so out of control. But still, she wasn't going to let Gabe know that, he'd tease her for days. So she pushed herself off with a pole, and tried to line her blades into his tracks.

"You're a train, Hol," Gabe shouted, waiting for her at the bottom. "Just keep in the grooves."

Her speed started to accelerate, the cool air rushing past her face. Gravity was pulling at her, trying to drag her down as quickly as it could. Her heart was racing too fast, matching the rhythm of her panicked breaths. She didn't like this at all.

And she was going to fall.

"Do a half wedge," Gabe shouted out. "Slow yourself down."

What the hell was a half wedge? Holly tried to lean back, bending her legs when she should be keeping them straight, as her arms started to windmill in panic as she attempted to decelerate her descent.

She could hear Gabe laughing, the bastard. If she had any breath left, she would have shouted at him. Instead, her teeth were clenched, her legs screaming, the air rushing through her ears like they were a wind tunnel.

"Turn!" Gabe shouted. "Watch out for the tree."

What tree? She looked up at the looming overgrown fir. *Shit*! She leaned to the side, but her feet kept heading straight for it, leaving the tracks that Gabe had made which circled to the right.

"Stop!" Gabe wasn't laughing any more. He was unclipping his skis and running up the hill. "Throw yourself down. *Do it now!*"

Her rapid breath caught, as the streak of green and brown got bigger. Then she did as Gabe said, and launched herself to the left. Her body hit the bank of snow, the air rushing out of her, powder spraying all around as Gabe reached her, panting.

"Are you okay?" He leaned over, frowning.

Holly lifted her head, winded.

He touched her helmet, nodding with satisfaction when he felt it was still firmly fixed to her head. "Anything hurt?" he asked.

She inhaled deeply, trying to regain her breath. "Just my pride," she managed to stutter.

Gabe laughed, relief washing over his face. "Dammit, Hol, I wish I'd been recording you." He reached for her hand. "Can you sit up?"

"Yeah." She let him pull her up until her back emerged from the snow.

He sat down beside her, rustling in his pocket until he brought out a flask. "Want some?"

"What is it?" She shook off her helmet, flakes flying everywhere.

"Whiskey. The good stuff. From the G. Scott Carter distillery."

"Only the best for you."

He loosened the lid and passed the flask to her. Holly took a swig, wincing at the burn. "You're gonna have some bruises tomorrow."

"I blame you for every one of them." She passed him the flask back and he took a sip, his eyes still sparkling.

"I told you to wedge."

"Remind me what a wedge is again?"

He started to laugh again. "Man, you need some lessons."

"Yeah, well I'm not planning on coming out with you again."

He bumped his shoulder against hers. "I'm glad you did. This is nice. We don't often spend time just the two of us."

She nodded, because he was right. This *was* nice. And despite the throbbing in every muscle she owned, it had taken her mind off things. Made her less jittery, if a little more bashed up. Gabe passed her the flask and she took another mouthful.

"So you and Gerber, huh?"

"Did North ask you to talk to me?" She gave him a half-smile.

Gabe tipped his head to look at her. "Nope. I just want to make sure you're happy."

"I am. Very happy."

"That's good." He nodded, looking into the distant valley. "So how are you going to handle this double crossing him thing?"

Holly frowned. "I'm not double crossing him. We're just trying to find a way to save this town. And anyway, we talked and agreed that business is business. He'd do whatever it takes to win, and so would I." Her stomach still gave a little twist, though. The sooner they got this over with, the better. She wasn't a natural liar. She hated deceit, even if it was for a good cause. "He's a businessman. He'll understand it isn't personal."

Gabe shrugged. "I guess."

Holly turned to look at him. "You don't think he'll understand?"

"I'm trying to put myself in his position. If it was a fellow snowboarder who I was in a relationship with but ended up double crossing me and winning a race, I'd be pretty pissed. No matter how hot she was." He pressed his lips together. "Not that a woman could beat me."

"You're a sexist ass."

"I meant because we don't compete in the same competition." Gabe rolled his eyes. "And anyway, we weren't talking about me."

"You're always talking about you." She was feeling grumpy, because he'd ruined her vibe.

"Touché." He chuckled. "Anyway, it's not the same."

No it wasn't. But it didn't stop three tiny lines from appearing in her brow. She and Josh were equals, she knew that. If he'd have won fair and square she would accept it. And he would, too. He had to, because otherwise it meant he didn't think she was as good as him.

She blew out a mouthful of air, watching the vapor dance before it dispersed. "Do you think I should tell him?"

"North would kill you if you did." Gabe gave her a sympathetic smile. "It'll be okay. Ignore me. If he loves you, he'll understand."

"Who said anything about love?" Her chest tightened.

Gabe twisted the lid back on his flask and stuffed it in his pocket. "You guys have been practically tied at the hip since he's been here. You bought him a tree. And let's not even get started on the way Dolores has been dealing with your coffee bills. Where do you see this thing going?"

She wanted to be with him. She knew that. But there was a truth in Gabe's questions that she didn't want to think about. What if saving Winterville meant losing him?

Holly exhaled raggedly. "Can we talk about something else? How about your love life?"

Gabe laughed. "You want the x-rated details?"

She wrinkled her nose. "Ugh, no."

"Then it'll be a short conversation."

She stood, dusting the snow from her ski pants. "In that case, I think we should start skiing again." At least the exertion would stop these confused thoughts from crashing through her brain.

"You sure you're okay to go on? We can turn around if you'd like."

Holly shook her head, reaching down to clip her skis back on. "I'm good. Throw all the downhills you can find at me." At least she could take her frustration out on the snow. None of this was her fault, yet somehow she felt guilty. Responsible.

"It's your funeral." Gabe shot her a wicked grin.

23

The elevator arrived with its usual swish, the doors opening to reveal the familiar polished mirrors. Josh pressed the penthouse button then leaned against the rail, watching as the numbers counted up.

When he stepped onto the executive floor of Gerber Enterprises, a feeling of surreality washed over him. His footsteps sounded wrong as he walked along the carpet, and it took him a moment to realize that's because he was wearing sneakers instead of the polished brogues he usually favored.

Willa looked up with a smile as he walked into the office. Her eyes gave the briefest sweep over his jeans and sweater. A look of surprise momentarily passed across her eyes.

"How was your trip yesterday?" she asked, regaining her usual calm demeanor.

"It was fine. A little snow along the way, but the blue skies appeared when I drove out of the mountains."

"Wouldn't it be nice if we had a white Christmas?" Willa said, looking wistful. Then she glanced over at Josh's office. "Oh, you have a visitor."

"Who is it?"

Before she could answer, the door opened. He wasn't surprised to see his grandfather standing there, his body supported by a perfectly polished cane. He was wearing a gray suit and red tie, a matching pocket square tucked jauntily into his jacket.

"I see standards have dropped," he said, taking in Josh's casual clothes.

"I'm only here for a couple of days. I figured I'd be more comfortable in jeans." Josh pushed the door open, worried about his grandfather's stability. "Would you like to sit down?"

"Not really." With slow, labored steps, his grandfather walked further into Josh's office. "So are you back for good now? Or are you still pretending to be Jimmy Stewart in some god awful festive movie?"

"I'm here to meet with Oren Stiles, then I'm going back to Winterville for Christmas." Josh grabbed a bottle of water from his refrigerator. "Would you like a drink?"

"I'm not here for drinks, young man. I'm here to find out if you're going to start doing your job."

Uncapping the bottle, he poured it into one of the cut crystal glasses on the wet bar. "I've been doing my job. There's this amazing new thing called the internet. You can make calls on it and everything."

"You know what I mean." His grandfather's voice was rough. "A CEO needs to be seen in his office. Otherwise the staff doesn't work the way they should. Especially at this time of the year. The finance department were all crowded around donuts when I walked in. I had to clear my throat for them to even notice me." His grandfather's lips formed into the smallest of smiles. "You should have seen them scurry when they did. Like rats off a sinking ship."

"It's the twenty-third of December. They're allowed to relax a little."

"It's the end of the year. They should be working harder than ever." His grandfather wobbled, and Josh shot forward to steady him, but the old man batted him off. "Anyway, I'm not here to talk about our employees, as much as they need some discipline. It's you I want to talk about. When are you going to come to your senses and let one of your staff handle that little town? You have more important things to deal with. Like Oren Stiles. He's been badmouthing us all over town, saying how unresponsive we are."

"Oren is impatient. He'll be fine after we meet today."

His grandfather stared at him through narrowed eyes. "Are you having some kind of breakdown?"

Josh started to laugh. He couldn't help it. Maybe it was the strangeness of being back in the office and not feeling like he belonged any more. Or perhaps it was the glorious exhilaration of his time with Holly. Either way, once the laugh started, it wouldn't stop.

And his grandfather's face became more and more red.

"You're a CEO, boy. Not a damn clown. Stop laughing."

"I'm not having a breakdown," Josh finally managed, his chest still shaking.

"Could have fooled me. You're almost hysterical." The old man snorted. "You should book in with one of those therapists. Use our Employee Assistance Plan. Or take some of those pills people are always talking about."

"I'm absolutely fine, Grandpa. In fact, I'm more than fine. I'm in love." Damn, it felt good to say it.

"What?"

"I've met the woman I plan to marry." Sure, she didn't know that yet. But he'd thought of little else on the drive from Winterville. He was addicted to that woman, and he'd do whatever it took to keep her with him.

"I think I need to sit down." His grandfather reached for a chair, slumping heavily on it. "Are you being bribed? Is she pregnant? So this is why you spent so long out of the office."

"I'm not being bribed. I'm happy. Maybe for the first time in my life. I've found somebody I care about, and I think she cares about me, too."

"You *think?*" His grandfather lifted a brow. "You don't even know if she feels the same way? You're putting this business in peril for a woman who might not even care about you?"

"She cares."

"Hmmph. Who is this woman anyway? She must be some kind of beauty to turn you into a sap."

"Her name is Holly Winter. She's Candy Winter's granddaughter."

His grandfather almost choked. "One of the idiots blocking the sale?"

Josh's lips twitched. "That's her."

"Well no wonder. It's a tale as old as time. Remember Salome and the dance of the veils? Samson and Delilah? She's seducing you to get what she wants, and you're falling for it. Thinking with your pants instead of your brain. I thought better of you, I really did."

Josh exhaled. His grandfather knew how to kill the good feelings. "I want to take a step back from the business."

His grandfather did a double take at Josh's change in conversation. "What do you mean? Who's going to run this business if you step back?"

"I will. But I'll take on more help. Recruit somebody who can take over the day to day running while I provide advice."

"This is a family business, Joshua. It's always been run by family. We can't let strangers take over. They won't have the loyalty we do. The drive to succeed. You're making a mistake. And if you were the only one who would suffer, that would be fine, but you're not. *I'll* suffer. Your grandma will, too. And your future children. Think of them. You're caretaking this business for them, don't throw it away."

"I've made my mind up." Josh met his grandfather's gaze. "I can't be dissuaded."

"Then I'm disappointed. Very disappointed."

They stared at each other for a moment. His grandfather's eyes were rheumy, his knuckles bleached where he still held onto his cane, even though he was sitting down.

"Maybe you should see a therapist," Josh murmured. "You could use our Employee Assistance Plan."

"Don't mess with me, Joshua."

"Knock knock."

A wave of relief washed over Josh as his grandma's smiling face appeared in the doorway. "Darling," she said, beaming when she saw him. "Willa just told me you were here. Are you joining us for brunch? We're going to Carter's Hotel."

Josh looked from her to his grandfather. "I don't have time. Are you two talking again?"

She laughed. "Kind of."

His grandfather stood slowly, his face grimacing as his bones set into place. "I'll wait for you in the lobby," he mumbled to his wife. "Think about what I said." He looked pointedly at Josh. "It's not too late."

When he was gone, his grandma embraced him warmly, kissing his cheek and patting his jaw. "Look at you. I swear the break has done you good."

"I haven't been on vacation, Grandma. I've been working."

"Then you should take a vacation. It suits you."

"What are you doing going out for brunch with Grandpa?" he asked her.

"Oh sweetheart, don't look so worried." She grinned at him. "I'm letting him woo me. It's quite sweet, really. He's been sending flowers and little gifts to my hotel room. Yesterday, I got this." She showed him a sparkling ring on her right hand. "I swear moths must have flown out of his wallet when he paid for it." She leaned on Josh's desk. "Anyway, I'm quite enjoying it. Plus, I'm an independent woman now. I have my own bank account and control of my own money. So any decisions I make now are from a place of power."

"You opened the bank account?"

"I promised your lovely friend that I would." Her eyes sparkled. "How is she?"

"She's..." An image of her laying naked beneath his Christmas tree flashed through his mind. "She's beautiful."

"Oh!" Her eyes widened. "Does that mean..."

"I'm in love with her." It was like a dam had broken. Now he wanted to say it all the time. Most of all, he wanted to say it to Holly, and hope to God she said it back.

"Josh." She hugged him hard, her eyes shining. "That's so wonderful. When can I meet her?"

"After Christmas. I said I'd spend it with her in Winterville. I'll ask if she'll come visit you after that."

His grandma beamed. "And she's okay with this thing about her home town?"

Another thing he'd been thinking about during his drive to Cincinnati. "She will be. I'm making a few changes to our plan. I'll be meeting with Kevin and Elizabeth later to discuss them."

"Do me a favor. Don't tell your grandfather about them until they're complete. He's got a bee in his bonnet and it's not good for his blood pressure."

"I promise not to tell him." Not until it was over. This decision was all his.

"Perfect. Now I'd better go before he terrorizes everybody in reception. Give me a kiss, sweetheart. And make sure you call me. Maybe you both can." Her eyes twinkled. "I'd like to talk with Holly again."

"We'll do that." Maybe on Christmas Day. And then, once this whole damn mess was sorted, he'd bring her here and introduce her to his family. If anybody could stand up to his grandfather, it was Holly Winter.

Not that he needed her to. He could stand up to the old man himself. He just had.

And boy did it feel good.

"So tell me about your day," Holly asked, her voice low and warm. There was a sleepy quality to it that made him want to be curled up next to her, kissing her neck the way she loved so much.

"It was busy. I saw my grandfather this morning. My grandma is talking to him again. Oh, and she opened up that bank account you suggested."

"She did?" Holly sounded pleased. "Good for her."

"She says she's letting him woo her. Whatever the hell *that* means."

"It sounds like she's in control. I like her already," she teased.

It had felt like a long day without her. After the unplanned meeting with his grandfather, and a catch up with his directors, he'd met with Kevin and Elizabeth – plus one of their lawyers.

And what he had to say almost floored them. But the lawyer drafted the papers as he'd instructed, and he'd explained the best way he could to Kevin and Elizabeth that he hadn't gone completely crazy.

He just wanted to change the direction of their acquisition.

And then he'd met with Oren Stiles, one of Gerber Enterprises' biggest investors, and Crystal Lang, their head of investment. As he'd suspected, Oren was only pissed at the lack of direct contact. He was high maintenance, but worth it.

That relationship was the first thing he'd delegate to the person he recruited to assist him in running the business. He wouldn't have time to do that. Not when he was busy wooing Holly Winter.

The sound of the old fashioned word made him grin.

"Ask me a question," he suggested. He didn't want to talk about work anymore.

"What's the best present you've ever gotten?"

"The LEGO *Star Wars* Millennium Falcon. It took me two days to build it."

"Did you get it for Christmas?" she asked him.

"No. For my eleventh birthday. I was a huge *Star Wars* nerd then. It was when episode one had just come out. Everybody wanted the Millennium Falcon. I hate to think how much it cost."

"Do you still have it?"

His breath caught. "No. I got rid of it a few days later."

"Why?" There was a frown in her voice. "I thought you said you loved it"

"The day after I built it, I took it to show my grandfather. He took it from my hands and told me that the Falcon was good, but if you took it apart you could build anything you wanted. And that I needed more imagination. Then he smashed it." He'd been distraught. In a fit of anger, he'd thrown it in the trash. His grandma had been furious.

"Josh..."

"It's okay. I think he was trying to teach me a life lesson."

"How could he do that to a kid?"

"I'm a big boy now, Holly. It was a long time ago."

"I'm going to buy you a LEGO set. And you can build them anyway you damn please."

He laughed. "That sounds good. So what have you been up to?"

"I went skiing with Gabe."

"I didn't know you skied."

"I don't very often. I ended up on my ass most of the time. I haven't seen him laugh so much in years. And then this evening I've been calming Everley down. She's panicking that there's going to be a snowstorm tomorrow. And even if there isn't, she's scared something will go wrong with the show."

"It's going to be great."

"You and I both know that. But she's in a whirlwind of panic. I don't think she'll sleep tonight."

"How about you?" he asked, his voice soft. "Are you going to sleep?"

"I hope so. My muscles feel like I've been in a boxing ring for ten rounds. I'm never going to ski again."

"I can talk you to sleep again if you want." He remembered how much he'd liked doing it last time. Talking until he could hear her soft breaths. It made him feel protective of her.

There was a smile in her voice when she replied. "That sounds good. Do you have the pebble with you?"

"It's in my hand."

There was a shuffle, as though she was turning in bed. "Are you in your pajamas?"

"I'm wearing shorts. It's warm in here." He cleared his throat. "I told my grandparents about you."

"You did?"

"Yeah. Is that okay?"

"Of course. My family knows about us, after all. What did they say?"

"My grandma is over the moon. She wants you to come

see her in Cincinnati. I think she already likes you more than me."

Holly laughed. "And your grandfather?"

"He'll get used to the idea."

"I guess there's going to be a lot of that going on."

He wanted to ask her how she felt about him. Wanted to tell her he loved her. That no matter what happened, he wanted his future to be with her. But it felt wrong to say over the phone. When he told her, he planned on seeing her expression. To make sure she felt the same way.

"I miss you," he told her. "This bed is way too empty."

"I miss you, too."

His heart warmed. "When I get home tomorrow, there's something I want to tell you."

"Did you just say *home*?"

He blinked. "I don't know. Did I?"

"I think so. But I'm tired and my ears are ringing from Everley's screams."

Josh laughed. "When I get to *Winterville* tomorrow, there's something I want to tell you."

"If it's that Santa doesn't exist, I won't believe you. People have tried to tell me that before. I know he's real." Her voice sounded thick and low. He wondered if her eyes were closed, her lips parted slightly the way they were when she slept.

Damn, he wanted to kiss those lips.

"Are you sleepy now?" he asked her.

"Getting there. Keep talking."

"How about I tell you about my drive yesterday? That should bore you to sleep."

"Sounds perfect. Thank you."

"I took a left out of my driveway, then headed through Winterville, and took a right onto the main road out of town." He carried on, telling her about the right he took onto the highway, then the descent from the mountains onto the

Interstate, a smile pulling at his lips when he heard her breathing become regular and soft.

"And by the way," he said. "I'm completely and totally in love with you."

Her breathing didn't stutter. It was okay, it was just a practice run. He'd tell her for real very soon.

❧ 24 ❧

And by the way, I'm completely and totally in love with you.

She woke to the memory of those words. He'd said them as she was falling asleep, and for a moment she'd wondered if she was dreaming. But then he'd carried on with his description of his drive, and she'd somehow managed to keep breathing.

But she hadn't said it back.

She'd wanted to. Because she'd fallen for him, too. But her chest had felt tight and the words were frozen on her tongue. She was afraid and she had no idea why.

Maybe they needed to get this thing with Winterville over and done with, for once and for all.

Yes, it was business. And yes, he'd agreed that whatever they did meant nothing to them as a couple. But she was still finding it difficult keeping a secret from him.

She wanted everything out in the open. Wanted there to be nothing between them except the feelings they had for each other.

Surely she'd be able to tell him she loved him then.

She walked out of the Inn, breathing in the cool outside

air. The sky above was a dull gray. It looked like they'd get a little snow today, but not the storm that Everley had been panicking about. It didn't stop her from worrying about Josh driving back from Cincinnati in bad weather though.

The sooner he got here, the better.

"Good morning," Dolores called out as Holly walked through the café door. "Usual?"

"Yes, please."

"No Josh today?"

"He's in Cincinnati. He's coming back later."

"Is he coming to the show?" Dolores asked. She looked pleased as punch at the idea.

"Yes he is. And to the Inn for Christmas."

Dolores caught her eye. "He's a good boy. Your grandma would have liked him."

It was the best kind of compliment, because there was a truth to it. Her grandmother *definitely* would have liked Josh, she did when she met him all those years ago, after all. Not just because he was good looking – although, Candy did have a well documented weakness for handsome men – but because he was funny, kind, and made Holly happy.

And that would have made Candy happy, too.

"It's going to be a hard Christmas without her," Dolores said. Holly nodded, her throat tight. "But at least we have tonight's show to look forward to. It's almost like there's a piece of her here still, isn't it? She would have loved all this fuss."

She would have adored it. She would've been fighting for her town the way Holly and her cousins were. There was nothing Candy Winter loved more than a challenge.

Dolores reached across the counter and squeezed Holly's hand. "It's going to be okay," she said, as though she could sense Holly's anxiety. "The show is going to be perfect, and tomorrow we save Winterville. You achieved everything you came here for."

"Thank you." Holly gave her a half smile.

"Now go warm up by the fire and I'll bring your coffee over. It's on the house."

"Oh no, I'll pay."

Dolores waved her off. "I get so confused over who's paying what, I figured I'd make my life easier today by paying for it my damn self."

Holly made a mental note to put a huge tip in the jar on her way out. She had ten minutes to drink her coffee before she needed to get over to the theater to calm Everley down. Alaska had already called her this morning to ask for her help. They needed their cousin to stop panicking and conserve her voice for that evening.

The fire was crackling and spitting as she sat down on the easy chair, wishing Josh was opposite her as usual. Dolores had put on an old Christmas playlist with some of Candy's most famous songs, her soft, throaty voice sounding melodic as it flowed from the speakers. Holly took a deep breath. It was going to be fine. Candy was so missed, but she'd want them to be happy.

She looked down at the message Josh had sent her first thing this morning.

I need to head into the office to pick something up, then I'm driving straight to Winterville. Can't wait to see you. – J

She couldn't wait to see him either. She'd been really good and hadn't called him this morning, wanting him to concentrate on the road ahead. He'd probably laugh when she told him, but that's because he was a hare and she was a snail.

And Holly was perfectly okay with that.

Her phone lit up again.

Holly? Are you almost here? Everley just checked weather.com and is in a full-blown panic. Come fast. We need you. Alaska xx

Holly stood and smiled at Dolores. "Can you make that coffee to go?" she asked.

Dolores nodded, grabbing a Styrofoam cup covered with pictures of reindeer across a red background. "Problems?" she asked.

"Nothing a little cousinly hug won't solve. Everley's panicking about the weather forecast."

Dolores nodded. "It's a little gray out there, but we won't be having much more than a dusting of snow today. And I know Charlie already has the plow ready in case he needs to clear the roads." She grabbed a bag and slid a few pastries inside. "Give this to Everley and tell her she needs to keep her energy up. And give her a big hug from me."

"I will." Holly nodded. "And thank you."

"It's going to be a good day," Dolores said, her voice warm.

Yes it was. A very good day, not least because Josh would be back in a few hours. Until then, Holly's job would be to keep Everley calm.

She could definitely do that. Because it was Christmas Eve, and everybody deserved to be happy.

The snow began as Josh drove around the town square, parking his car so he could head into the Jingle Bell Theater. It was a little more than a dusting, but it made everything look pretty. He walked around the white stucco building, smiling when he saw the huge banner strung at the front.

Winterville Presents For One Night Only
A Very Candy Christmas

He opened the stage door and a cacophony of sound and vision rushed over him. People were shouting at each other, a band was tuning up, and there were roadies dressed in black walking to and from the trucks parked at the rear, their expressions set as they carried equipment and scenery into the main auditorium. Josh kept close to the walls of the snaking corridors as they pushed past him, looking in each room in an attempt to locate Holly.

The last time he'd been backstage in these hallways was the day he'd presented their vision of Winterville's future to the town. This was where he'd confronted Holly after she'd heckled him during their question and answer session.

It felt like a lifetime ago.

He'd been attracted to her even then. Had been from the start. But he'd been fighting that undeniable pull. Telling himself it was just the energy she created because she was pissed with him.

And now he was in love with the woman who'd stood up and denounced him in front of Winterville.

"Oh my God!" Holly ran toward him in a rush of movement, slamming into his body so hard he was almost winded. He caught her in his arms, laughing despite the lack of oxygen in his lungs. His heart warmed as she grinned up at him, her eyes shining as they met his. "I missed you," she told him, kissing his neck. "Don't go away again."

"I missed you, too."

She ran his hands over his hair. "Is it snowing already?"

"Only a dusting." He pushed a stray tendril of hair from her cheek.

"Well we need to get rid of the evidence. If Everley sees that she'll have another fit." Holly grimaced. "She's convinced there's going to be a storm and we'll have to cancel the show."

"Classic displacement." He smiled at her warm expression. "Worry about the weather instead of the important stuff."

"Right? Alaska's removed the weather app from her phone, and I've been keeping her away from the windows. They're about to do the sound check, so that should keep her busy." Holly traced the line of his jaw with her warm fingertip. "How was your drive?"

"Long."

"But fast. Am I right?"

"Faster than a snail, yeah." He kissed the tip of her nose. "Damn, it's good to see you."

"Holly, do you know where the set lists are?" Alaska ran in, breathless. "Everley's put hers somewhere and can't find it."

"I printed a whole bunch up and put them by the lighting equipment. You can grab one there."

"Thank God for you." Alaska blew her a kiss.

"I should go so you can work," Josh said, reluctant to let her go.

"You could stay," Holly suggested hopefully.

"I have a little work to do myself. Plus I want to wrap your gift before tomorrow. Then I need to shower and get ready for your mom's cocktail party."

Holly let out a low sigh. "About the party..."

"Don't try to get out of it."

"But Everley needs me."

"No she doesn't," Alaska said, running past Holly with a fistful of printed papers. "We'll be fine. Go."

Josh smirked. "It'll be okay." Spending an hour at her mom's couldn't be any worse than telling his grandfather he was taking a step back. And the truth was, he wanted to know her family. Wanted to be accepted by them.

"Okay. But only for an hour. Then we come straight back here."

"Of course. I'll pick you up at the Inn at four."

Holly nodded, looking pale. "You owe me for this, Gerber."

"I'm pretty sure I already know how to make it up to you." He kissed her lips, her jaw and then her neck, where it always made her sigh. "It'll be fine. I promise."

She tangled her fingers into his thick hair, her head tipping back as she let out another sigh. One that had nothing to do with her mom, and everything to do with the heat from his mouth.

"I'll see you in a couple of hours," he said again, stepping back. Holly blinked, her gaze glassy.

"Okay," she whispered. "But I demand retribution tonight."

Holly caught a glance of her reflection in the mirror beside the Winterville Inn's inglenook fireplace. She looked okay, considering she'd gotten ready in a huge rush. Her dark hair was swept into a low, smooth bun, and her lips were painted scarlet. She was wearing a simple black cocktail dress, the lace bodice and short skirt clinging to her curves. It was understated and elegant, set off with a pair of diamond earrings and necklace that once belonged to Candy.

"You look beautiful," Josh whispered in her ear, kissing the exposed curve between her neck and shoulders.

She felt beautiful, too. Not just because this dress fit her perfectly, or that her hair had behaved for once, but because of the way Josh was staring at her in the mirror.

"We could skip the party," he murmured.

"No way." She met his gaze in the mirror, amusement pulling at her lips. "You're the one who insisted on this."

"But I didn't know how delectable you were going to look. How quickly can you drink a cocktail?"

She leaned back against him, inclining her head so she could kiss his jaw. "Really, really fast."

"Thank God."

"And then we'll head straight to the theater before Everley has a complete breakdown."

Her mother's sweeping driveway was full of expensive cars as Josh slowed to a stop. There was a big 'for sale' sign at the front of the gravel drive. Holly blinked at it but said nothing. Though her mom's – and uncles' – houses were outside the Winterville city limits, she guessed they were ready to move on. It made sense, because her mom spent hardly any time here. She much preferred the warmer climate of the Mediterranean.

They walked up the stone steps, and the door was opened by a maid, "May I take your coats?" she asked.

Josh slipped Holly's dress coat from her shoulders and passed it to the maid, thanking her as he shucked off his own jacket. He was wearing a dark gray suit, with a white shirt and blue tie. It fit his broad, muscled body perfectly.

"I'd forgotten what you looked like in a suit," she said to him as they walked into the main living area. A waiter passed them two non-alcoholic cocktails.

"My grandfather thinks you've corrupted me into wearing jeans and sweaters."

Her eyes sparkled. "I'm so bad."

"He thinks you're seducing me to get your town back," he teased.

She lifted her brows. "Perhaps I am."

"Darling, you came." Her mom walked over, a glass of champagne in her hand, and air kissed Holly before smiling at Josh. "It's a pleasure to have you here, Mr. Gerber. I guess you'll be heading back to Cincinnati soon?"

He slid his hand into Holly's. "Not too soon."

"Which is good," Holly said softly to him. "Because I only just got you back."

Her mom frowned, as though she wasn't sure what to say next. "Um, let me introduce you to my husband. Garrick?"

An elegantly dressed sixty-something man walked over, taking her mom's hand in his and lifting it to his lips. "Yes, my darling?"

"This is Holly, my daughter. And her... friend? Josh Gerber."

The silver-haired fox tipped his head to the side. "Surely not, my angel. You're too young to have a daughter that age."

Her mom laughed, the tinkle so shrill Holly was amazed her glass didn't shatter. "Oh Garrick, you know how to flatter a lady."

Garrick kissed her on both cheeks, then shook Josh's hand. "Why are you drinking non-alcoholic cocktails?" he asked them. "I'm mixing some amazing Martinis right now."

"I'm driving," Josh said, shrugging.

"And I have to help Everley with the show. I need a clear mind."

"Wait a minute. Josh Gerber? Aren't you the one who bought the town from my angel?" He stroked her mom's arm.

Josh nodded. "That's right."

"And you're here with Holly? I thought you two were on opposing sides."

Josh shrugged. "We are , but we're keeping business separate from pleasure."

"You don't mind about the new plan?"

Her mom turned pale. "Garrick, perhaps you should go work on those cocktails now."

"Of course, my darling." He nodded at Josh. "I love these modern relationships. You young people are so much more laid back than my generation." He inclined his head. "We would have felt emasculated if our girlfriends bought a town out from under us."

Josh's smile didn't waver. "Holly hasn't bought the town."

Garrick laughed. "So true." Holly's mom was tugging at his arm, but he was ignoring her, as though on a roll. Holly felt her stomach shoot through the floor. "Still, it's a cunning plan, isn't it? Find some old deed and use it to buy up some buildings."

Holly felt herself freeze. She couldn't look at Josh.

"Garrick!" Her mom widened her eyes. "We need those drinks, now."

Josh cleared his throat. "I don't understand. What old deed?"

Garrick blinked, as though realizing for the first time that he'd said the wrong thing. "Um, I really should make those cocktails."

"What do you mean?" Josh asked again, his voice low. Holly inhaled a ragged breath, because she could feel the tension wafting off him.

Garrick looked from Josh to her mom, then back to Josh again. "Oh dear, it seems I've put my foot in my mouth.

Ignore me." He cleared his throat. "Two virgin cocktails, was it?"

"Holly?" Josh looked at her. There was no emotion in his eyes at all. "What's he talking about?"

This was it. There was no getting out of it. And it wasn't how she'd planned to tell him at all.

She was going to do it tomorrow, when they were alone. When he had time to listen and understand.

But then Garrick started talking again, and she wanted to pull his damn tongue out and wrap it around his neck.

"He really didn't know?" he murmured to her mom. "Oops."

"Of course he didn't know," she hissed. "I guess he does now." Her mom looked at Holly with sympathy. "I'm so sorry. Dolores told me. I didn't think to tell Garrick it was a secret."

"What secret?" Josh persisted. A mixture of hurt and anger flashed across his face.

Holly swallowed hard. "We found a way to stop you from redeveloping Winterville."

🦋 25 🦋

His grip on Holly's hand was so tight it was cutting off her circulation, but he couldn't loosen it. He was afraid she'd run away if he did.

Holly was pale and silent as he attempted to find somewhere they could talk. Somewhere away from the infernal Christmas music and the low level chatter, and Holly's new stepfather who looked like he was about to join Holly in tears.

Somewhere that he could figure out what the heck was going on.

The third door he pushed open revealed an empty room. There was a huge gleaming table in the center, surrounded by plush velvet chairs.

"Sit down," he said, pointing at the nearest chair.

"I can't." She shook her head. Her fingers were trembling in his grasp.

"Why not?"

"Because you look so angry, and I'm scared."

He tried to neutralize his expression. He didn't want her to be scared of him. He just wanted to know what was happening here. She was acting like he was some kind of mass murderer. Taking a deep breath, he tried to calm the rush of thoughts in his brain, and slow the pounding of his heart against his ribcage.

"I'm sorry. I have no idea what your stepdad is talking about. It's like everybody knows but me."

"I was going to tell you." Her voice was imploring. "I really was. I just wanted to wait for the right time."

"So tell me. Somebody needs to." He was trying really hard to keep the hurt from his voice, but from the way she winced, he was clearly failing.

"I found some handwritten deeds from when my grandma first created the town. There was a clause that allowed tenants to buy their houses and buildings at market value. For cash only. We've had them valued and the documents drawn up and we're having them sent to your office tomorrow."

Josh blinked. "My office is closed tomorrow."

"I know." Holly inhaled raggedly. "That was part of the plan. To catch your team off guard, give us more time. I'm sorry, so sorry, Josh. I was going to tell you tomorrow, I swear. I wouldn't have let you walk into that unprepared."

There was a stabbing pain in his heart. It felt like she was plunging a dagger between his ribs.

"You were going to tell me tomorrow," he said dully.

"Yes." Holly nodded. "I really was."

"On Christmas Day." The day he'd been looking forward to ever since she'd invited him to spend it at the Inn with her. He'd been expecting singing and food, not her telling him she'd been lying.

Holly bit her lip. "I wanted to tell you before somebody else did."

"So on Christmas Day you were going to tell me you've been lying to me for weeks." He tried to keep his voice steady. "Isn't that, I don't know, *cruel?*" About as cruel as smashing a

LEGO Millennium Falcon he'd been working on for days. No, it was crueller, because he believed in her.

And she'd decided to hurt him on the day she loved most.

She winced at his words. "I wanted to tell you before. We talked about this. We agreed we'd keep business and our private lives separate."

"You could have told me at any time. I wouldn't have stopped you." And wasn't that the bitch? He was in love with her. He'd let her do anything. "But on Christmas?" No, not then.

"I promised the others I wouldn't." She was blinking back tears. "It's been horrible, keeping this a secret. And I'm so sorry you're hurt. I'll make it up to you, I will."

Josh gripped the table behind him. She was right, they had agreed not to talk about the future of Winterville. But he hadn't agreed to be lied to. Kept in the dark. Treated like he wasn't important at all to her.

And that's how he felt. Insignificant. Unwanted. Like he was a stranger in the town all over again, and everybody knew something he didn't.

"You promised the others you wouldn't." He ran his fingers through his hair, raking it from his face. "Because your family is more important to you than I am."

"That's not true." She shook her head. "You're the most important thing to me." She took his hand. He let it hang limply against her palm. "I've fallen for you, Josh. Now that this is all out in the open, we can start to plan our lives."

He pulled his hand away from hers. She blinked to stop the tears from falling. How was it possible for a heart to physically ache so damn much? "I was going to give it to you."

"Give me what?"

"The town. It's one of the reasons I went to Cincinnati, to get the contract drawn up. I was going to give you the town to run the way you wanted to. That's your Christmas present."

A loud sob escaped from her lips. "That's... oh God, Josh. That's beautiful." A tear rolled down her cheek. "I'm so sorry I ruined it."

"It doesn't matter either way, does it? You got what you wanted." He stepped back, trying to give himself some distance. Building a wall around his heart, brick by brick. His grandfather's words echoed in his mind.

She's seducing you to get what she wants, and you're falling for it. Thinking with your pants instead of your brain. I thought better of you, I really did.

Was he right? Had he spent the past few weeks falling for this beautiful woman in front of him, while she'd spent the same time planning his downfall?

"I need to go," he muttered. Because he had this stupid ache in his chest and he had no idea what to do with it. He felt like a wounded animal seeking its home, where he'd curl up to die.

But he didn't have a home. He had a rented house in a town that didn't want him. Near a woman who chose everybody over him.

Holly grabbed his hand again. "I'll come with you."

He pulled it out of her grasp. He couldn't bear her to touch him. "I fell in love with you. Did you know that?"

She nodded, her breath hitching. "I heard you tell me last night."

"And you didn't say it back." Another stab. This one felt fatal.

"I wanted to." Tears were pouring down her pretty cheeks. "But I couldn't say it until you knew the truth about all this. I didn't want my words to be tainted once I told you the truth."

"Then say it now." His voice was full of grit.

She looked up at him, her eyes red, her lips trembling. "Josh..."

"Say it." For some reason he had to hear it. Wanted to watch her lips form the words. Even if it killed him.

"I can't. Not while you're looking at me like that."

"Like what?"

"Like you hate me."

He shook her hand away. "So you can't say it." She couldn't even give him that. "I get it now. You don't trust yourself to say it because you're afraid. Not of me, but of yourself. You're afraid of giving yourself to somebody. Afraid of ending up like your mother. So much better to be a fucking ice queen than to admit that you have feelings for somebody."

Her face crumpled. A long, slow sob escaped her lips. And he hated himself, because he'd made her hurt, too.

Damn, she was beautiful, even with red ringed eyes and a trail of mascara smudging her cheeks. He wanted to rub his fingers over her soft skin, to make it pristine again. Just like he wanted to forget any of this had happened.

But he couldn't. He hurt too much, and he didn't trust himself to do anything right now. Everything was only getting worse.

"Can you get one of your cousins to pick you up and take you to the theater?" he asked her.

Holly blinked. "Why?"

"I need to go back to my house." He nearly said home.

"We can go together."

"No. I need some time to be alone. To think." And yeah, maybe to scream a little. Because that might take away the hurt. "You need to think, too. About how you really feel about me."

"I know how I feel about you, Josh."

He held his hand up. "I don't want to hear it now. Not like this. I'm messed up and hurt and angry. And I need to find some damn peace and quiet to think about what's happening here. We're going in circles and it's helping nobody. You have a show to help run, and your family needs you."

"I don't give a damn who needs me."

"No. You don't get to say that. Not after you've broken my damn heart by siding with them. Give me a chance to lick my wounds, and really think about what you want from me. If you feel the same way I feel about you, come find me after the show."

She let out a long, ragged breath. "Josh..."

"I mean it. I'm not ready to talk now. I need to be alone." He ran his finger along the trail of her tears. "You'll probably want to wash your face before you go."

Another tear fell. "I will."

Nodding, he took a deep breath, but the tightness of his chest stopped him. He turned away, not wanting her to see the shininess of his own eyes. Grown men didn't cry.

Even if he was about to.

He walked toward the door, as she sobbed again. He didn't dare turn back, afraid he'd give in and hold her until she stopped.

And he couldn't. Not if he wanted to emerge from this with some dignity.

"I do love you, Josh," she whispered, as he walked into the hallway. "I love you so much."

He grit his teeth, wincing at her words, and carried on walking toward the front door.

The auditorium echoed to the sound of "The Christmas Song", Gray Hartson's low, gritty voice singing about chestnuts roasting around a fire. And it made Holly's heart hurt, because that was the song she'd played the morning she laid naked beneath Josh's Christmas tree.

Everything made her think of him. Maybe that's why she kept crying.

"You hanging in there?" North nudged her. They were standing in the wings, each holding a running order as they took over from Everley so she could get ready for her appearance on stage. Alaska had gone with her to the dressing room, saying she'd need help with her outfit, but they all knew she was trying to keep her big sister calm.

Gabe was at the front of the theater to help with the lighting. They'd flickered a few times, and Everley had panicked about that, too.

Now Holly was alone with North.

"I'll be fine." Just as soon as this was over and she could drive to Josh's house and tell him exactly what a fool she'd been. Her heart had been battering against her ribcage ever since he'd walked out of her mom's house, and her hand was cramping from holding her phone so tightly. Just in case he decided to reply to her messages.

She lifted the phone up. He hadn't sent her anything. But she knew he'd received hers from the two little ticks next to them. It hurt to know he wasn't responding, but it hurt even more to know why.

Because she'd hurt him. Made him think she didn't care. She should have told him the moment she knew she was in love with him. Should have shouted it from the rooftops. He was right, she was afraid.

And she hated it.

Maybe she should send one more text, just to tell him she loved him?

"Don't even think about it," North said, taking her phone from her. "He said he wanted time to think. And you need it too, Hol. He doesn't want a panic response. He doesn't want you to throw yourself at his feet. He wants you to *really* think about this. To go to him willingly. To open yourself to him. Show him that you've taken the time to realize just how much he means to you."

Holly blinked, her mouth agape.

"What?" North frowned.

"Where did you come up with all that stuff?" She sniffled.

"I spend a lot of time with Amber." He shrugged. "She's even worse with relationships than we are. And when they go wrong, I have to sit and watch movies with her."

"What kind of movies?"

"Sad stuff. I dunno." He shrugged. "But the advice still stands. Us Winters aren't exactly great at relationships. We didn't have good role models. And you're even worse because you spend your life mopping up other peoples' relationship messes. No wonder you're cynical."

"You think I'm cynical?" Her heart throbbed a little bit more.

"I think you wear cynicism like a comfort blanket." North smiled to take the sting from his words. Not that it helped. "Because when something goes wrong, you can claim you knew it would all along. Somehow that makes you feel safer."

Wow, that hurt. But there was so much truth in his words. "I guess I learned a long time ago that the only person I could rely on is me."

He gave her a sad smile. "I hate that for you. For us. We had Grandma, and she was wonderful, but we deserved better parents. All of us. Have you looked around and wondered why we're all still single at our age?"

Holly pulled her lip between her teeth. "We've had relationships. Everley got married. Alaska falls in love with pretty much everybody she meets. Even you date sometimes."

"I date but I never get involved." He pressed his lips together. "For exactly the same reasons you don't."

"Wow."

"What?"

"I'm having a deep conversation with North Winter. Who would have thought it?"

He snorted. "You have a very low opinion of me."

She grabbed his hand, squeezing it. "I really don't. I was born hero worshipping you. We all were. Remember all those snow fights when we were kids? We'd spend hours arguing over who got to be on your side. And look at this place," she said, pointing out through the wings. "None of this would be happening if it wasn't for you. We wouldn't all be here, saving Grandma's town. I have the highest opinion of you."

His lips curled. "You're kind of sweet, really. So let me ask you a question."

"Okay?"

"If you had to choose between saving Winterville, and loving Josh Gerber, which would you opt for?"

Holly's brows knit. "I guess I already chose, didn't I?"

"No, you didn't. Until earlier you thought you could have it all. You were going to tell him tomorrow, and you thought he'd understand. But right now you know he doesn't. So I'll ask again, if you had to choose, which way would you go?"

She swallowed thickly. Cold fingers of fear were prying her ribs apart, one by one. And her heart – the one she'd tried to keep safe from sadness for all these years – felt raw and exposed.

And by the way, I'm completely and totally in love with you.

She should have lifted the phone to her lips and told him she loved him, too. Should have told him about Winterville and found a solution together.

She should have trusted him. Trusted her judgement of him.

Instead, she'd pretended not to hear.

"Him," she whispered roughly. "I'd choose Josh."

North nodded, looking completely unsurprised. "That's what you need to tell him. I think that's what every guy needs to hear. That they're the top of your list. That you choose them."

Her eyes watered. "I should have chosen him all along. Because that way I would have been choosing myself."

"I'll drive you straight there after the show."

"I can drive there."

"You've been crying for two hours. You can hardly see out of your swollen eyes. I think it's safer if I do the driving. Think of it as my gift to you. For helping you mess things up."

"I didn't need much help," she mumbled.

"No, but I still made you promise not to tell him. And that's on me. So let me help you tonight."

She nodded, her words caught in her throat. "Thank you," she managed to croak.

Gray Hartson was finishing his song, and the whole audience was standing, swaying to the music. Damn, he was a good looking man. His wife and children were on the other side of the stage, smiling at him like he was some kind of Rock God. Everley had introduced them earlier, and Holly had found them to be so warm and kind. Maddie Hartson had hugged each one of them, and promised to come visit Winterville with the family once the upheaval was over.

He hit the last note, and the audience began to scream. Feet stamped and hands clapped. Gray lifted his hand in salute to them all, then glanced at the wings for direction. North nodded to him.

"Ladies and gentlemen, before I leave I'd like to sing you a couple more songs. But this time I'd like a little help. Anybody know somebody who can sing like Candy Winter?"

"Everley!" a voice shouted. "You should ask Everley."

"Yeah! We need Everley Winter," somebody else agreed.

Suddenly, the theater was filled with chants for her to come to the stage. Everley walked into the wings, her face as pale as the snow.

"You ready?" Holly asked her. She hadn't told Everley a word about her problems with Josh. She was too highly strung for that.

"Not one bit," Everley admitted, frowning when she looked at Holly. "You okay? Your eyes are red."

"Gray Hartson always makes me cry," Holly lied. "Now enough about me. You need to get out there."

Gray shouted out, "Ladies and Gentlemen, please raise your hands for the one and only, Everley Winter!"

The volume of cheers increased, making Holly's ears throb. Everley hugged Alaska and North, then grabbed Holly's hands. "It'll be okay, right?"

"It'll be wonderful. You're fantastic. Now go out there and have fun."

Everley took a deep breath and walked onto the stage, and the audience erupted.

"She's been pacing the floor of her dressing room," Alaska whispered to North. "I've never seen her this nervous. I guess performing here means a lot to her."

Gray was kissing Everley's cheek, and she was beaming out at the audience, as though she didn't have a care in the world, let alone that she'd been full of anxiety moments before. Holly had forgotten just how much of a natural entertainer her cousin was. She'd inherited Candy's star quality, that was for sure.

"Well, what are we going to sing?" Everley was asking, raising an eyebrow at the audience. "One of your songs?"

"I was thinking we should sing one of yours."

"But I don't have any songs," Everley pointed out. "I'm not a mega superstar like you."

The audience laughed at her sassiness. She was so good at this.

"In that case, let's sing a Christmas song. I have the perfect one all lined up." Gray nodded at the pianist. The low plaintive notes of "Fairytale of New York" struck up, and Gray leaned into the microphone, singing about Christmas Eve in the drunk tank.

The audience sighed as Everley sang back to him, all playful and cheeky, telling him about all the Christmas promises he made her that he didn't fulfill.

Holly blinked back more tears. Because her cousin was so damn beautiful and deserved to be on that stage. She was holding her own with a rock superstar, keeping the audience on the edge of their seats as she told him he was a scumbag and a maggot.

Then the lights flickered, and she held her breath until they came back on again.

"Where the hell is Gabe?" North muttered.

"I'm here." Gabe stalked over to where she and North were standing. "And we have a huge fucking problem."

❈ 26 ❈

"What kind of problem?" Holly frowned at Gabe. He was shifting his feet like he couldn't stand still. The lights flickered again.

"You know the storm we promised Everley wouldn't happen? It just reached Marshall's Gap." That was the next big town. "Took out their power. They're working on getting it back up, but of course everything's so damn slow because it's Christmas Eve."

"What does that mean for us?" North asked, running his thumb along his chin.

"The storm's heading this way. It's likely to take our power out, too, and since we rely on Marshall's Gap for backup, it isn't going to happen.

"The storm's coming here?" Holly shook her head. "I thought it was headed south of here."

Gabe grimaced. "It's already snowing like crazy out there. The winds are picking up. It's only a matter of time before the eye hits us."

"Shit." North looked out at the stage. "We have all these people who have to get home."

"Should we stop the performance?" Holly asked. "Give them a chance to get out of here?"

"It's too late." Gabe's voice was grim. The lights flickered once more, this time staying dark for five seconds before they came back on.

"Can somebody put a dime in the meter?" Everley yelled from the stage, and the audience laughed.

Gray Hartson started singing again, and the murmurs from the audience quietened.

"Okay, let's think." Holly put her hand to her temple. Her brain was mush. It was hard to form a coherent thought. "Um, the Inn has a generator, right?"

"Yep. And a few of the houses do, too."

"So we get as many people as we can to safety. Between the Inn and the local houses we should be able to take care of most of the audience. We could even get some heaters and cots into this place as an overspill if necessary."

North nodded. "I'll make an announcement as soon as they finish their song. We need to get people out while the power's still working."

"Alaska and I will head over to the Inn now," Gabe said. "Get things as ready as we can for an influx of people."

Holly let out a lungful of air. "I need to get to Josh's cottage."

Gabe and North exchanged a look. "You can't drive in this weather, Hol. You'll kill yourself."

"I've driven in snow before."

"Not this kind of snow." North shook his head. "Seriously, we'll have to wait it out. You can go to Josh in the morning."

"But he doesn't have a generator. We need to get him to the Inn." Panic gripped her.

"Holly, you can't go out. People will follow you. Hell, *I'll* follow you. And we'll all end up getting hurt." Gabe put his hands on her shoulders. "Call him and tell him about the storm. I'll give him some tips for keeping warm. Then as soon as it passes, we'll go get him, okay?"

She let out a long breath, taking her phone from her pocket. "Okay."

Bringing up her contacts, she pressed his name, lifting the phone to her ear.

"Hi, this is Josh Gerber. Leave a message."

"It's his voicemail," she mouthed at Gabe.

"Tell him about the storm then pass it to me," he told her.

"Josh, this is Holly. There's a storm coming. You need to get ready for it, because nobody can get to you right now. Gabe's going to tell you exactly what you need to do to be prepared, but stay safe, okay?"

She passed the phone to Gabe, barely listening as he listed the things Josh could use to bunker down and keep warm. He'd be all right, she knew that. He had a fireplace and there had to be candles somewhere. And the storm would pass soon, wouldn't it?

Gabe finished rattling off instructions. "Okay, man. Stay safe. We'll get you when we can."

He passed her the phone. Everley and Gray were still singing about the Boys of the NYPD choir, their voices rising to a crescendo that thrilled the audience.

Then the lights flickered again, before plunging them all into darkness, and people started to shout and scream.

Holly turned on her phone's flashlight. Gabe and North did the same.

"I need to get on the stage and tell them what's happening." North frowned.

But then something magical happened. One by one, everybody in the audience turned their own flashlights on, holding them up in the air and swaying them from side to side.

Everley started to sing again, and Gray joined in, the two

of them performing without a back track or mics, until they ended the song and everybody applauded.

North was by their sides as soon as they finished singing, whispering into their ears. Everley nodded, and turned back to the audience.

"Friends," she shouted out. "I'd like to ask each and every one of you for a favor. Please stay seated and listen carefully to my very handsome and clever cousin, North Winter."

Gabe slid his hand into Holly's, squeezing it tight. She squeezed back, thankful he was here.

"Hello everybody," North said, yelling so he could be heard at the back. "We have a little problem. A winter storm has decided it wants to join in the festivities. But I don't want you to worry, because we have a plan. Listen carefully, and stay seated until we evacuate you row by row. It looks like you'll be spending Christmas Eve with us in Winterville this year."

Josh couldn't sit still. He'd been pacing the floor of his living room for what felt like hours, thinking about *her*.

Holly laughing with him while they ate dinner together.

Holly kissing him when he was supposed to be working.

Holly naked under the tree the day he had to leave for those damn work meetings.

He'd thought those moments had meant as much to her as they did to him. Thought they were on the same page. He was in love with her. And it hurt.

It hurt.

Love wasn't supposed to make you feel this bad, was it?

He let out a sigh, raking his hand through his hair. It had started snowing again. And now he was worried about her driving here after the show. He picked up his phone and opened up his messenger app, wincing when he read her words.

Don't drive tonight. The weather is bad out there. We can talk tomorrow. Josh x

He waited for the two ticks to arrive, to let him know she'd received it. But they didn't come. He frowned and resent it, then a little red dot appeared.

Unable to send message.

He tried calling her instead, even though he wasn't sure he was ready to talk to her. But instead of connecting, all he could hear was static. Frowning, he looked at his service bar.

But it wasn't there.

And then all the lights in the house went out.

The fire was still burning, casting an orange glow across the living room floor. He walked over and flicked the light switch up and down again, but it was futile.

The electricity was gone. Along with the phone service and god knew what else.

He walked to the front door and pulled it open, and a thick curtain of snow rushed in. The icy cold air stunned him, before he pushed it closed again, leaving a blanket of snowflakes on the wooden floor.

Damn!

It was a snowstorm. An honest-to-goodness white out. The kind they rarely got in Cincinatti, thank god. And even if they did, his condo had generators, and it was a short walk to the nearest shop or café for help.

But here he was alone. He looked at his watch. It was almost nine o'clock. The show was due to finish in the next ten minutes. Was it snowing this heavy in Winterville, too? If it wasn't, it would be soon. It was only a couple of miles away.

What if Holly tries to drive here anyway?

A cold shiver snaked its way down his spine. The last words he'd said to her had been unkind. She'd hurt him, and he'd taken it out on her. Then he tried to get her to tell him she loved him, before rejecting her.

He was like a wounded animal, lashing out because he didn't know how to deal with the pain.

Truth was, he still had no idea how to deal with it. Holly was the only person who'd ever gotten beneath his skin. He'd fallen for her in the biggest of ways. He was in love with her.

He'd spent a lifetime building up defenses to keep him safe from pain. He'd become a successful businessman because that was what he knew. But then she came along, and everything changed.

She was the only one who knew him. And if he was being honest, that's why she was able to hurt him so much. He'd let himself become vulnerable and her hiding things hit him at the deepest, tenderest part of his heart.

He'd spent the last two days figuring how he could give the town back to her. To give her the greatest gift he could think of.

And all the time she'd been hiding the truth from him. She didn't need him to give her the town. She'd already gotten what she wanted.

His chest clenched, the pain making him wince. He wanted to hit something, to lash out. To do anything to take this hurt away.

He leaned his head against the hallway wall, closing his eyes as he remembered her tear-stained face.

I wanted to tell you before. We talked about this. We agreed we'd keep business and our private lives separate.

He *had* agreed. Maybe he was even the one who suggested

it, he couldn't remember now. And she hadn't done anything wrong. Not really. She'd done exactly what she said she would.

Kept things separate.

He was the one who'd begun to mix them up. He'd decided to gift her the town instead of doing what a good businessman would. He'd thought that she'd be so grateful, and he'd get to be the knight riding in on a silver steed.

But she didn't need a knight. She was her own knight. That was the beauty of Holly Winter. She never stopped fighting. She never gave up. She loved fiercely, even when she couldn't admit it.

And she'd taught him how to love. Something he never thought he could do. And now that he'd had a taste of it, he wanted more.

He wanted her.

Wanted to wrap her in his arms, to tell her it was going to be okay. To kiss away the tears he'd caused until her lips curled in a smile again.

He wanted her to be happy. To be the one who made her happy.

Wanted to love her. To show her that no matter what happened, he would be there for her. That she could rely on him the way she hadn't relied on anybody else.

The wind was whipping around the house, making the windows and the door rattle. He looked at his phone again. Still no service.

But he couldn't stay here. Not knowing that she might be out there, trying to drive to his house because he demanded she did.

He had to get to her before she got hurt. He grabbed his phone again, wincing when the 'no service' icon appeared at the top of the screen. Running his fingers over the keypad, he quickly typed out a message, knowing it wouldn't be received.

. . .

Don't drive anywhere. I'm coming to you. Stay in Winterville, I'll be there as soon as I can. - J

The Inn was full of people everywhere you looked. Even Gray Hartson and his family were settled in on a sofa waiting for the storm to pass. The staff was doing their best, passing around hot cups of cocoa and coffee, along with pastries and sandwiches they'd quickly whipped up. Alaska was at the desk, allocating bedrooms to those who needed them most – children and the elderly, while Gabe and Everley were searching through the linen closet, piling up pillows and blankets for those who would be sleeping in the lobby and dining room.

Even though there was a whiteout outside, everybody was in good spirits. Alaska had put on some Christmas music, and people were singing along, their voices echoing through the lobby. In a corner, somebody had gathered up all the children and was reading *'Twas The Night Before Christmas* to them, as they all stared up, their sweet faces full of excitement, because this was so much more fun than being made to go to bed and wait for Santa.

"Are you okay?" Dolores asked, as Holly stared out of the window, wincing at the force of the wind as it pelted snowflakes against the glass.

"It's bad out there," Holly said.

"It'll be fine in a few hours. You know what these storms are like." Dolores patted her arm. "Hang in there, honey."

"Josh is stuck at his home. He won't have electricity." She hoped he'd had the sense to get firewood in before the storm got too bad. It was the only way he could keep warm.

"He isn't here?" Dolores asked, her brows pinching. "Why not?"

Holly pulled her lip between her teeth, her eyes stinging. "We had an argument."

"Oh honey. No wonder you're worried." Dolores patted her arm. "It'll be okay. You should be able to get to him in the morning. He's a sensible man. He knows how to keep warm."

Holly let out a long breath. "Yeah." But it didn't stop her from checking the weather every few minutes. Or from wishing she hadn't lied to him.

"Everything okay?" Charlie Shaw asked, passing Dolores a cup of cocoa. "I put a little something extra in it," he told her, patting his pocket, where an outline of a whiskey flask revealed itself.

Dolores gave him a thankful smile. "Holly's worried about Josh. He's stuck at his place."

"Ah, it'll be cold but he'll be fine." Charlie winked at Holly. "You and this Josh fella, you're a thing, huh?"

Holly swallowed hard. "Kind of." Or they were, until she'd hurt him. A fresh stab of guilt cut at her tender heart.

Charlie patted her arm. "He'll stay inside. That's all you gotta do in this weather."

"I told her that." Dolores took a mouthful of cocoa and winced. "What the hell did you put in here?"

"A little bit of my moonshine."

Dolores widened her eyes. "I'm already seeing two of you."

"Two of who?" North asked, appearing behind Holly.

"Charlie's sharing his moonshine." Dolores's voice sounded slurred. "Want some?"

North grimaced. "I think I'll pass." He bumped his shoulder against Holly's. "You hanging in there?"

"Maybe I should go outside," Holly looked out of the window again. "I guess I could walk to his house."

"Hell no. You'll find your death out there. And anyway, how will you see where you're going? You're more likely to walk into a tree than you are to find his house." North shook his head.

"He's right." Charlie nodded. "I'll clear the road in the morning. We all just need to stay put until then."

Somebody was singing "Silent Night". The plaintive notes made her heart ache.

Then a rally of beeps started echoing through the lobby.

"We have service," somebody shouted out.

"My phone's working!"

Oh thank God! Holly pulled her phone out to call Josh. She held her breath as her screen lit up.

Don't drive anywhere. I'm coming to you. Stay in Winterville, I'll be there as soon as I can.

Oh no. No, no, no. Her heart started to clammer against her ribcage. "He's gone outside," she said, her voice full of horror.

"What?" North bent to look at her screen. "Why the hell has he done that?"

Dolores and Charlie exchanged a worried glance.

"I don't know." Holly shook her head. She could feel the tears threatening again. She swallowed hard, trying to push them away because now was not the time to be crying. She needed to have a level head. To figure out what to do.

Because the man she loved was out in this storm, trying to get to her.

"Gabe?" North called out.

"Yep?" He lifted his head and walked over to them. "Wassup?"

"Josh is out in the storm. Can you call mountain rescue?"

Gabe pulled his phone from his pocket. "I can, but they won't come out. Not in this weather."

"Call them anyway," North said. "Log his disappearance."

Holly stared out the window again. Snow was pelting

against it, sticking to the glass. "What can we do?" she murmured, shaking her head.

"Only one thing we can do," Dolores said, pressing her lips together. Her words weren't slurred any more. Funny how an emergency could sober a person up. "We need to call a town meeting."

Walking in a storm like this was turning out to be a bad idea. Even in a thick padded coat and boots, with his snow gloves and hat firmly covering any exposed skin, save his face, Josh could still feel the cold seeping through. The wind was noisy and unrelenting as it blasted down the side of the mountain, snowflakes slapping against his face like they had a personal beef with him.

He took a deep breath in, forcing his body forward, taking slow but steady steps as his boots crunched in the snow.

He could only see a couple of feet ahead. Enough to make out that he was still on the road, thanks to the gap between the trees, but he had no idea how far he'd walked, or how far there was still to go.

Josh hadn't seen a single car, either. He wasn't sure anybody could drive in this weather and actually make it to their destination safely. There was already two feet of snow on the road, with more on the sides as the wind banked snow up until it was four or five feet high.

If Holly had gotten into her car, then she must have stopped somewhere. She had a blanket in there, he thought. She was intelligent enough to know she needed to stay where she was.

Yeah, and you're intelligent enough to know you should have stayed at home, idiot.

He blinked at the vehemence of his own thoughts. Thanks, brain. Even that had turned against him.

That's because you're a complete dickwad. Have been since you left Cincinnati this morning.

Was it only this morning? He blew out a mouthful of air. He hadn't realized how steep the hill into Winterville was when he was driving it. Now that he was on his feet, it felt like he was climbing Everest.

Except only dickwads climb Everest in a storm.

Snow was sticking to his eyelashes, making his vision blurry. He blinked them away, trying to focus on the road ahead. It was shrouded in darkness, the same way it had been since he'd left his house. When was that? An hour ago? Two? He'd lost all sense of time and distance. He pulled his phone out of his pocket, blinking when he saw he finally had service.

Then the phone slid out of his hands into the snow. He dropped to his knees.

His mittened hands were useless as he dug into the snow to get his phone, but he didn't dare take his gloves off. Sure, he was an idiot – his brain had established that much – but he didn't have a death wish.

When he finally extracted it, the phone was covered with snow. He dusted it off, praying to God that water hadn't gotten inside. When the screen lit up, he grinned, because at last something was going his way, even if the wind was still a bitch as it whipped his face.

Then, as if by a Christmas miracle, it started to ring, Holly's name lighting up the screen.

He grinned, swiping the accept call with his nose so he didn't have to take his gloves off.

"Holly?" He had to shout to hear his own voice over the wind.

An unintelligible buzz was his only reply.

"Holly? Where are you?"

This time there was silence. And damn if this wasn't worse than no service at all.

"Holly, wherever you are, stay there. It's a nightmare out here. Whatever you do, don't go out."

There was no connection. He couldn't hear anything at all. When he looked at the screen it was black.

He tried to switch it with his nose again. Nothing. Then, in frustration, he shoved the phone back into his pocket.

She was alive and using her phone. That's all he needed to know. Now he was going to keep walking until he found her.

"Well there's nothing for it," Dolores said, as the townsfolk gathered around in the dining room. "One of our own is in trouble. We have to help."

There were murmurs of agreement. Now that Holly had called Josh and confirmed he was out in the storm, they had to make a plan. She bit down on her lip to ward off the emotion because they were all being so lovely. She'd lost count of how many of their friends had hugged her or told her it was all going to be okay.

Even if it felt like it wasn't okay at all.

"When do you think you can get the plow out?" North asked, running his finger along his jaw.

"First light. I checked the forecast and the storm should be died down by then." Charlie let out a sigh. "I could try before, but it'll cause more problems than it solves."

"So what do we do?" Holly asked. "Since he's out there, we need to get him."

"The snowmobiles?" Alaska suggested. "We have a couple in the shed."

"If there's no visibility we're likely to end up head first in a tree." Gabe shook his head. "We can use them once it dies down but not before. The only option I can come up with is if North and I put our skis on. We can cover the distance in about half an hour if the weather doesn't get any worse."

"What if it does?" Everley asked, her voice quiet.

"Then it'll slow us down."

"Skis it is." Holly nodded. "I'm coming with you."

"That's not a good idea." Gabe glanced at her from the corner of his eye. "You're not a seasoned skier. We know that much from the last time I took you out."

"I did okay apart from the downhills. And I can't sit here and do nothing."

Her jaw was set. She knew she could ski. Sure, she fell going downhill with Gabe, but she'd picked herself up and kept going. Plus there was the fact that Gabe and North always skied too fast. This way she'd be able to make sure her cousins were safe, too.

North licked his lips, eyeing her carefully. "If we say no..."

"I'll come anyway."

A ghost of a smile passed his lips. "I thought so." He glanced at Gabe. "How quickly can we be ready?"

"Five minutes. You guys get dressed and I'll get the supplies. But you have to agree to listen to what I tell you to do, okay? And we keep to the road at all times. That's the most likely place he'll be, and if he isn't... well..."

Well, then they'd never find him. Not until the storm had passed and visibility had returned.

"He'll stay on the road." Holly's voice was low. "We'll find him."

"That's my girl." North patted her back. "Come on, let's get ourselves ready for some skiing.

They all jumped into action. Alaska knew exactly where everything was, locating the warm snowsuits and skis they loaned out to interested guests within a couple of minutes.

Gabe filled up two backpacks with essentials – emergency warming blankets, flashlights, and foldaway shovels, along with flares in case they needed more help than they realized.

"Here, take this," Charlie Shaw said, passing his flask to Gabe. "It's saved me in more than one emergency."

"Are you sure you want to go out there?" Everley asked Holly, looking out at the snow. "I thought you were never going to ski again."

"I'm sure." Holly nodded. She was going to ignore that fear inside of her. Because Josh needed her.

Just like she needed him.

And she couldn't take another moment of sitting around and not seeing him.

A few minutes later, they were skiing down the driveway, snow wooshing past them as they moved forward steadily, Gabe at the front, Holly in the middle, and North at the back. She knew they'd done that deliberately. Gabe would make the tracks that Holly could follow, while North would be there to make sure she didn't stumble or fall.

Her heart clenched with love for her cousins, because they were doing this for her and for Josh.

She lost count of the number of people who'd slapped their backs and wished them luck as they'd walked through the lobby carrying their skis and backpacks. It was as though they were going out to fight a war, rather than ski a few miles up the road. They were so lucky to have so many people caring for them.

And when she found Josh, she was going to tell him just how many people cared about him, too.

They made it to the road, and Gabe turned to the right, keeping to the middle of the open, snowy expanse, as he propelled himself forward.

"Be ready to pull to the right if we see something coming." His voice was almost lost in the wind.

He was skiing steadily. She knew that was for her sake. If she wasn't here, her cousins would probably be careening down the hillside, whooping and laughing at the heady sensation.

Still, she kept pushing forward, making herself go as fast as she could. There was no time for fear or for being overly careful. They needed to get to Josh.

And the first thing she was going to do was tell him she loved him. No pauses, no fears, just throwing herself toward him and opening herself up.

She was sick of being afraid. Fear had made her almost lose the man she loved. She needed to be as brave for herself as she was for everybody else.

"There's a slope ahead," Gabe shouted. "You okay with that, Holly?"

"I'm good." Her voice was grimly determined. "I'll wedge the shit out of it."

Gabe's laugh carried back to her on the wind.

Less than a minute later she was following him down the hill, feeling the wind slapping against her face. Snowflakes clung to her skin, before melting against her. Her heart was speeding as fast as her skis, her breath short as she concentrated on her form, keeping her skis wedged to control her descent.

By the time they made it to the next flat, she was exhilarated. If only it was all downhill, they'd get there so much faster. North skied up beside her, shooting her a grin.

"You aced it. Gabe said you were terrible at hills."

"I'm a fast learner."

"I can see that." He bumped her shoulder. "You're a Winter, after all."

They skied on, and the road was hauntingly empty. No humans to be seen – no animals either. They were all sensibly staying safe, sheltering from the storm.

All of them except the four people who should know better.

They'd taken another downhill when Gabe let out a shout, the echo deadened by the layers of snow covering the ground and the trees.

"There's somebody ahead."

She squinted her eyes, because right now all she could see was the white of the snowflakes as they careened toward them. Then something shifted. It was dark and difficult to make out, but whatever it was, it was moving.

"Josh?" she shouted, the wind swallowing up her voice.

She pushed herself faster, shortening the distance between her and Gabe. Her breath was puffing through her lips and her thigh muscles were aching, but with every slide forward she felt something she hadn't since she'd left her mom's house.

Hope.

She felt hope.

"It's human," Gabe shouted. She could hear North's skis whooshing as fast as hers as he skied alongside her, not bothering to use her tracks.

"It's him!" she shouted at her cousin. "It's definitely him." She'd know that thick coat from anywhere. And that determination in his gait. Out of nowhere, tears stung her eyes because she was so damn relieved.

He was alive. He was walking. He was here.

"Josh!" she shouted out again.

"Holly?" his low shout came in reply.

"I love you. I love you. I love you." She had to take a breath. "I love you, dammit."

"I think he gets the message, Hol." North was laughing now. He reached for Gabe's shoulder, and they both stopped, letting Holly cover the rest of the distance between her and Josh.

And then she was in front of him. This man she'd fallen for in spite of herself. This man who loved her enough to give her a town for Christmas.

This man who set her world on fire.

"I love you," she said, reaching for his mittened hand with her own. "I love you, Josh Gerber."

His teeth were chattering, but somehow he managed to smile. "I love you, too. So damn much. And I thought I told you not to come."

"I wouldn't have, except some townie was stupid enough to go out in the cold." She wanted to laugh, because relief was washing over her. He loved her. And it was everything. In that moment, nothing else mattered.

The snow. The town. Or the fact that she was so cold her face was stinging.

"This is really nice," Gabe said dryly, skiing to a stop beside them. "Very romantic, and all that. But there's a storm raging and we have to get inside."

"Josh doesn't have skis," Holly pointed out.

"I know." Gabe smiled. "It's a good thing he's only made it just over a mile from his house."

"A mile?" Josh frowned. "That can't be right. I must have gone further."

"We'll explain the concept of snow blindness later." Gabe patted his arm. "But now we need to get you back. Do you have electricity at your place?"

"It went out before I left."

"You have blankets and a fire?" Gabe looked hopeful.

"Yep." Josh nodded. "And plenty of wood."

"Then let's go."

North and Gabe stayed with them until the wind died down, and the snowfall had lightened up, looking less like Armageddon and more like Christmas Eve. They'd found blankets and towels, each of them drying off by the fireplace, then they'd boiled a pan of water and made hot chocolate.

Now they were standing at the door, and Holly was hugging them both. "Are you sure you have to leave? Maybe you should wait until morning."

"Alaska and Everley need our help at the Inn," North told her, looking at his phone. "Apparently, Charlie's talking about bringing more moonshine over from his garage. I need to shut that down and get him to sleep. We need him up to plow the roads tomorrow."

"You guys could come, too," Gabe suggested to her and Josh. "I don't know when you'll get the power back here. We have the generator at the Inn."

"We have the fire," Holly said, giving him a smile. Gabe nodded, getting the message.

She and Josh had some talking to do. Alone.

And maybe when they were done talking, more of other stuff, too.

"We'll see you tomorrow. As soon as Charlie's sober enough to drive." North ruffled her hair. "Bye Hol. Bye Josh."

"Thank you for taking care of her." Josh shook North's hand. It made her heart clench to watch the two main men in her life connecting once more. This time in a much less violent way.

"We had no choice. If Holly decides to do something, she does it." North chuckled. "Anyway, she's all yours now."

Her cousins left, North letting out a whoop as he threw a snowball at Gabe's back, then skied past him like a lightning streak. Holly rolled her eyes and turned back to Josh, who was looking at her with a smile on his lips.

"Come lay by the fire," he said, sliding his hand into hers. In the living room, he had laid blankets out in front of the hearth, piling cushions up so she could lay down and let the flames warm her. He settled in behind her, pulling her close against his body, then pulled another blanket up to cover them both.

"Are you warm enough?" he murmured.

"Toasty."

She let her head rest on his chest, smelling the smoke wafting in from the fire, and the masculine scent of this man with his arms wrapped around her. Somehow they'd made it back together, despite the odds.

And despite the way she'd hurt him.

"I'm so sorry," she told him. "I shouldn't have hidden our plan from you."

He kissed her head. "I overreacted. I should have listened to what you had to say." He splayed his hand out over her stomach, pulling her closer, until they were two spoons warming in front of the fireplace. "The truth was, I wanted to be your knight in shining armor. To give you this wonderful gift on Christmas morning. To see your face when you realized that the town was yours."

"And I spoiled it. I'm sorry."

"No, *I* spoiled it. A gift shouldn't be given with any expectations attached to it. It should be given freely and with love. But I got all butt hurt because you didn't need my gift. You'd already gotten what you needed for yourself."

She turned her head, her eyes shining as they met his. "I should have told you I loved you the night you told me."

He swallowed, his throat bobbing. "Why didn't you?"

"Because I was afraid." She pulled her lip between her teeth. "I told myself it was because I needed to wait until you knew the truth about the town. But I don't think that was it at all. I was afraid to open myself up to you. So scared that you could hurt me. But instead I ended up hurting us both by staying quiet."

"Are you still afraid?" he asked her.

"I'm afraid of not being with you," she whispered. "I'm afraid that you won't want to be with me because I hurt you."

"I do want to be with you." He brushed his lips against her cheek. "So much."

She let out a lungful of air, her body sagging with relief. "We were all so worried about you. We had a town meeting about how to rescue you."

A smile played at his lips. "You did?"

She nodded. "Yeah. You've got a lot of fans in Winterville." Including his biggest one, who happened to be in his arms. "Even if you're an idiot who goes out in the snow when he knows better."

"Takes one to know one." He kissed her cheek again. "I told you to stay put."

"I know. But I needed to be with you."

"Back atcha." He brushed her hair over her shoulder and pressed his lips to her neck. "I would have made it to the Inn. Eventually." He didn't sound so sure.

"We can go tomorrow. When the roads are cleared," she said, closing her eyes, because his mouth felt so good.

"Or the next day. Whatever."

She turned her head again, so he could capture her mouth with his. His kiss was warm and gentle and made her stomach turn to jelly.

"I can't believe you tried to give me a town for Christmas," she said, smiling against his lips.

"I didn't try. I did it. The contracts are signed."

"I can't accept it."

"Yes you can. It's what you've been fighting for all this time. And it's easier than sending lawyer's letters and buying some buildings from me."

"But what about your business? Your investors?"

"The investors will be repaid. And the business will be fine. Eventually." He didn't sound worried at all. There was too much heat in his voice for that. His hand slid down her side, cupping her hip and pulling her harder against him.

She could feel just how hot he was getting. She was feeling the same way. But she wanted to see his face, to look into his eyes. Squirming in his grasp, she managed to turn onto her other side, reaching up to touch his hair, his face, his lips.

"Hello." She smiled at him.

"Hi." There was so much warmth in his eyes as he stared at her. It made her heart ache. This man who'd given up a town for her. Who'd risked his relationship with his grandfather to make her happy.

The man who went out in a snowstorm because he was afraid she might injure herself trying to get to him.

"I have a gift for you, too," she told him, sliding her hand down his arm, feeling the steel of his biceps beneath his sweater.

"I was hoping you did." He lifted a brow and she laughed.

"Not that." Although it did sound appealing right now. "It's at the Inn. We have to go there tomorrow to pick it up."

"I like the other gift better."

She snickered. Then he kissed her neck and the laughter died in her throat, replaced by a soft sigh as his warm hands slid down her sides.

"Tell me you love me again," he whispered, kissing the corner of her lips.

"I love you."

He rewarded her with the warmth of his mouth capturing hers, his tongue smooth and soft as he deepened their connection.

"Again."

"I love you."

This time he slid his hands inside her sweater, his thumbs feathering the peaks of her nipples until her breath stuttered in her throat.

His fingers were deft as they unfastened her pants, sliding them down her smooth thighs. He sat on his knees, looking down at her. "Again."

"I love you."

"That's what I like to hear." He tugged at her panties, throwing them over his shoulder until she was bare before him, on the bottom half at least. The top was still cozy warm, as though he didn't want her to freeze.

She loved it. She loved him.

"For the record, I love you too," he murmured, running his fingertips up her thighs. There was an intent expression on his face. He was a man on a mission. "So damn much."

Just as he buried his head between her thighs there was a loud crack, then the lights flashed on. The clock on the kitchen let out a loud beep, then the phone did the same. The heating system began with a whoosh of air.

"You're a magician," Holly whispered.

He looked up, a grin on his lips. "It's the electricity between us. Even a storm can't beat it."

"I was kind of liking the darkness and the fireplace." She pulled her lip between her teeth. "It felt like we were the only people in the world."

"You want me to turn the lights out?"

"Yeah, I would." Just for a few hours. Enough for it to be just the two of them and nothing else. No worries about her family or his business, or this town that brought them together after tearing them apart.

Just Holly and Josh and the feeling of his skin pressing against hers.

"Don't move," he whispered. "I'm going to flip the fuses."

It was like he could read her mind, and she loved him for it. So much it felt like she might burst.

For so long she'd been afraid of this feeling, and she couldn't imagine why. Because it was perfect.

Just like Josh, who was walking back into the living room, his face illuminated by orange flames. He glanced at his watch and lifted a brow. "It's midnight," he told her.

"It's Christmas," she breathed, watching as he pulled his sweater off, followed by his t-shirt, revealing his muscled chest.

"It is." He unbuckled his belt, tugging his pants and shorts off. "And now I definitely want my gift."

❦ 28 ❧

They were still laying by the fire when Holly awoke. At some point in the night, Josh must have turned the power back on, because she could hear the low hum of the heating system. The fire had burned down to black embers, though the smell of it still hung warmly in the air. The two of them were laying on the floor, under soft wool blankets, her head on Josh's chest.

At first, the sound was almost imperceptible above Josh's gentle, rhythmic breaths. But then it became louder. A trill of bells, and music, along with a low roar of an engine. Was Charlie Shaw actually playing Christmas music as he plowed the roads? Maybe he had drunk too much moonshine after all.

Holly carefully extricated herself from Josh's warm embrace, pulling on her panties and Josh's discarded t-shirt, before padding over to the living room window. She pulled the curtain open an inch or two, looking out at the blanket of snow covering Josh's driveway and lawn. The early morning sun reflected against it, sparkling like diamonds.

There wasn't a cloud in the sky. No trace of the storm that had taken place the night before. It was a beautiful Winterville morning.

The rumble of the engine increased, and she could hear the music clearer, too. It was "Jingle Bells" she could hear playing. She grinned at the jauntiness of it all.

Then Charlie Shaw's snowplow turned into Josh's driveway, pushing snow to the sides of the blacktop path, and she felt wistful because it meant they were no longer cut off.

But that thought rushed out of her mind as she saw the cavalcade of trucks and cars following behind.

"Josh?"

"Huh?" He sat up, rubbing his eyes. The blanket fell around his hips, revealing his bare chest.

"We have company. You might want to get dressed."

"Company?" He frowned. "Who?"

"All of Winterville, by the looks of it."

She looked out of the window again. She could see North and Gabe in the first truck, with Alaska and Everley hanging out of the back windows, grinning like idiots.

Then there was The Cold Fingers Café truck, driven by a laughing Dolores. More vehicles followed behind, belonging to the local businesses. Then there were four wheel drive cars. The line stretched back along the road from Winterville.

Josh pulled on his shorts, then blinked at her. "I need my t-shirt back."

She grinned. "Oops." Closing the curtain, she pulled it off, loving the way his eyes darkened at the sight of her body. There was a hint of regret in his expression.

Within a minute they were dressed. She was flattening her hair into submission as Charlie began honking his horn, then all the other cars and trucks joined in.

"Is it always like this on Christmas morning?" he asked her.

"If you'd have stayed eight years ago, you would have found out."

He kissed her temple. "Worst mistake of my life."

She laced her fingers through his and led him to the door. As she opened it, cold air rushed past them, making her gasp.

"What's going on?" she asked, looking over at her cousins.

"It's Christmas morning," North shouted. "We can't start the celebrations without you."

Everley jumped down from his truck. "He said we can't even open our gifts until we brought you back to the Inn." She looked at Josh. "Both of you."

Holly squeezed his hand, and he squeezed back, and it made everything feel right. "You could have called," she said. "Josh has a car." She couldn't help but grin. Because her beautiful family and gorgeous friends were crazy.

"You would have ignored us." Gabe walked up the step and hugged her, then shook Josh's hand. "Don't tell me you wouldn't."

"Maybe until lunchtime."

"Yeah, well I can't wait until lunchtime to open my gifts. So you're coming back with us now." His eyes flickered to Josh's. "Okay?"

"Works for me." Josh's voice was thick. She looked over her shoulder at him, and his eyes were shining. As though he loved that they were including him in this.

He deserved it. Winterville owed it to him. More than they knew.

She pressed her lips to his cheek. "Come on, let's go."

She'd given him a LEGO Millennium Falcon for Christmas. Josh still had no idea how she'd tracked it down in twenty-four hours, let alone how she'd gotten it to Winterville in time for Christmas morning. When he asked her, she'd smiled enigmatically and told him to build the damn thing.

So that's what he was doing right now. Putting bricks together, or rather, showing the six kids who'd run over as soon as he'd opened his present how to build the Falcon, listening to them as they talked excitedly about Darth Vader and Luke Skywalker and all the things he used to love so much.

It felt as though the entire population of Winterville were still hanging around the Inn. Half of them were in the kitchen, cleaning up after the huge breakfast they'd served. That was where Holly was right now, though when he'd tried to follow her she'd shooed him back.

"You're a guest, for now. Next year you can help clean up."

Next year. He liked the sound of that.

"So, hey." North sat down on the bench beside him. One of the kids moved the half-built Falcon a few inches to the left, as though afraid North was going to butt in on the building.

"Hey." Josh gave him a tight smile.

"I wanted to apologize to you." North tapped his fingers on his thigh.

"What for?"

"For hitting you eight years ago. And for treating you like the enemy for the past month."

"I guess I was the enemy." A ghost of a smile flickered across Josh's lips. "Or at least it must have seemed that way."

"Yeah, well it doesn't matter. I was brought up better than that. If my grandma could have seen me." North winced. "We welcome everybody here in Winterville. Even when they've just bought it."

"Apology accepted. On both counts."

North's gaze met his. "Holly's important to us all. She has this tough exterior, but inside, I don't know. She's kinda soft."

"I know." Josh nodded. "And you don't need to worry about me hurting her. I won't be doing that ever again."

"Does that mean you'll be sticking around?"

"I'm planning on it. I have a few things to take care of in Cincinnati, but this month has proved I can work remotely a lot of the time. Plus I'm recruiting someone to take over the reins there."

North gave him a look of respect. "That'll make Holly happy."

"Not as happy as I'll be."

The door to the Inn opened, and they both turned to look at the new arrival. Holly's mom swept in, wearing what looked like a white fox fur coat, her blonde hair cascading over her shoulders.

"Cruella's arrived," North murmured. The next moment, they both stood up. Then they looked at each other and laughed.

"Were you about to protect Holly?" North asked him.

Josh nodded. "Yeah. You?"

"Yep. But she doesn't need our protection, does she?"

No she didn't. Holly Winter could kick ass all on her own. She could drive grown businessmen into submission, and save towns without losing her breath.

And she definitely didn't need his help dealing with her mom.

"I might just head over there anyway," Josh murmured, his eyes following the streak of white fur as Susannah searched for her daughter.

"Good idea. If you need me, holler."

By the time he reached the kitchen, he saw that Susannah had found Holly. The two of them were standing in the corner by the back door. She looked up and saw him, her lips curling into a smile.

And damn if that smile didn't hit him right in the chest.

"You okay?"

"I'm fine." She nodded.

"I'll be around if you need me." He gave her a wink.

"Please stay," Susannah said, looking over at him. "I want to apologize to both of you for last night. Garrick didn't mean to let the cat out of the bag. He's devastated it caused so many issues."

Holly pulled her lip between her teeth. "Why did he say it in the first place?"

"He thought he was building a relationship with you both. He knows it's important for me to get to know you better, and he thought he was helping." Her mom sighed. "He knows he wasn't now. He'd like to apologize to you himself. If you'll let him."

"I don't know." Holly rubbed her temple with the heel of her hand.

"And I want to apologize to you, too. For everything." Her mom's voice was soft. "I really thought this year would be the time we could rebuild our relationship. I made so many mistakes, Holly. For so many years. I hate that you can barely bring yourself to look at me."

Holly blinked, her eyes glassy. "It's not that I can't look at you. It's that every time we talk it ends in an argument."

"I didn't know how to love you," her mom whispered, wringing her fingers together. "From the moment you were born, I was afraid. And my mother was there, knowing exactly how to take care of you. How to feed you, how to rock you to sleep. I should have fought harder for you. But the two of you were always so content to be together. I was young and foolish and felt excluded."

"I wanted a mom. All my life I wanted nothing more than a mom." Holly's voice was thick.

"And I thought I couldn't be who you wanted. Until that summer in Italy. Remember how much fun we had? For the first time I thought we could build a relationship again."

"And then you turned your back on me. It hurt." Holly blinked back the tears. Josh clenched his teeth, knowing they needed to talk. But it didn't stop him from wanting to hold Holly in his arms.

"I was so selfish," her mom whispered. "When your grandma arrived and whisked you away the day of your wedding, it felt like your birth all over again. You two had this special relationship that I couldn't penetrate. When you were hurt or in pain you always looked for her."

"Because you were never there." Holly's expression was stormy.

"I know. I was selfish. I thought that motherhood was like in the movies. That I could swoop in and you'd love me unconditionally. But I now know that I was wrong, and it's too late now because you've grown up and you don't need me anymore."

"I needed you when Grandma died." Holly's eyes welled up.

Susannah nodded. "I didn't think that you wanted me. Look at you, sweetheart. You're an amazing woman. You have a wonderful career, and so much success. And that's all down to you and my mom. I wish I had something to do with the person you've turned out to be, but I don't." She sighed. "All I ask is that maybe you'll give me a chance to get to know you all over again. I want to be your friend, not your enemy."

Holly looked at Josh. There was a lost expression on her face. Like she was the child she used to be, hoping for some-body to make it all better. He walked over to her, kissing her on the temple. She curled her arm around his waist.

"Okay?" he murmured.

She nodded, melting against him. "Can we talk about this later this week?" she asked her mom. "Maybe we can come over for dinner or something?"

Hope flashed in her mom's eyes. "I'd like that very much." She pulled open her purse, rifling in it until she found what she was looking for. "I have a little Christmas gift for you," she said, passing the wrapped present to Holly.

"I didn't get you anything." Holly turned the silver box over in her hand.

"You did." Her mom smiled. "You gave me hope." She patted her daughter's hand, a smile on her lips. "Now open it."

Holly tugged at the ivory ribbon, then tore into the silver paper, revealing a blue velvet jewelry box. As she opened the lid, she gasped when she saw what was inside.

A silver butterfly locket, the wings embellished with diamonds. With shaking hands she pressed at the wings, swallowing hard when they opened to reveal a photograph.

Josh leaned over her shoulder, taking in the tiny picture of Candy, wearing a red Santa suit, her hair perfectly coiffed and a big smile on her face. On her lap was a little girl of six or seven, smiling widely to reveal a toothless gap.

Holly. She looked beautiful even as a kid.

"It's lovely," Holly whispered. "Thank you."

"You're welcome. Now I should go." Impulsively, her mom leaned forward and kissed Holly's cheek. "Merry Christmas."

"Merry Christmas, Mom." Holly leaned against Josh, watching as her mother walked out of the kitchen. She leaned her head against his shoulder, and he smoothed the hair from her face.

"You okay?" he murmured.

She tilted her head to look up at him. "Yeah, I am." She slid her arms around him, breathing softly against his neck.

"You should be. You're amazing. The strongest woman I've ever met."

She pressed her lips to his throat. "Are you for real? I keep wondering if it's eight years ago and I'm having some kind of weird psychedelic flash forward."

"Completely real. Pinch me if you don't believe me."

She did, and it hurt his nipple like a bitch, but he'd offered, after all. "Okay. So we've established I'm real and we're both adults. And I don't have to rush off to London for a year. So what happens next?"

Holly looked up at him, her eyes so full of emotion it made his heart clatter against his ribcage. "Let's go for a walk in the snow," she whispered.

It seemed like symmetry to bring him back here of all places. To the little cabin in the snow where he'd first kissed her all those years ago.

And now they were kissing in here again. His hands tangled in her hair, her body wedged between his and the wooden walls, as his tongue slid and danced against hers.

He'd ruined her for any other man, and she didn't care a bit. Because nobody else existed for her.

"I have another gift for you," she whispered. He grinned and she shook her head. "No, not that, you dirty minded man. A proper gift." She pulled it out of her pocket. A flash of white caught his eye.

"My pebble?" he asked, seeing the stone in her hand.

"No. Not yours. It's a new one."

He took it between his fingers, inspecting it closely. A butterfly was painted on the surface in lilacs and blues. It caught the light shining through the window. "It looks almost the same."

"I found the pebble and asked Alaska to paint it. She's artsy that way."

"I love it." He slid it into his pocket, then pulled his old one out. "I guess two's a crowd, huh?"

"You can keep the old one, too."

He shook his head. "No. That's the one I used to touch to remember you existed. I don't need that memory anymore. You're here." He reached out to cup her cheek. She leaned her face against his palm. "Let's leave it here in the cabin."

She nodded. "We could put it in the fireplace."

They leaned down together, nestling the old white pebble among the dark embers of a long-extinguished fire. "I have one more thing for you," Holly told him.

He shook his head, amused. "You have to stop with the gifts. They're making me feel inadequate."

"Inadequate? You gave me a town. Imagine trying to top that?"

He smiled smugly.

"Anyway, that's kind of what I want to give you." She unfolded a piece of paper. There was handwriting at the top, followed by five signatures and Kris's name printed at the bottom.

"We hereby gift Joshua Gerber one seventh of Winterville." He blinked at the words he'd read out loud. "What's this?"

"You gave us Winterville, but we want you to be part of it. We all agreed. Even Kris, who wasn't very pleased because he was sleeping off his Christmas dinner when we called him in England." Holly smiled at Josh's confused expression. "We don't want to do this without you. You can be as involved as you want to be, but you get to own a part of this town, too."

"You all want me to be part of this?" he murmured, looking at the signatures again. They'd signed in age order.

North, then Gabe. Everley and Holly. At the end was Alaska, and Kris's name with a cc next to it.

"I won't do it without you." Holly lifted her chin.

"I thought we agreed not to mix business and pleasure." He still looked bemused, as though he was trying to take it all in.

Holly took a deep breath. "The thing is, I want to do everything with you. I want to fall asleep with you at night and wake up with you in the morning. I want you to know every part of me. The brave parts and the scared parts. The laughter and the sadness. I don't want secrets or lies or things that come between us. I won't do that again. So if I'm going to do this and try to turn this town around, I want to do it with you. Whether you play a big role or a small one, I want you to be part of it. With me. Us."

He swallowed, his warm eyes still on hers. "You want me here?"

"Every part of you, Josh. And I know you still have a business to run. So you can be a silent partner if you prefer."

"I engaged a recruitment firm yesterday to start searching for a new CEO." He pressed his lips to her head. His voice was soft, emotional. "I'll still be part of Gerber Enterprises, but it will free my time up."

"To be here?"

"Yes. To be with you."

"Does your grandfather know?"

He nodded. "Yeah, and he's not impressed. But he'll come around." He didn't sound as though he cared either way. "The business will survive, and so will he."

She lifted her head, both it and her heart so full of emotion she could burst. "I love you," she told him.

"And I will never get bored of hearing it. Not ever."

She pressed her lips to his cheek. "That's good, because I plan on telling you a lot."

"Say it again," he whispered.

She grinned against his cheek. "I love you."

"And I love you." He swept his lips over hers. "Now let's go spend the rest of Christmas with your family."

EPILOGUE

Winterville looked so different in the high heat of summer. The lawns – covered with snow until March – were now the deepest green, and the fir trees that lined the slope down toward Marshall's Gap stood proudly snow free, though Holly thought they looked a little naked without their little caps of white. The sun was shining, and there wasn't a cloud in the glorious blue sky. It was the perfect day to reopen Winterville after a spring of renovations.

She was standing with her cousins and Josh on a podium they'd erected in front of the Winterville Inn. Everley was wearing a pretty pink summer dress, and Alaska – who'd been dragged reluctantly from her favorite position behind the reception desk – was wearing a light blouse and red shorts – the new summer uniform for all that worked in the Inn. Gabe and North were wearing jeans and polo shirts – their tan, muscled arms making all the women sigh.

And next to her was Josh.

Her Josh.

The man who'd begun a new life with her here in Winterville.

He was wearing a suit, though the heat of the sun had made him shuck off his jacket and remove his tie. She knew it was neatly rolled up in his pocket, in case he needed it later. His sleeves were pushed up to just below his elbow, revealing his strong, muscled forearms that did strange things to her.

Gray Hartson was here, too. The famous singer and his family had come in for the opening day of the season. After spending Christmas Eve in Winterville, they'd struck up a bond with the Winter family, and had been regular visitors while the renovations were taking place.

And now he was here to sing Candy's songs once again. This time to a crowd of people lining the lawns in front of the Winterville Inn, ready to celebrate Christmas in June.

She'd kind of stolen it from Hallmark, but made it one month early, because June was the start of their vacation season.

"Yeah, we're ready."

Josh squeezed her hand as she walked toward the microphone. She'd argued with North and Everley that either of them would be better than her to make a speech at the opening ceremony. But somehow she'd ended up with the short straw, and she was trying to take it like a champ.

A really nervous, anxious champ.

"Hello everybody." She forced a smile onto her face as she leaned toward the mic. The crowd let up a big roar. Scanning the front, she saw her mom and Garrick standing there, smiling up at her. The two of them had stuck around while the renovations were taking place. Garrick had even dirtied it up with the guys, helping to lay tiles and paint walls so they could get everything ready as quick as possible.

And her mom? Well, she'd done her best to build bridges. And Holly had, too. It was an ongoing process. You didn't solve years of hurt with a few months of friendship. But she liked her mom being around.

"The Winter family would like to extend a huge welcome to you all. As you can see, the town has been freshly renovated this year. We've upgraded all of our hotel rooms and renovated our cabins. We've refreshed the Jingle Bell Theater, which I'm delighted to announce has a brand new director, in the form of Miss Everley Winter." She grinned at Everley, who blew out a lungful of air. "We have a brand new season of summer shows coming your way, and we very much hope you'll come back this holiday season, when we'll be restarting our Winter Revues."

Another cheer rippled through the crowd. Thank goodness everybody looked happy. Well, *almost* everybody. She spotted Josh's grandparents sitting in a little shaded area to the right. His grandma was smiling at her, of course. She and Holly had been in regular contact since Christmas, and Holly had visited Cincinnati a few times with Josh. He only drove back occasionally now, when there was a big meeting his new CEO couldn't handle.

But boy, the reconciliations more than made up for it.

Josh's grandfather was more taciturn. Holly wasn't sure if it was because he was wearing a full, wool suit with a vest, or because they'd proved him wrong. The Winterville Inn was already fully booked. Not just for the summer season, but for the holiday season, too. Josh and North were talking about buying more land to build a second Inn.

"During your stay here in Winterville, we very much hope you'll enjoy the newly remodeled Cold Fingers Café, run by our very own Dolores." She grinned at the café owner. "And for dinner, if you don't want to eat at the Inn, we highly recommend our brand new restaurant in town, Candy's Canteen. And for those of you over the age of twenty-one, why not stop by to try out the bar there?"

She glanced down at her notes. "Oh, and while you're here, please make sure to visit our amazing gift shops. Since we celebrate Christmas all year round, why not stock up on all your gifts and decorations? You'll be the envy of your friends having Christmas wrapped up by the end of summer."

She glanced over her shoulder at her cousins and Josh, wondering if she'd forgotten anything. But they were all staring proudly at her. Taking a deep breath, she nodded at Gray Hartson, who nodded back.

"So without further ado, let me introduce the wonderful Gray Hartson and his band. They've kindly agreed to play for us today, and we are so grateful to them."

The crowd went wild. Gray was a big deal, not just here but all over America and the World. His low, rough voice and his heartfelt songs made women go weak in the knees. And men want to save them from falling.

Gray winked at her, then walked up to the mic, kissing Holly on the cheek. "Ladies and gentlemen, please give a huge cheer to Holly Winter and her cousins, North, Gabe, Alaska, and Everley. Without them, none of us would be here today."

Everybody was raving about the concert Gray and his band had put on. Staff dressed in their summer uniforms were handing out glasses of champagne and orange juice, along with popsicles for the children. Josh slid his hand into Holly's and looked out at the throng of guests.

"Are you happy?" he asked her with a soft smile. She looked beautiful today, in a white summer dress, and a thick brown belt that accentuated her slim waist.

"So happy. How about you? Did you make the right decision?" She pulled her lip between her teeth. She'd asked him this before.

Was he sure he wanted to be here in Winterville and not in Cincinnati?

Was he certain he was ready to leave his business in others' hands?

Was he okay with pissing his Grandad off, even if the old man had forgiven him since?

The answer to all three was yes. Moving here with Holly was the best decision of his life. How could he regret it when it had given him the one thing he wanted.

Her.

"I absolutely made the right decision," he murmured. Happiness bubbled through him. "I'm part of this. Right along with you. And I'm so happy. I am."

"So am I." She leaned her head against his shoulder.

He pressed his lips to her brow. "Can I make you even happier?"

She looked up at him. "Is that a come on?"

He laughed. "No. But maybe later. I just want to show you something." He slid his arm around her waist. "Come for a walk with me."

She gave him a quizzical look, but walked with him anyway. Around the back of the Inn toward the newly renovated cabins that lined the slope down the mountain. This had been his project. The cabins had been ten years old when he'd started to work on them, and their age had been showing through. Now each one was gleaming new, with all modern conveniences inside. They were able to rent them out for a premium, both in summer and for the winter ahead. He was damn proud of that.

"Where are we going?" Holly asked him, as they passed the cabins and made their way down the hill beyond.

"You'll see." He took a left, then smiled because she let out a little gasp.

"You didn't knock it down?" she asked, her voice filled with wonder. She was staring at her old cabin, though it didn't look old anymore.

"Nope." It had taken an act of will to stop her from coming down here to inspect the cabins while they worked on them. Thank goodness he'd gotten her cousins to distract her. Because he hadn't wanted Holly to see her old cabin until it was ready.

And now it was, and her eyes were shining with tears.

"I worked on this one myself." With his own two hands. And the work had taken him about three times as long as it would have a builder. But he wanted it to be special. To be theirs and theirs alone.

Holly walked toward the cabin, reaching out to touch the wooden door. Above it, he'd hung a hand painted sign.

Holly's Cabin.

"You're going to need to change that," she told him, looking over her shoulder. "Your name should be there, too."

"Holly and Josh?" he asked her.

"Josh and Holly." She smiled, remembering Everley's couple name for them. "Jolly."

He laughed. Because the contraction of their names was just so damn apt. Better than Bennifer and Brangelina and Kimye. Not that any of them had lasted.

Jolly, on the other hand, was here for the duration. They would last forever.

"Go inside."

She pushed the door open, revealing her one-room cabin. He'd repaired the roof and cleaned out the fireplace, then laid a new floor and painted the walls.

And then there were the beds. Two of them with butterfly coverlets.

"It looks the same, only better."

He smiled, pleased. "That was the plan."

"You did this for me?" she asked him, her voice cracking.

"For us. Because this is where we started. And maybe for our kids, when they're older and they want to get away from us. It's the perfect hideaway."

"Kids?" She grinned goofily at him.

"One day." He nodded. "Right?"

"Right." She twirled, looking around the cabin again. "Hey, you cleaned out the fireplace."

"Yep. It's in full working order."

"But what about the pebble?"

"The pebble?"

"Your old butterfly pebble. We put it in there on Christmas Day." She blinked, the smile melting from her lips. "Don't tell me it's gone."

He swallowed. "Look in the grate."

She walked over to the fireplace, dropping to her knees. "It's here." She sounded relieved. "There's something else, too. What is it?" Her voice trailed off as she picked her discovery up from the grate. "Josh?"

When she turned to look at him, he was already on one knee. She was holding the ring in her palm, looking at it with surprise.

"Holly Winter. You beautiful, intelligent, amazing woman. I pinch myself every day when I wake up and see you in bed next to me. I keep waiting for you to run, but you never do. And now that I've got you, I want to keep you forever. So will you do me the honor of agreeing to marry me?"

She shuffled toward him on her knees, a tear rolling down her cheek. "You planned all this?"

"Yeah." He'd thought of it months ago. "Keeping it a secret has been a bitch. North's had to stand on Everley's feet about five times today to shut her up."

Holly laughed. "I saw that! She was cursing North to hell. She told him if she couldn't dance again, it was his fault."

Josh smiled, because he loved Holly's cousins. Working alongside North to get everything ready had given him a grudging respect for him. And Gabe always kept everybody amused when he visited. Everley and Alaska had always been on his side – and for that he was grateful.

"So what do you say?" he asked her. "Want to take a chance on a city boy like me?"

Her eyes sparkled just like the diamond on her palm. "Yes, I really do."

He breathed out heavily. He hadn't even been aware he was holding his breath. "Thank God." He took her hand in his, sliding the ring onto her slim finger. Then he pulled her close, his lips capturing hers, and she wrapped her arms around his neck, kissing him back with so much love it made his heart ache.

"Let's make it a short engagement," he whispered, sliding his hand through her hair, tracing the line of her spine through the fabric of her dress.

"How short?"

"A week?"

She laughed. "Give me a few months at least. I want to get married when there's snow on the ground."

"Here?"

"Definitely." She kissed him again, delight making her skin glow.

"November," he agreed. "When the first snow arrives." He could wait until then. If he had to. Because, let's face it, Holly Winter was worth waiting for.

He'd done it for eight years, he could do it for another five months. And while they were waiting, he'd keep kissing her and loving her and pinching himself every morning.

"I love you," he whispered, taking her hand in his. She was still clutching his old pebble. It made him smile.

"I love you, too," she told him.

And there was nothing better in his life than hearing that.

Later that year...

"She looks beautiful," Everley whispered to Alaska, as Holly and Josh kissed beneath a floral arch, Josh's hands tangling into her tumbling curls. As bridesmaids, she and Alaska were wearing red velvet dresses, white roses woven into their blonde hair. Alaska was openly crying, tears smearing mascara over her cheeks. Everley smiled and hugged her sister tight, blinking back her own tears.

One of them had to be strong. And it was usually her.

The pianist started to play a beautifully slow version of "Have Yourself A Merry Little Christmas", and Josh took Holly's hand in his, a smile pulling at his lips when he touched her new wedding ring. Then they walked down the aisle, smiling at their family and friends, though their gazes kept returning to each other.

Everley let out a little sigh, because Holly and Josh deserved to be happy. They'd fought hard to be together, after all. And they'd fought hard for this town, too. Everybody here loved them.

And she thought she might love them most of all.

As Josh and Holly made it out of the ballroom and the wedding party followed, the guests stood and followed them down the aisle. Alaska and Everley waited with their cousins. Gabe had agreed to be Josh's best man, and North had walked Holly down the aisle. Now they were welcoming the guests as they walked into the lobby. Kris hadn't been able to make it over. Though they were still hoping he might make it back stateside in a few months.

It had been way too long since their sixth cousin had made it home.

"Um, Ev?" Alaska sounded wary.

Everley pulled her gaze from her cousins. Alaska was frowning as she looked over her shoulder. "What's up?"

Alaska's voice was tight. "Have you seen who's with Charlie?"

"Is it Dolores? I swear those two have a thing going."

Alaska slowly shook her head. "Not Dolores. Look at the back of the line."

A shot of electricity prickled down Everley's spine as she turned to look in the direction Alaska was indicating.

Sure enough, Charlie was standing there, talking rapidly to somebody next to him, his arms gesticulating as though he couldn't keep control of them.

And that's when her gaze caught *his*. Pale blue eyes she knew all too well. Dark hair, cut short, revealing a line of paler skin above the tan he must have gotten from all his time working in Africa.

Dylan Shaw. Charlie's son.

Her childhood sweetheart. Her first love. The one who left her all those years ago.

Her ex-husband.

She hadn't seen him in years. It had felt like a gift from God that he'd been working for Doctors Overseas in Africa. Because dammit he was still as beautiful as she remembered.

Maybe more so. The years had definitely been kind to him.

"What's he doing here?" Alaska asked.

"I have no idea." But whatever it was, her heart needed to calm down. Right now it was doing a loop the loop behind her ribcage. "Just stick with me, okay. I don't want to talk to him."

Alaska nodded. "Of course. I've got your back."

Everley swallowed, lifting her shoulders back to regain her poise. She was an actress, a performer. She could feign nonchalance. Even if her body was screaming that it was very much *not cool* with this situation.

The guests shuffled through, shaking their hands one by one. And with each moment, she could feel Dylan getting closer.

What would she say? Would he touch her? Could she deal with it? She took another deep breath.

This was Holly's wedding. She'd *have* to deal with it.

"I wish they would hurry up," Gabe said, oblivious to her turmoil. "I don't want the champagne to run out."

It took another minute for Charlie and Dylan to reach them. Charlie shook North's hand, then Gabe's, before leaning to kiss Alaska's cheek.

"Sweetheart," he said gruffly, pulling Everley against him.

Once upon a time he'd been her father-in-law. For such a short time. But even before that, they'd been close.

"Thank you for coming," she murmured as he released her.

Then Dylan was standing in front of her. All six-foot-two of him. He was wearing a blue suit, with a white shirt and yellow tie. And dammit, he still smelled good. Too good.

"Hello. Thank you for being here. Please go through and grab a glass of champagne." She kept a smile on her face, despite the best effort of her muscles.

"You look beautiful." His voice was smooth and deep. "How are you?"

Her heart hammered against her chest. "I'm good. Real good."

He nodded. "I'm pleased to hear that." He leaned forward to kiss her cheek, and she had to squeeze her eyes shut. Her heart did another three-sixty leap. "Can I talk with you later?" he asked her. "In private?"

Alarm bells clattered in her ears. "I don't think I'll have the time today. I'm the maid of honor. I have a lot to do."

His gaze flickered to hers. "It's important."

She frowned. "It can't be *that* important. I haven't seen you for years."

Dylan exhaled heavily, his beautiful lips parting. "It's really important, Evie. We have a problem we need to sort out."

Evie. Only Dylan had ever called her that. She felt her cheeks flush.

"What kind of problem?"

He leaned closer, his breath tickling her ear. His voice was low and smooth, and made her shiver. But not as much as his words did. Because they were the last thing she expected to hear as his sweet voice caressed her skin.

"A really big problem. We're still married."

DEAR READER

Thank you so much for reading Josh and Holly's story. If you enjoyed it and you get a chance, I'd be so grateful if you can leave a review. And don't forget to keep an eye out for **HEARTS IN WINTER**, Everley and Dylan's story, coming later this year.

I can't wait to share more stories with you.

Yours,

Carrie xx

ALSO BY CARRIE ELKS

THE WINTERVILLE SERIES

A gorgeously wintery small town romance series, featuring six cousins who fight to save the sound their grandmother built.

Welcome to Winterville

Hearts In Winter (releases late 2021)

Leave Me Breathless (releases 2022

ANGEL SANDS SERIES

A heartwarming small town beach series, full of best friends, hot guys and happily-ever-afters.

Let Me Burn

She's Like the Wind

Sweet Little Lies

Just A Kiss

Baby I'm Yours

Pieces Of Us

Chasing The Sun

Heart And Soul

Lost In Him (releases 2022)

THE HEARTBREAK BROTHERS SERIES

A gorgeous small town series about four brothers and the women who capture their hearts.

Take Me Home

Still The One

A Better Man

Somebody Like You

When We Touch

THE SHAKESPEARE SISTERS SERIES

An epic series about four strong yet vulnerable sisters, and the alpha men who steal their hearts.

Summer's Lease

A Winter's Tale

Absent in the Spring

By Virtue Fall

THE LOVE IN LONDON SERIES

Three books about strong and sassy women finding love in the big city.

Coming Down

Broken Chords

Canada Square

STANDALONE

Fix You

An epic romance that spans the decades. Breathtaking and angsty and all the things in between.

ABOUT THE AUTHOR

Carrie Elks writes contemporary romance with a sizzling edge. Her first book, *Fix You*, has been translated into eight languages and made a surprise appearance on *Big Brother* in Brazil. Luckily for her, it wasn't voted out.

Carrie lives with her husband, two lovely children and a larger-than-life black pug called Plato. When she isn't writing or reading, she can be found baking, drinking an occasional (!) glass of wine, or chatting on social media.

You can find Carrie in all these places
www.carrieelks.com
carrie.elks@mail.com

ACKNOWLEDGMENTS

I've had the idea for Welcome To Winterville for a long time, but it's taken until now to put Holly and Josh's story to paper. It's partially inspired by a trip I took with my family back in 2006 (what a long time ago) into the mountains at Gatlinburg and Pigeon Forge, and to the amazing theme park at Dollywood.

Now, Winterville isn't Dollywood. There's no theme park (yet!) and Candy Winter may have a lot of success, but she's not Dolly either. Though she was a kick ass, strong woman, and Dolly is certainly that.

All this is to say that an idea is only the start of a book. So many people have helped me bring it to life, and I'm very grateful to all of them.

Rose David is my editor and she's amazing. Mich from Proofreading by Mich catches my oopses like a ninja. And Kirsty from the Pretty Little Design co always knows how to bring my books to life - she's a genius.

Marian is my beta reader, and she' s fabulous. Her suggestions are always little nuggets of gold.

Thank you to my agent, Meire Dias, of the Bookcase

agency, and Flavia who always gives me so much support and kindness.

My PA, Amanda, is amazing. You rock, lady!

To my family - thank you for accepting me for who I am, even when I'm mentally in another world where cooking and cleaning don't exist.

And to my reader group, The Water Cooler, thank you for all your support and appreciation. We have a lot of fun, and it's my favorite place to blow off steam.

Finally to you, the reader. THANK YOU for picking up this, and any of my other books. I hope I helped you escape for a little while. I'm grateful for you giving me a chance.

Keep smiling!

Carrie x

Made in the USA
Middletown, DE
21 November 2021

53029431R00187